REMAKING MOTHERHOOD

By the Same Author
With Patricia Lone
Working Woman: A Guide to Fitness and Health

With Dr. Laurence Balter
Dr. Balter's Child Sense

REMAKING MOTHERHOOD

How Working Mothers Are Shaping Our Children's Future

ANITA SHREVE

Viking

VIKING
Viking Penguin Inc., 40 West 23rd Street, New York, New York 10010, U.S.A.
Penguin Books Ltd, Harmondsworth, Middlesex, England
Penguin Books Australia Ltd, Ringwood, Victoria, Australia
Penguin Books Canada Limited, 2801 John Street, Markham, Ontario, Canada L3R 1B4
Penguin Books (N.Z.) Ltd, 182–190 Wairau Road, Auckland 10, New Zealand

First published in 1987 by Viking Penguin Inc.
Published simultaneously in Canada

Portions of this book first appeared, in different form, in
The New York Times Magazine and *Redbook.*

Grateful acknowledgment is made for permission to reprint excerpts from
the following copyrighted material:
Dr. Balter's Child Sense by Lawrence Balter with Anita Shreve. Copyright © 1985
by Lawrence Balter. Reprinted by permission of Simon & Schuster, Inc.
Reproduction of Mothering: Psychoanalysis and the Sociology of Gender by Nancy
Chodorow. © 1978 Regents of the University of California, University of California Press.
Daycare: The Developing Child by Alison Clarke-Stewart, Harvard University Press.
Reprinted by permission.
"Maternal Employment and the Young Child" by Lois Hoffman in *Parent-Child Interaction
and Parent-Child Relations in Child Development* edited by Marion Perlmutter, The Minnesota
Symposia on Child Psychology, Vol. 17. By permission of Lawrence Erlbaum Associates.
Beyond Sugar and Spice: How Women Grow, Learn and Thrive by Caryl Rivers,
Rosalind Barnett and Grace Baruch. Reprinted by permission of The Putnam Publishing
Group. Copyright © 1979 by Caryl Rivers, Rosalind Barnett and Grace Baruch.

LIBRARY OF CONGRESS CATALOGING IN PUBLICATION DATA
Shreve, Anita.
Remaking motherhood.
Bibliography: p.
Includes index.
1. Working mothers—United States—Psychology.
2. Children of working mothers—United States—
Psychology.   3. Work and family—United States
4. Role conflict.   I. Title.
HQ759.48.S55   1987   306.8'743   86-40428
ISBN 0-670-80722-2

Printed in the United States of America by The Book Press, Brattleboro, Vermont
Set in Avanta
Designed by Amy Lamb

FOR JOHN AND KATHERINE

Acknowledgments

There are many people who contributed to this book, but I would especially like to thank Ed Klein, editor of *The New York Times Magazine,* in whose office the idea for this book (then in the form of an article) was originally conceived; Bob Stock and Michaela Williams, who edited the article "The Working Mother as Role Model," which appeared as the cover story of that magazine on September 9, 1984; my supportive agent, Ginger Barber, who was responsible for turning the article into a book; Pat Mulcahy, my excellent editor at Viking, who gave me the freedom to shape the book as I wanted and who provided an astute critical eye when the manuscript was completed; Dr. J. Brooks-Gunn, Dr. Patricia Knaub, Dr. Lawrence Balter, Dr. Michael Bulmash, Dr. Sam Ritvo, Dr. Kirsten Dahl, Dr. Phyllis Cohen, Dr. Nancy Close, Dr. Carol Galligan, Dr. Martin V. Cohen, Dr. Sylvia Feinberg, Laurice Glover, Charna Levine, Rena Merkin, Susan Weissman, Mary Anne Weinberger, Ellen Galinsky and many other professionals who gave of their time, expertise and data; feminist author Betty Friedan, who was generous with her thoughts regarding the subject matter of this book; Leonard D'Orlando, principal of Reading High School, who allowed me to interview the students there; Elizabeth Cooper, who helped to arrange interviews with other students; Frances Burck, who arranged interviews for me and read some portions of the manuscript; and Gail Olsen, who provided prompt and accurate transcriptions of scores of interviews.

The heart of this book is the testimony of the mothers, fathers and children who shared their lives with me, and I am most grateful to them for the time they gave.

My special thanks, however, go to my husband, John, to my daughter, Katherine, and to my parents.

Contents

REMAKING MOTHERHOOD

1

"Am I Doing the Right Thing?"

Katherine was three. It was four o'clock in the afternoon. I was carrying a bundle of laundry from my bedroom to her closet when I saw her in the hallway between our room and hers. She was sitting at a small wooden drafting board that my husband and I had set up for her under a window some weeks earlier. It had a stool that allowed her to reach the surface comfortably, and we had thought she might use it to scribble in her coloring books or to draw pictures. A winter sun poured in over the drafting board and illuminated in red-gold light her tiny body bent over her task. Arrested by the scene and also by her frown of concentration, I stood there and watched. She was cutting up pieces of paper with a pair of child's scissors and was pasting some of these bits onto other larger pieces of paper with Scotch tape. The leftover scraps were periodically dispatched with a gesture that made me smile since it was a part of my own repertoire, a luxurious sweep of the arm that caused the debris—rough drafts, junk mail—to rain onto the floor, to be picked up all at once at day's end. When she had the larger papers as she wanted them, she began "writing" on them, occasionally stopping to consult her "computer"—a Speak and Spell game she had received for her birthday. Beside her on the "desk" was a light blue telephone that a year earlier had been on its way to the dump before my husband rescued it and gave it to her.

"What are you doing?" I asked quietly behind her.

She looked up, startled. "I can't talk to you right now," she said in a voice full of authority and purpose. "But as soon as I'm finished my working, I can. I have a lot of hard working to do. I have to write a article and I am going to have important phone calls, and you can't talk to me while I'm having them."

My eyes widened in amusement and surprise. I turned away quickly before she could see. But for a few changes in grammar, she had it right. The words were my words, I realized with some chagrin, the work was my work. As I had done countless times, she was writing an article and she was announcing that this was a moment when she could not be disturbed.

After that afternoon, there were many incidents that struck me with the same incompatible mix of feelings—a kind of giddy delight at her earnestness and her sense of importance, a smile at the charm of a three-year-old trying to imitate her parent, some mild embarrassment when expressions I had used in a crisis or on deadline to buy time or silence came back to haunt me, a puzzlement as to how she perceived me and my endeavors in the world, and the first stirrings of curiosity as to what it all meant. She had the persistent belief, for example, that whenever I left the house, even if I was going to a movie, I was going to my "work." She said often that she was going to grow up to be a writer ("like Mommy") and use a "typo-writer," and this occupation for many months was rivaled only by that of Supergirl. She understood that work generated income and once asked me when my husband and I were going out to dinner, "When you go get the monies, can I stay home with Daddy?" (this in lieu of a babysitter).

Presently she began to ask for an "office," which her father built for her as part of a loft-bed arrangement, and to go to it with the same frequency as she played house with Cheer Bear or went out to her swing in the backyard. She would often say, "I'm working at my office [or "my computer"] just like Mommy," and would "write" and make things while there. It wasn't so much the fact that she aped me that I found intriguing (all children imitate their parents—pretending to be "shaving" in the mirror, scolding their dolls in borrowed tones of voice); it was the nature of the activity. "Mommy works; therefore, if I want to be like Mommy, I work, too," she seemed to be saying. I found it especially interesting that although she saw me "working" at other tasks—and surely carrying heavy bags of groceries or digging up a garden might appear to be more arduous than writing an article—she never referred to these chores as "work." Work was something you did when you went to your office and wrote things and had phone calls.

One day a friend of mine came to dinner. She was the mother of an eight-year-old boy who, although exceptionally bright and engaging, had never been particularly adept at entertaining himself. And so it did not escape her notice when Katherine, seeing that we mothers were momentarily involved in meal preparation and with news of each other, went off to her "office" and began cutting and pasting and writing and drawing—or as Katherine was fond of putting it, doing her "working."

"Do you think," asked my friend, returning from a visit to my daughter's room, "that Katherine's ability to play by herself at her desk stems from seeing you creating 'work' out of unstructured time?"

I didn't know the answer, but I liked the question.

I am a working mother.* I belong, in fact, to a working mother boom. The majority of mothers in this country now work outside the home. In 1948, only 26 percent of mothers with children under the age of eighteen were in the labor force. Today more than half of that group are at the workplace. The most startling increase, however, has occurred among mothers of preschool children. In 1960—just twenty-five years ago—only 15 percent of mothers of children under the age of five had paid work outside the home. Today two-thirds of the mothers of these young children now leave their sons and daughters in the care of others and join the labor force. It is estimated by the U.S. Department of Labor that less than three years from now 75 percent of two-parent families will have both parents employed. And by 1990, it is projected that as many as half of all families in this country may be headed by

---

*I am aware of the misuse of the term "working mother." It has been said by many before me that to refer only to mothers who work outside the home as working mothers does a gross injustice to millions of mothers who rightly feel they are working quite hard in the home. The problem is a semantic one, however, and to refer constantly to "women who work outside the home" is stylistically awkward. Therefore, I try to refer, where appropriate, to "working mothers" and "at-home mothers" and to avoid the term "nonworking mothers," which seems to me to be particularly offensive.

a single parent, 90 percent of whom will be women—almost all of them working out of necessity, if not by choice. If these figures are correct, that means that by 1990, between 80 and 85 percent of all the children in this country will be growing up in the homes of working mothers. This huge outpouring of mothers from the home into the workplace is the most remarkable change in the U.S. labor force—and in the American family—in recent years.

Like other working mothers, I am concerned about the effects of my working on my child. "Am I doing the right thing?" has been for me, as it has for so many of my generation, the question of the hour since my child was born. For reasons which will be explored later, many of us have been plagued with guilt, conflict and anxiety about this un-proven path that we have taken. Because so few of us have had working-mother role models ourselves, we have felt like pioneers in an uncharted landscape. If we have been fairly sanguine about the benefits to our-selves—economic, psychological and social—of remaining in the work-place while we have families, we have been less confident about the effects on our children. On our best days, we convince ourselves that we are, at least, not harming them; in our worst hours, we are beset by gut-wrenching fears. You can get divorced and live to tell about it. You can miss out on a promotion and try again next year. You cannot, however, fail at child-rearing and sleep at night.

Perhaps that was why my friend's question was so intriguing. It stimulated me to formulate one small thought: Was it not possible that there were some *benefits* to my child—besides the obvious economic ones—of my working?

In the months that followed, that question begat many others. Al-though my curiosity stemmed initially from personal incidents in my relationship with my daughter, I soon began to wonder about an entire generation of children who were growing up in the homes of working mothers. My relationship with Katherine is not a pure example, nor do I intend for us to be neatly representative (my job does not require me to be away from her for eight or more hours a day, for instance), but we are, without question, part of a phenomenon that is changing the shape of American society as we know it.

Much has been written and said about working mothers. And most of this discussion has focused on the *absence* of the mother from the home: "How does the absence of the mother from the home affect a young child?" My concern, however, is with her *presence:* Does the *presence* of a working mother in the home have an impact on her child, and at what age and in what way is this impact expressed? Does a working mother, for example, shape the way a child perceives what mothers and women do in the world? Does her presence affect a child's cognitive, psychological and social development? Does the changing concept of motherhood affect a child's formation of his or her sex role? Will sexual stereotypes be erased or reinforced by the presence of a working mother in nearly two-thirds of American families? And are the effects on children different if the mother works part-time as opposed to full-time?

The questions that prompted this book began as small signposts on well-worn paths, when almost at once I found myself in a maze of unfamiliar trails, some interconnecting—indeed, leading to new avenues of thought—and others, like *cul de sacs,* with no clear answers at the end. I began to wonder that if it were true that the traditional mother model had prepared girls for subservient roles in society, would the nontraditional working mother encourage a daughter to adopt an achieving, competent, nontraditional role? Would it alter how that girl thought of herself in relation to male children and ultimately to men —and would it enhance her self-esteem? If the current generation of working mothers grew up believing that becoming a breadwinner required adopting a male role model, would their daughters see becoming a breadwinner as incorporating a female role? Do working mothers beget more working mothers, and will these daughters, as they mature, experience less of the guilt and conflict regarding the combining of working and mothering that have so plagued our generation?

And what of the effects on boys? Will sons who grow up with a working mother accept it as a given that women work, and will that construct make them, as men, more aware at home, in the workplace and in the political arena of the needs of working mothers? As working mothers pursue success in the workplace (and as fathers take on more of the childcare tasks as a consequence of the mother's working outside the house), will children come to regard male and female roles as interchangeable—indeed, will the parental role become to a large degree an androgynous one? Will sons of fathers who share parenting tasks grow up to be more nurturing men themselves?

The notion of a more androgynous parental role led to a particularly compelling path of speculation: Will children pattern themselves after their mothers and fathers in a way they never have before? Will motherhood be perceived as being closer to our current notion of fatherhood? Will children begin to experience their mothers in the same way a previous generation experienced their fathers?

Inevitably some of the questions necessitated several detours. If the working mother presents her child with more options, will he or she be able to meet the challenge of having so many choices? May not a child be overwhelmed by having to live up to the standards of two achieving parents? And if the mother is largely absent, will it matter to the child if others are able to provide loving and nurturing when she is away? Finally, do the potential benefits of having a working mother *present* in the home outweigh the consequences of her *absence* for eight hours a day?

In the end, I discovered that all roads led to one central question: *Will today's children grow up with fundamentally different notions of mothers, fathers, women, men, self, society, work, home and family than any generation before them?* What exactly will these notions be, and will they make our children better persons, parents, bosses and workers than we are? Will these changing perceptions create a healthier society? Will the world as we know it be recognizable in thirty years' time? Twenty years' time? Ten years' time?

In 1984, when Katherine was four and in nursery school, her teacher asked the class what they thought were the proper roles of men and women, mothers and fathers. Katherine's answers were as follows: Dad cooks the meals; Dad goes to the supermarket; Mom drives; Dad mows the lawn; Mom does the laundry; Dad gets the kids dressed; Dad's job is taking photographs; Mom's job is getting the money; Dad changes diapers; Dad fixes doorknobs. Had I had to answer the same questions when I was four (which would have been in 1950), my answers would have been these: Mom cooks the meals; Mom goes to the supermarket; Dad drives; Dad mows the lawn; Mom does the laundry; Mom gets the kids dressed; Dad's job is getting the money; Mom's job is taking care of the house and the children; Mom changes diapers; Dad fixes doorknobs. It wouldn't have mattered whether or not you were asking me to respond solely in terms of my own family or for all families, such as I understood them to be. My answers would have been the same.

In 1950, my answers would have been unremarkable and quite common to my generation. I was born in 1946, the first year of the "baby boom." I grew up on a very average middle-class street in a middle-class suburb of Boston. Most of the houses on the street were small bungalows or variations of the two-bedroom Cape Cod.

My mother had worked briefly in a bank during World War II, but did not work outside the home ever again once she was married. She had three daughters, myself the eldest, and considered her role to be that of mother and homemaker. (During our childhood years she made custom drapes for a short time in order to earn extra money, but she did this work at night after we had gone to bed.) My father was an airline pilot, a profession he pursued until he retired at age sixty. He was the breadwinner in the family and did not participate in routine homemaking or child-rearing tasks, with the exception of assuming the traditional male role of being a teacher of morals and values, and of being a disciplinarian. We three girls considered my father (as we did my mother) to be quite special, and we had a lot of fun with him as kids, horsing around and going camping with him; but to my knowledge he never changed a diaper, fed a child a bottle, put a load of laundry into a washing machine, or dressed a child for school. Once he gave me a bath (a memorable occasion on which he used a scrub brush instead of a washcloth) and once he cooked a meal when my mother was in the hospital having my younger sister—which he has yet to live down, as he made a macaroni-and-cheese dinner (from a box) using bacon fat instead of butter. My father was a good pilot, a gifted artist, a remarkably hard worker and a talented handyman, but in the realm of "women's work," as it was then known, he was notoriously incompetent. Interestingly, however, we thought little about this, if at all. The fact that he was incompetent—or, more to the point, nonparticipatory —in household tasks never even registered, since fathers just simply *didn't do* that sort of thing. Likewise, it never even occurred to us that my mother might be ambitious enough to want to pursue a successful career. She kept a clean house, she cooked tasty meals, she was always there in the afternoons when we came home from school with our needs and with our stories, and although she had a great many talents and a keen interest in politics, her active endeavors related, without exception, to the keeping of the home and the rearing of the children. For much of my childhood, she did not even drive a car.

What is interesting about this portrait is that it was completely uninteresting at the time. Everyone on the street was doing the same thing. All of the fathers went off to work and all of the mothers stayed home. The fathers were the breadwinners and the achievers, and the mothers were the nurturers. Income came by way of the father's job or not at all. As children of the 1950s, we clearly understood this division of labor. Little girls would grow up to be mothers and home-makers, and little boys would grow up to have jobs and careers. Fathers didn't cook meals and mothers didn't go off to earn money. For the most part, this pattern on my street was repeated throughout my town. There were no working mothers of the children in my first-grade class or throughout my elementary years, and, indeed, I never met anyone who had a working mother until the eighth grade, when I made friends with a girl whose mother worked as a part-time salesclerk in a dress store *during school hours only.* Although, as I shall discuss in a minute, there have always been working mothers in the working class, and although there have been exceptions to the norm among all classes, this was the pattern, by and large, in middle-class homes throughout the entire country.

As girl children, we were encouraged to do well in school, particularly after 1957, when *Sputnik* was launched and the country entered a panicky race to "catch up" to the Russians. But it was understood that if you did well in school, your options were limited. You could be a teacher, a nurse or an "executive secretary." To the best of my knowledge, not one girl in my high school graduating class of over three hundred students in 1964 ever even entertained the notion of becoming an engineer or a lawyer or a doctor—and certainly not a mail carrier or a telephone lineswoman or the head of a corporation.

Moreover, we were not expected to make a lifelong commitment to work in the way that boys were. (In fact, in some families of both boys and girls, it was not uncommon for the boys, and not the girls, to get the college education.) Instead, we were expected to make our lifelong commitments to husbands and children. As a result of this notion, when I got to college, I had two goals. One was spoken and one was unspoken. The spoken goal was that I had to have a teaching certificate by the time I graduated. The unspoken goal was that I also had to have a husband—or at least the prospect of one—before commencement. During my four years of college—from 1964 to 1968—I also developed literary interests and was witness to a maelstrom of growing political activity. As a result of all these expectations and interests and forces, I found myself, the last semester of my senior year, pursuing four simultaneous endeavors: I was student-teaching at a suburban high school to gain my teaching certificate; I was madly reading Thoreau for an honor's thesis on that author, though I had no plans to continue my studies; I was following with keen interest the events at Columbia in the spring of 1968 as well as those of the new SDS chapter at my school; and I was preparing for a wedding that would take place, believe it or not, the day after I graduated from college. I tell this bit of personal history not because it was exceptional, but, to the contrary, because I think I was quite typical of my generation. My activities during my last semester in 1968 strike me now, in retrospect, as a perfect example of someone caught in the wringer of social change.

I am part of a cohort (as sociologists like to call such groups) of women who were children in the 1950s and 1960s and who came of age in the late 1960s and early 1970s. Much has been written about the size of the baby boom and its resulting impact on education, politics, economics and the media. The most salient fact about this group to which I belong, however, is that we matured during a period of head-spinning social revolution. We were brought up in homes that promoted the notions of a domestic life for women, of male superiority in the home and in society, of the validity of the male-dominated workplace and of limited options for female children. In the twenty years that intervened between 1960 and 1980, however, this group either participated in or was witness to the civil rights movement; the war in Vietnam; the political protests of the late 1960s that stemmed from these two events; the erosion of confidence in what came to be called "establishment" practices as a consequence of both the Vietnam war and the Watergate scandal; the pervasive consciousness-raising of the women's movement; the sexual revolution; the disintegration of stability in marriage, the resulting high divorce rate and the realization that marriage no longer offered economic security; the erosion of the economy and the subsequent rise of the two-paycheck family; the expansion of career and work opportunities for women; the loss of support for female domesticity; the flooding of women into the work-place, and into previously male-dominated fields; the delaying of child-bearing until the thirties, and, finally, at the tail end of the 1970s, the working-mother boom. Little girls who thought they would have four kids and grow up in a house just like the one on "Father Knows Best" now have one child, a job and the economic necessity to bring home a paycheck in order to make mortgage payments on a house that is smaller than the one they grew up in. Daughters who were told that if they did exceptionally well in school they might grow up to be teachers now run corporations. Women who thought they would have marriages like their parents that lasted for fifty years are now twice-divorced and single-handedly raising their own children. The majority of an entire generation of girl children who grew up with fixed traditional expectations gradually found a familiar world turned upside down and are now struggling to find a comfortable and productive place in a new and different society. Most of them are combining mothering and working. And they have had few, if any, role models to show them how to do it. For this group, "Change is a dominant motif," says Kathleen Gerson, assistant professor of sociology at New York University, in her book, *Hard Choices:* "[The women of this cohort] found themselves leading far different adult lives than the ones they had imagined as children. Although they had expected and planned for motherhood and domesticity, social circumstances intervened to push these women off a traditional path. . . .

"The combined effect of all these changes has a number of important implications for women's lives. Most obvious, a growing proportion of women—even among those who were raised to prepare themselves for a life centered around full-time mothering—are increasingly likely to find their lives centered as much on the workplace as on the home. Personal independence and commitments outside the home will continue to take on greater importance in women's lives, and motherhood is not likely to command the central place in the vast majority of women's lives that it did thirty years ago."[1]

In a study of this group of women she undertook to better understand what caused them to make their life choices, Dr. Gerson found that the vast majority of them had been raised to assume a domestic lifestyle, but most of these women had forsworn this traditional path in adulthood. "Among these women who began their adult lives with traditional (if sometimes vague) notions of domesticity as their ultimate goal, two-thirds developed nondomestic orientations as their lives proceeded. Over time, these respondents developed strong ties to the workplace and usually high ambitions as well. . . . This group, above all others, exemplifies the processes and structural underpinnings of the subtle revolution now occurring in women's lives."[2]

Dr. Grace Baruch and her colleagues, Dr. Rosalind Barnett and Caryl Rivers, also documented this revolution in a study of women they conducted and reported on in their book *Lifeprints*. "When the women in our study were growing up, working women were the 'deviant' group, and they often felt isolated and stigmatized. Today, however, it is the homemakers in our sample who often feel alone and misunderstood by those around them, while working women are experiencing a newfound sense of support. These trends are not likely to be reversed in the years ahead. . . ."

The women themselves are not unmindful of this revolution. As one working mother of a six-year-old from Boston put it, "I think it's analogous to how I perceived the Vietnam war. It was a tremendously significant transitional period in our lives, but I didn't realize it at the time. Now I see it, ten years after the fact. I have a feeling the same thing is happening now, with this boom in working mothers. I have this sense of being an individual in this very important whole. And only later will we really see the magnitude of it all."

A thirty-five-year-old editor in New York—the mother of two pre-school girls—agrees. "What we're going through now—all these changes, the way this is going to affect our children—it's huge. It's colossal."

Most of the mothers of the current generation of working mothers stayed home to have children and to care for those children until they left the nest. By contrast, most mothers today dress in business or work attire in the morning, share cornflakes with their children, kiss them good-bye, and go off to jobs as factory workers, doctors, policewomen, guidance counselors, lawyers, politicians, bureaucrats, secretaries, corporate executives and waitresses. Sometimes the children understand the nature of the job and sometimes they don't (in the same way we, as children, grew to have a better understanding of what our fathers did as we matured), but most understand that the mother is going to her work and that she will come home to them.

If both mother and father work full-time, the child is in another person's care for at least eight hours. The mother may arrive home, at the babysitter's or at the day-care center at about 6 P.M. For the two and one-half or three hours remaining until the child's bedtime, the role the mother will perform will be a nurturing one, and if there is a father in the home, the parental roles may be interchangeable. Both parents may help to prepare the meal. Both parents may play with the child. The parents may take turns giving the child a bath and reading to her or him. Often both parents are present for the bedtime ritual. Even on weekends, both parents may share child-rearing and meal preparation (yet, as we shall see, women still perform more household tasks than do men). Although the child will know that the parents have different personalities, likes and dislikes, he or she is aware that both parents work and that both parents are nurturers. More to the point, she or he will be aware that the mother performs two functions: She leaves the house to work, and then she comes home to take care of the child—a fundamental perception that differs markedly from that of the children of a previous generation.

Unlike their own mothers, who defined themselves primarily as wives and mothers, this generation of working mothers defines themselves as mothers and workers (rarely as wives), and sometimes as professionals with high ambitions. Many of these women pursue what they think of as careers with commitment and the special kind of self-identification that having a career entails. Others who might not necessarily define themselves as having a "career" take pride in their work, and find satisfaction in its economic and social compensations. These notions of pride, competence and achievement (and their counterparts of stress, frustration and disappointment in the workplace) are not lost on the children.

2

But Mothers Have Always Worked...

*T*hroughout history, women have always worked—both inside and outside the home. In traditional, nonindustrial societies, women have been a central part of hunter-gatherer and agricultural economies. They have grown crops, gathered firewood, tended farm animals, built houses, made cloth, fashioned utensils, traded goods, sold produce, earned cash and, of course, tended to the home and children. In some rural societies of Africa, it is still possible to see this traditional way of life in operation. Rural Kikuyu women in Kenya, for example, are the mainstay of their agricultural economy. They grow maize and beans for subsistence and for market, harvest the crops, build mud-and-wattle huts, make their brightly colored clothes, take their produce to market and aggressively sell it there, carry great burdens of faggots gleaned from the woods to fuel their fires, and sometimes walk for hours, and even days, to fetch water for their families. The women depend for childcare upon extended family members, their own older children and other women in the community. In direct contrast to most Western societies, the women, for the most part, support the family. No longer needed as hunters or warriors and not yet having secured a place in post-colonial Kenya, men in the rural areas often pursue one of two paths: They either leave their families to work as servants and factory workers in Nairobi, sending home from time to time portions of pitiful wages; or they sit under baobab and acacia trees, trading yarns with other "unemployed warriors," much like retired cronies might gather around a chess table in an urban park. Many of them drink to escape the boredom.

Although certain aspects of this rural Kikuyu society are unique to the twentieth century (the superannuated role of the male, for example), the role of woman as worker is not. Prior to the Industrial Revolution, woman's place may have been in the home,[1] but that home was an economic hub, a mini cottage industry in which both the man and the woman—and all but the very youngest children—contributed to the economic well-being of the family unit. (Girls, in fact, were routinely trained by their mothers for the adult world of work.)[2] It was not until the Industrial Revolution, when paid work outside the home was offered, that the home and the workplace were irrevocably separated. Even so, in the early years of the Industrial Revolution, women and children worked alongside men in the factories until wages increased enough to allow a man to support his family.[3] Many women, of course, were never able to leave the factories, and there has always—ever since the Industrial Revolution—been a significant portion of women from the working class who have worked outside the home in low-paying jobs.[4]

The notion of the middle-class home, in which the woman's role is primarily that of a support to her husband and children, is a relatively recent phenomenon. It wasn't until the mid-nineteenth century that a woman's exclusive job became that of caring for men and children in the home. (By the turn of the century, only 20 percent of American women worked outside the home in paid jobs.[5]) Men were expected to support the family financially, and the woman's sole occupation was to be wife, mother and homemaker. As a result of this division of labor, a peculiar ideology emerged: Women, and women only, were uniquely morally qualified to raise children and to protect the home from the corruption of society. This belief was soon translated to mean that mothering was a woman's highest priority.[6] So entrenched, in fact, was this ideology that during the Victorian era women came to be defined by the milestones of their reproductive years—puberty, marriage, childbearing and menopause[7]—the legacy of which we are not entirely free from, even today.

Despite this burgeoning belief in the sanctity of motherhood, however, women have always been shuttled in and out of the labor force as the economy has decreed. They were shuttled in when needed during World War I and forced out by the Armistice in 1918. They were hired back in large numbers during World War II (the image of Rosie the Riveter comes to mind), both to fill jobs vacated by men and to take on the increasing numbers of pink-collar jobs (clerks, typists, secretaries and receptionists) that were developing as a result of post-industrial capitalism.[8] By the end of World War II, six million women were in the work force.

By 1946, however, women were again back in the home, this time ensconced in a landscape specifically designed for the post-war family —suburbia. They were not needed and not wanted in the work force —except in pink-collar jobs—and the old ideology that woman's place was in the home (and that children could be raised only by at-home mothers), which had proved so successful in keeping them there in Victorian society, once again became a nearly patriotic imperative for American women. In 1947, barely 30 percent of American women worked outside the home, and nearly all of these women were either unmarried or in low-paying blue-collar or pink-collar jobs. During the late 1940s, the 1950s and most of the 1960s, the concept of the nuclear family—with its at-home mother, its breadwinning, absent father and its evenly spaced children—became an American ideal, and, for the most part, an American reality. This was the era that gave birth to the baby boom, fostered the notion of a child-centered household and legitimized, indeed sanctified, the concept of the full-time housewife-mother.[9] This was also the era during which most of the women who are working mothers today came of age.

It wasn't until a particularly powerful combination of economic and social forces in the late 1960s and early 1970s merged that women began entering the work force again in any substantial numbers. Historians say that a number of factors contributed to these social changes: the expansion of the pink-collar pool (the housewife of the 1950s was well qualified—she was trained to take orders from men)[10]; the rise of a consumer society and the subsequent inability of one paycheck to pay for appliances, furniture and two cars—not to mention college educations for growing children; runaway inflation; the post–World War II

higher educational attainment of women; the tendency to delay childbearing and to have fewer children; and the political, social and psychological changes that followed in the wake of the publication of Betty
Friedan's *The Feminine Mystique* in 1963. These same historians,
however, do not agree on the relative weight to give to the various
causative factors. Some believe that economic motives spawned the
women's movement; others vehemently maintain that without the
women's movement, women would never have entered the work force
in such large numbers—and certainly not in formerly male-dominated
occupations.

Whatever weight one ultimately assigns to the reasons for women
entering the work force, fifty million American women were working
full-time by October 1984. It is estimated that 90 percent of the girls
now coming of age in this country will both work in the labor force and
have families—and most of them expect to perform these tasks simultaneously.

WOMEN HAVE ALWAYS WORKED, BUT . . .

Although it is accurate to say that women have always worked, the
recent boom in working mothers differs both in magnitude and character from any era prior to this one. Never before have so many mothers
worked outside the home in nondomestic tasks. The percentage of
mothers with children under eighteen who are employed has risen from
26 percent in 1948, to 35 percent in 1970, to 49 percent in 1975 to
well over 50 percent today.[11] The largest increase in women workers
since 1950 has been among married women, mothers with children at
home and women between the ages of twenty-five and forty-four.[12] As
I mentioned earlier, the most dramatic demographic change has involved women with children under the age of three. While in generations past it was acceptable to work only once the children were in
school (and then necessarily only part-time), we have recently wit-
nessed an unparalleled increase in the number of women leaving their
young children in surrogate care while they themselves go off to work
for eight or more hours a day. The biggest surge of mothers of preschoolers into the work force dates from 1979–80. Susan Weissman,
director of the Park Center day-care centers in New York City, who

began her centers in response to what she saw as an explosion of working mothers with young children, is among those who date the working-mother boom to 1980. "It's just since 1980 that these abrupt changes [among mothers of preschool children] have happened," she says. "When I was doing my marketing research in 1979–80, I was astounded by what appeared to be an incredible boom in the number of women with young children who were returning to work." According to Census Bureau figures, the number of working women with children under the age of five increased from 4.7 million in 1977 to six million in June 1982. Moreover, 52 percent of women over thirty who had given birth the previous year were in the work force in June 1984. In 1976—just eight years earlier—the comparable figure was 28 percent.

Of equal importance to the magnitude of these social changes, however, is the character of them. Unlike women's work of previous eras, women's work in America today does not center primarily on the home. The women who consider themselves workers today do not perform tasks, as do the Kikuyu women, that are home-based and home-centered. Aside from earning cash to support the household, the contemporary working mother differs as much from these traditional women as she does from the pre-Industrial Revolution woman who worked at a variety of tasks, but whose work was home-based. Today's mother leaves the home to go to work, in the same way that men ever since the Industrial Revolution have left the home to go to factories and corporations.

Not only does she leave the home in a manner once reserved for men, but the working mother is entering (and has entered) professions and positions in the work force that were once the exclusive province of men. No longer is a working mother almost certain to join the work force in the service professions (teachers, nurses or social workers), as a factory worker or as a secretary. Instead she is joining as a mail carrier, a typesetter or a lawyer. In the spring of 1986, women surpassed men in the professions. Women now make up 25 percent of the work force in such male-dominated fields as accounting and computer science. From 1972 to 1982, the number of women lawyers increased fivefold. From 1962 to 1982, the proportion of women among engineers rose from 1 percent to 6 percent; mail carriers, 3 to 17 percent; physicians, 6 to 15 percent; insurance agents, 10 to 26 percent; and college teachers, 19 to

25 percent. Moreover, the nature of the relationship on the part of women to their work has changed. Women now resemble male workers in the strength of their commitment to the workplace and in the nature of their steady, full-time employment. Today, work-life expectancy of women is only ten years behind that of men. In 1959, work-life expectancy for women was nearly thirty years behind that of men.

Perhaps one of the most important ways in which the character of the working mother has changed relates to her self-perceptions about her work life. No longer defining herself solely in terms of her reproductive capacities and her homemaking abilities, today's working mother sees herself as both a breadwinner and mother. Never before have so many women pursued what they think of as careers. Many have social ties to the workplace (in the same way that men do) that often rival their ties at home. They think in terms of upward mobility, and they have career goals for which they strive and which they communicate to their families. They see themselves as lifelong workers who will continue to work even when their families are grown.

Women who work in working-class trades and jobs also think of themselves as having "careers." If a career is a chosen path or life work, then many working-class women can be said to have careers—and, in fact, do define themselves that way. Thus a secretary becomes a "promotion coordinator" or a "business manager" by self-definition. A typesetter may look forward to the day when she will be a supervisor. There are entry-level positions and for some the possibility of forward movement. There may be a sense of a lifelong commitment either to the development of skills, the enhancement of one's professional position, the improvement of one's salary or to the company itself. There may be the recognition of important social ties and of work-related benefits. Even women who do not think of themselves as ambitious have a changed self-image as a result of being in the work force. Both the women's movement and the publicity that has surrounded the recent full-scale entry of women into the workplace have combined to enlarge the range and number of self-defined "careers" for women. Working mothers who, in years past, would not have considered themselves as having a profession now define themselves in much the same way that men in previous generations did. And, as we shall see later, it is the woman's *perception* of her work life that matters most in terms of the effects of that mother's work on her children.

This isn't to say that equality has been achieved in the workplace, or that all women can take pride in their work. Hundreds of thousands of working women remain underpaid and undervalued. As a whole, women still earn only sixty-four cents to the dollar for men, and at least half of all women today still work in either clerical, service or sales jobs. Yet even with this pervasive inequality, the changes that have taken place, both in real terms and in self-perceptions, have been dramatic. A woman whose mother never worked, but who is herself an administrative secretary with a lifelong commitment to remain with her company, perceives her life as being very different from her mother's. A saleswoman at a department store, who has her eye on the position of department manager or buyer at some point in the future, perceives herself, despite her low-paying position, as having a career in retail sales. While the women of this generation have often compared their financial positions and job opportunities to those of men and have come up short, they have also compared their financial positions, job opportunities, work commitment and increased skills to those of the women of previous generations, and have felt pride in their accomplishments.

The character of mothers working also differs substantially from that of previous eras because of the prevalence of working mothers. Today most mothers work, and the stay-at-home mom is increasingly becoming part of an elite group. According to Lois Hoffman, a research scientist at the University of Michigan and one of the foremost experts on working mothers today, "The role of the present-day nonemployed mothers may be as new as the role of the majority of present-day mothers who are employed."[13] A majority of both working (59 percent) and at-home (57 percent) mothers surveyed by *Newsweek* in 1986 said they thought it had become less socially acceptable to stay at home with children. Seventy-one percent of the at-home mothers said they would like to work.

When a pattern becomes the norm, its potential for harmful effects on any given individual diminishes. The effect on a child whose mother works when the pattern is rare is significantly different from the effect on that same child when the pattern is pervasive. Thus working mothers feel more comfortable about working today than working mothers did in previous generations. Likewise, the child who shares his first-grade classroom with other children of working mothers feels more

comfortable than the child who is the only one in his class with a
working mother.

At the same time that women have been committing themselves to
lifelong work outside the home—in stark contrast to women of previous
generations—they have also been committing themselves to children.
Although the birth rate has declined since 1960, and although women
have demonstrated a tendency to delay childbearing (between 1972
and 1982, the rate of first births for women in their thirties rose 50
percent; the rate of first births for women in their late thirties rose 83
percent), women still expect to raise families. Among women ages
eighteen to thirty-four, 90 percent expect to have children, thus quash-
ing the idea that today's woman puts work before children. In fact,
according to one study, the role of employee becomes primary only
when the roles of wife and mother are absent from the woman's current
life. In this study of Chicago working women between the ages of
twenty-five and fifty-four, only 14 percent put work before children on
the scale of priorities.[14] Rather, the contemporary working mother sees
herself, again in contrast to the majority of women in previous generations, as being both a worker and a nurturer, a breadwinner and a
mother, and these dual roles define her life.

That women's commitment to children is stronger than that to work
is not surprising, given the expectations that this generation of women
grew up with in the 1950s and the intimate and powerful nature of the
mother-child bond; but to commit oneself to children *instead* of work
does not reflect the reality of a woman's life. The female child growing
up today can look forward to a life span of nearly eighty years. The time
she will spend bearing and raising children will account for no more
than a quarter of those years. To render herself unemployable either
during those years or after them is becoming increasingly risky. Few of
the girl children being raised today will be able to afford to turn their
backs on the work force.

THE BACKLASH . . .

At the same time that we are receiving evidence from all sides that our
daughters must be prepared for a life of work, however, we find ourselves in the midst of a backlash against working mothers. A relatively

recent phenomenon—and perhaps the natural reaction to any controversial sociological development, or possibly a part of what appears to
be a growing conservative movement in this country—the backlash is,
nevertheless, distressing and unnerving in the obstacles it presents to
the forward momentum of women in the workplace.

On a recent popular morning talk show, televised nationally, a woman
who had written a book extolling the virtues of mothers remaining in
the home with their children rather than entering the work force
shared the stage with six "experts" in childcare, all of whom promoted
the belief that working mothers were harmful to children. In an atmosphere of fervor, passion and righteousness, during which no studies
were cited, working mothers were blamed for juvenile delinquency, the
breakdown of the American family and chartreuse Mohawk hairstyles,
not necessarily in that order. (I am not aware that the similarly disrepu-
table "D.A."—or "duck's ass" haircut—so prevalent in my childhood
was ever blamed on the fact that almost all mothers then stayed home.)
    The notion that women might reasonably be able to combine work-
ing and mothering has been assaulted as "mythic" and dangerous in
a plethora of magazine and newspaper articles, television and radio
shows and books. Women who have tried to do both have been accused
of attempting the impossible—wanting to be "superwomen"—and of
being selfish, self-obsessed and an integral component of "the culture
of narcissism." Proponents of these ideas suggest that women not only
can't do both (which is referred to, more often than not, as trying to
"do it all," as though women were greedier than men), but that they
shouldn't even be trying. Blame is assigned to the mother, whose reach
exceeds her grasp, but not to the employer or to her male partner, both
of whom have been remarkably slow to facilitate her entry into the
workplace and to ease the burden of domestic chores. "Women today
. . . are considered unmotherly if they demand day-care centers, [and]
greedy and unreasonable if they expect help from husbands," writes
Nancy Chodorow, author of *The Reproduction of Mothering.*
    Although current data show a clear trend for women's commitment
to work to converge soon with that of men's,[15] it is still considered
"normal" for women to remain at home with young children. Despite
a great deal of evidence to the contrary, there is a pervasive belief in
this country that working mothers are harming their children. In a

recent survey conducted by the Public Agenda Foundation, a nonprofit organization headed by Daniel Yankelovich, 63 percent of working men and 52 percent of working women said that having a mother who works outside the home is bad for children less than six years of age. According to Dr. J. Brooks-Gunn, a senior research scientist at the Educational Testing Service in Princeton, New Jersey, the notion of the mothers of preschool children working outside the home provokes negative reaction even on the part of some social scientists who have read the evidence to the contrary. "You have to ask yourself why, in the face of everything we know about the effects of working mothers on children, people still persist in thinking that it's wrong," Dr. Brooks-Gunn says. "I have colleagues who will say to me, 'Yes, I see the evidence, and I've read it, but somehow *in my heart,* I can't believe that it's right.' "

Two possibilities have been put forth for the contradiction inherent in these passionately held—but not intellectually held—beliefs. The first is attributed to the social conditioning of the person holding the beliefs. Most adults today were raised to believe that a mother's place was in the home, and that a father's place, and his alone, was in the work force. These ideas, because they were presented to us during our formative years, remain potent, despite later rejection of them intellectually. The second is a suggestion made by Dr. Lawrence Balter, professor of educational psychology at New York University: "As children, we often feel that we don't have enough of mother. All children feel this way to a greater or lesser extent. These feelings often lie dormant until we have children ourselves, when many feelings that have been buried since childhood are suddenly triggered. When this feeling of not having had enough of mother is triggered, instead of recognizing it as pertaining to ourselves, we project this feeling onto our children. Therefore no matter what we do, we often feel that we aren't giving them enough mothering. This feeds into the guilt of the working mother and may serve to bolster the opinion on the part of some men that mothers of young children should not work."

There has been a persistent refusal on the part of male partners to share the domestic "servant" tasks with working mothers. Although more men now share more child-rearing tasks than they used to, in fact women continue to bear the burden of household chores. In a study of 651 employees of an unidentified company, conducted by Boston

University's School of Social Work, researchers found that women work twice as many hours on homemaking and child care as men. This was true even of women whose income was equal to or greater than that of the spouse. Married female parents spent eighty-five hours per week at work and family tasks. Married male parents spent sixty-six hours per week. This unequal burden has resulted in a focus on the stress and frustration of trying to juggle the dual roles of worker and mother, but one which fails to assess appropriate blame for the problem. The unwillingness of men to participate in domestic chores or to relinquish the superior nonservant position in the family has contributed to a feeling of nostalgia for the "good old days" when Mom was in the kitchen instead of at the office.

There has been an equally persistent and pervasive refusal on the part of corporate America to facilitate flexible scheduling, part-time work or job-sharing—all schemes that would better allow both men and women to share parenting tasks adequately when young children are at home. Moreover, there has been relatively little support for corporate-sponsored childcare. Programs which have been proposed—on-site day-care or flexible benefits which allow an employee to use benefit money for childcare rather than duplicating a spouse's benefits—have been slow in coming to fruition. Rather than blaming themselves for failing to acknowledge that half their work force has the primary responsibility to bear and raise children, the reaction within American corporations has been one of a backlash. Working mothers who will not work ten-hour days, who request part-time work during their children's infant and toddler years or who stay home when their children are sick are often regarded with annoyance and disdain by managers and colleagues alike. Worse, for all their struggles, they are accused of setting back opportunities for other women at the workplace. At the heart of this reactionary attitude toward any special needs that working mothers might have is the suggestion that women ought not to be trying to combine work and mothering. Thus women are made to feel guilty for not fitting into a corporate situation that was never designed for them in the first place and has made few alterations to accommodate them.

Working mothers have become complacent in thinking that the rights and opportunities that women have won for themselves cannot be taken away from them—or put another way, that women will never go home again unless they choose to do so for their own reasons. But women in the past have been shown to have remarkably little free will when it comes to entering and leaving the work force. If this nascent backlash gathers momentum, women risk losing not only everything they themselves have struggled so hard to attain, but worse, they run the risk of shutting off, before their children have even had a chance to sample them, a wide and fulfilling range of choices. If daughters grow up believing that working and mothering cannot be successfully combined, they may turn their backs on either the world of work and the fulfillment there, or on one of the greatest joys life has to offer— that of giving birth and of raising children. Love and work have long been thought to be essential to one's mental health. How remarkable, then, that women were excluded from this prescription, and that now that they've begun to fill it, they may have it snatched away from them. In *Lifeprints,* referred to earlier, the authors documented the funda- mental importance of both love and work—those twin pillars of mental and emotional well-being—to women. In a study of three hundred women, the authors found that in order to feel good about themselves, many women needed to understand and develop *both* aspects of their lives. (Of course, "work" in this context is not inclusive of situations in which a woman does not enjoy her job or feels exploited or like a mindless drone in a dehumanizing environment. The love-plus-work axiom presupposes that one's job inspires positive internal responses and fosters an attractive self-image.)

The backlash against working mothers promotes the idea that such mothers are a disaster for children, and it blames a host of society's ills on the phenomenon. But the evidence simply doesn't lend support to the idea that working mothers are harmful. To the contrary, the evi- dence suggests that the working mother is a necessary and not un- healthy addition to the American family, that the benefits of her working *for herself and for her children* outweigh the disadvantages, and that she has the potential, by her very presence, for promoting a more egalitarian society in which both men and women will have available to them a wider range of options.

A MORE POSITIVE LOOK . . .

Until recently, developmental psychologists were not as concerned about the effects of the parental role on young children as they were about other matters, such as sleep patterns, visual development and auditory stimulation. It is only in the last decade that professional journals have begun to reflect an interest in how a working mother shapes a child's psychology and personality. This research has begun to focus on the areas of self-esteem, cognitive development, verbal development, I.Q., reading ability, aptitude and achievement, egalitarian role orientations, traditional and nontraditional career choices and educational attainment.[16]

Prior to this research, working mothers were not thought to enhance a child's life in ways other than providing additional family income. The only benefits that were cited were to a working mother herself. Children were viewed as either holding their own despite their mother's absence or as victims of maternal deprivation. At best, all a working mother could hope for was not to do any serious damage.

Today we know that this bleak view is not a correct one. To the contrary, there is a considerable amount of research supporting the idea that the children of working mothers do not just hold their own—they do quite well. Preliminary evidence, which this book will examine critically in later chapters, appears to suggest that both daughters and sons benefit from having a working mother. Daughters of working mothers, for example, appear to be more independent, outgoing, have more ambitious career aspirations, attain a higher level of educational achievement, have a wider range of career options, admire their mothers more and have more respect for women's capabilities. Independent and achieving mothers engender similar qualities in daughters, and the girl children of working mothers, say researchers, have a greater sense of mastery and power than their counterparts.

Although the findings for daughters are almost always more dramatic than the findings for sons, the sons of working mothers have been found to have less stereotypical ideas about men and women and their own future role in society than their peers who live in homes with at-home mothers, to regard nurturing as a viable option for a male and to be more sensitized to the needs of working mothers. Both sons and daughters of working mothers appear to show positive differences in cognitive development, and across the board they are reported to be more independent and reliable.

Children's perceptions of mothers and women are markedly different than they were for a previous generation. Both sons and daughters today are being socialized to possess characteristics that will help them in the work force as well as in parenting. And they are, as a result of having a working mother in the home, growing up with a sense of the value of working. Child specialists also believe that as more children grow up in the families of working mothers, both boys and girls will find it easier to balance their masculine and feminine characteristics than their parents did. Says Dr. E. Kirsten Dahl, an assistant professor of anthropology at Yale University's Child Study Center: "No one, even in more traditional families, is totally masculine or feminine. We all have within us these two forces. The recognition of certain masculine traits troubled women of my generation. But the children of this generation may not see feminine and masculine traits as being so irreconcilable."

These same child specialists also suggest that the next generation of women, as a result of being less troubled about pursuing both "masculine" and "feminine" endeavors, will be able more easily to combine career and family life—a juggling act that is difficult for many women today and often leads to feelings of inadequacy, stress and guilt. "The daughters of women today are more assertive and have a clearer sense of themselves," says feminist author Betty Friedan. "They will have both their careers and their children without guilt."

In addition to certain specific effects on individual children in individual families, there is a ripple effect from the presence of the working mother in the home. The father who, unlike his own father, discovers the pleasures of active participation in the care of his children (because he was either encouraged to or required to by the exigencies of having a working spouse) is enlarging the scope of possibilities for his own son, and giving him something many of the men of my generation never had—a certain innate comfort with the nurturing role. Children who grow up with parents who are both breadwinners and nurturers may adopt less rigidly stereotypical roles as they mature themselves. "The thawing of stereotypical parental roles makes the androgynous image more real and more prevalent for the child," says Dr. Kyle Pruett, clinical professor of psychiatry at the Yale Child Study Center, and the author of *The Nurturing Father*. "A generation ago, such an image was considered dangerous and frightening. Today, however, it is seen as attractive—even chic."

Typically the concerns that child psychologists and other personnel who work with children have about toddlers and preschoolers are more dramatic than the issue of role models; child abuse, sexual abuse or the gross neglect that occurs in a small minority of families are far more urgent concerns, for example. The impact of the new mother model is a relatively recent area of investigation, quietly giving rise to speculation about the future of the next generation. And yet it may turn out, in the end, to have the most far-reaching consequences of all. If the children in so many families across the nation are growing up with the notion that women work as a matter of course, that women are just as competent as men and that girls will be workers when they grow up (or, in the case of boys, that they will marry women who will work), won't the future society that they shape be markedly different from our own?

I am a journalist and a reporter, not a researcher or a psychologist. The questions that I raise, and the answers I present, stem from interviews with (or my reading of) child specialists, as well as historians, social scientists, psychologists, political economists and many others whose work deals either centrally or peripherally with the issue of the working mother in our society. But though this book will contain primary research and facts gleaned from talks with dozens of experts, it has been my experience that if you want to know what is happening to mothers and children, you begin first by going directly to the source.

3

Mothers and Daughters: Voices

Sue, 31, Typesetter*

I am committed to my work. First of all, since I'm almost divorced, I have to be committed: I have to support myself, my children. We have to have a roof over our heads. That's my main motivation. For myself, I do find I like to have somewhere to go each day. I like to be stimulated. Self-esteem is part of it. You learn something, you try to use what God gave you and you try to develop it. I do enjoy my work, and that to me is very important. I anticipate working the rest of my life, and so my work had better be something I like. Actually, right now, I'm training on some new equipment. It's sophisticated and challenging. I'm really hoping this will turn into a good career for me. Being a typesetter, you can get to know the machine better, train other people, write formats or be a supervisor. I'd really like to learn the machine very well and excel at it and make a better wage. I've brought my daughter, who is four, and my son, who is five, in with me to work on Saturdays. They sit at the typesetting machine and type away. It gives them an idea of what I do.

---

*Some of these interviews have been edited to reflect, in this chapter, only those comments dealing directly with the relationship between mother and daughter. Portions of the interviews dealing with sons or with the stresses and strains of the working mother will appear in subsequent chapters.

My own mother didn't work until I was twenty. All the mothers were home then. Anybody I knew, their mothers were home. The daddy went to work and the mommy took care of everybody. My kids know that it doesn't work that way. They're liberated. All the friends they have, their mothers work. Day-care has really become a way of life. In fact, in this family, it's kind of funny. I think my children sometimes think that only mothers work and that it's the father's job to stay home. Their father works nights, and so he is there most of the day to see them off to school and to be there when they get home from school. And my father, who is retired, babysits for them, and cooks and cleans because my mother now works. So my children know that a woman's place is to work and a father's place is to stay home.

I think I'm a positive role model for my daughter in that I'm letting her know that a woman just doesn't get taken care of in life. She really has to go out on her own and make her own life. She has to make her own happiness. She shouldn't depend on anybody to take charge of her. When I was growing up, I was raised to believe that you're going to meet Prince Charming and be swept away, and it's going to be okay just because you're in love. And you know, that's not the way it is, and it's very hard when you find that out. I don't want my daughter to grow up under that illusion.

I would like to raise her knowing her own worth, and what her capabilities are. But I don't want to mold her into anything. Maybe she'll want to stay home and raise a family, or find work she can do in her own home. I would encourage her to do all that she can with herself and not take a backseat to somebody and devote her life to some man. Her life should be devoted to doing what she can with herself and making all the things she cares about mesh together.

I'm happy with what I'm doing in my work, and that's important for my children to see. The time that I'm with them is good time. We're happy. I teach them responsibility. I'm a good role model for them in the sense that I've sort of taken control of things. They see me as a strong, independent person.

I hope they will grow up with the idea that there's nothing a woman can do in the home that a man can't do, and that there's nothing in the world of work that a man can do that a woman can't. I would like that to be the case. To me, there's no reason for otherwise. There's no reason why a man can't be cooking dinner, picking up after the kids. The traditional Mom and Dad—Dad works, Mom stays home—that's changed. It just seems that in the past the cost to the woman was too much. I don't like those stereotypes. They're not for this family.

Phyllis, 41, Librarian

I had a role model of a mother who didn't work. And I had a very strong feeling that she was very lonely. She'd finish her housework very early and pounce on us for company. My father was the breadwinner, but we could have used her income. Finally, when my younger sister was in junior high school, she went to work, and she was a lot happier.

When I was a child, I was taught to look for happiness in a man. Although I wanted to be a librarian since I was twelve, and had a good job, the expectations I had growing up made me feel unfulfilled. By the time I was twenty-five, I felt I should be married. For years I always felt I was just nothing. I hope my daughter will want to marry someday, but I hope she won't feel that she's nothing if she doesn't have a man. I think it's very important that girls grow up with the idea that they'll work and have careers. Too many women are left penniless—either divorced or widowed, and they have no profession or trade. It's not enough to be under the shadow of a man.

I think my daughter accepts it as a given that women work. She's four now, and she's seen me working all her life. I've taken her to the library with me, and I'm always bringing a lot of books home. She has good care, and she seems very secure.

I would hope that she'd want to emulate me and want to have a profession. She sees that I'm happy in my work and that having my own money makes me feel more independent. I'm proud I'm a working woman and I think she knows that. I do hope, however, that she'll go into more of a man's field. I'm still in a woman's field—one of the "helping professions," like being a nurse or a social worker. I've been working for twenty years, and my salary is still ridiculous. I'd like to see her become a doctor, something more lucrative. I never wanted to do that because it just wasn't ever a possibility for girls when I was growing up.

Mayra, 29, Financial Comptroller

My daughter, Giselle, who is four, likes to talk about her future. "I'm going to have a baby," she said to me last week, "and I'll take her to the Montessori School [where she goes] and then to the babysitter, and you know, Mommy, I'm not going to be like you because remember when I would ask you to stay home and sometimes you stayed with me, I don't think I'm going to do that because you really didn't have to. I think I'll just bring her quickly to the babysitter and she will know that I have important things to do and she will be fine when I leave."

It's cute. She thinks she has everything planned. She wants to have a family, but she wants to do important things. I asked what important things she had in mind. She considers having a career very important. "Well, I want to have a good secretary like yours and I want to do reports and I want to have meetings and then I want to come home and be with a baby." I told her that she didn't have to have the same profession as me, and even that she didn't really have to work if she didn't want to, and she said, "Oh, no, you don't have to tell me. I want to do this." The way I see it, I don't think she is going to have the same problems that I have in terms of "Am I doing the right thing?"

Two years ago, although she has always thought of women as workers, she thought of them as teachers and secretaries. Doctors and astronauts had to be men. All that has changed now. Recently she asked me if there were any female doctors, because her pediatrician is a male, and I said, sure, the person that delivered you was a woman doctor, so I took her to see my ob/gyn. At first she didn't believe me that there were women doctors, but we went to the office and she saw her and she spoke to her, and they talked about how the doctor delivered her and that really meant a lot. It was an important experience for her.

I believe Giselle is very independent. Her teacher tells me that when she compares Giselle to the other children that she is much more independent than the kids whose mothers are at home. The teacher told me that she herself wishes she had done what I am doing. She said, "Mayra, never feel guilty about what you have done because it is working much better. Giselle is a very, very happy child. She is one of the happiest children I have ever known. So obviously you must be doing something right."

Recently, I took her to work with me. We went on a Sunday morning to the office, and she had the greatest time. She really enjoyed it. She played with the computers. She sat at the desk and called different people on the telephone.

I think one of the reasons why she has the perceptions that she has is that, at home, her father and I share everything. There is really no distinct role for either of us. I do the wash. He does the wash. I do the cleaning. He does the cleaning. I take care of her. He takes care of her. Whoever is able to takes off from work when Giselle is sick. I truly think that she believes there are no roles that aren't interchangeable.

My husband and I never really discussed having interchangeable roles. We were married for four years before we had Giselle because we really wanted to do a lot of traveling. We were getting our careers under way. We never really discussed the role of a woman or a man. It was just that this was our household and we both did the things that needed to be done. We'd both get home from work late and share.

In general, I think these children are going to have a much easier time because they are going to be more independent, have more self-assurance and more direction, which is coming from within themselves. They know the options, they know what is available to them. I think it is going to be much easier for them to decide: Do I want to be a homemaker or do I want to have a profession? It's going to be much easier for them to make a decision than it was for us.

Celeste, 38, President, Design Firm

I remember from the time my daughter, Elizabeth, was a very young child encouraging a certain amount of independence in her. I did this both because I'd never had it as a child and wished I had, and also because I had just started working and I simply didn't have the time to hover over her. Even at a very young age, I remember her climbing to the top of the jungle gym and jumping off. It was such a feat of daring. Instead of scaring me for her safety, it pleased me. She seemed to have a willingness to go out and meet the world that I was just beginning to experience as an adult. She appeared to have none of the timidity that I felt. I encouraged her to be what I hadn't been because I wasn't always there for her to rely on. As a result she developed a fearlessness and tenacity that I felt would stand her in good stead.

As a working-mother role model, I have this feeling that I have allowed her to see that she has a myriad of possibilities open to her. She could do or be whatever she wanted to be. I don't ever remember as a child thinking that there were a lot of possibilities open to me. To the contrary, one assumed that one grew up and got married, and I found that frightening. In the last two years, she's decided that she would like to become an architect. I take pride in the fact that she will go me one further. It's a field of endeavor that's similar to mine—but it's pushing further into a more masculine field. It's more intellectually rigorous than my career. I gave her a set of drafting tools for Christmas. I've taught her to use an architect's scale the way my mother taught me to bake cookies. This is something special I can give her.

Elizabeth, 17, Student (Celeste's Daughter)

My mother is a role model in terms of career aspirations. She's an interior designer. I'm looking into architecture. She's a resource I can refer to. I can go to her and ask questions about architecture and she can guide me.

My father is a dentist, but my mother is the stronger role model. My father had his route all planned out, but my mother had to make more sacrifices. She's also a role model in terms of career and family. She's never given up on me or on her career. She's had to make sacrifices, but she's never quit. This isn't to say that she's a superwoman, nor is she telling me that I have to be a superwoman. She's just saying that I can try to have a career and a family, too.

I had a dream recently. In the dream I was in Italy for the Milan Fair. I was an architect. My husband and two children were with me. My husband had a career that wasn't directly involved with mine, but we could communicate. I think he was in real estate. I think this shows that I will probably get married and have children. That's inferred from the culture. It's a given. The fact that I will have a career is more my own wish. But I also think that if I'd been in a home where the mother never worked, and I didn't have any kind of a social life that brought me into contact with mothers who had careers, I wouldn't have the desire to have a career. I wouldn't know any better.

Almost all my friends at school have working mothers. My friends want to be psychiatrists, doctors, biochemists. I don't know anyone who isn't planning on having a career. We talk about what jobs our parents do. There's prestige attached to having a mother who has an interesting job. I like the fact that my mother is an interior designer. My friends want to know what she does, and I tell them, and they say, "That's neat." One time one of my friends was talking to her mother on the phone. Her mother manages a chain of restaurants. When my friend got off the phone, she said, "She sounds so much happier now that she's got a better job. She's worked so hard for it." That's one thing. You really know how hard your mother's worked.

Johanna, 29, Personnel Manager

When I was growing up, I really wanted to go to college. But I didn't. I had a brother, and there was only enough money for one, so he got to go. Meanwhile, he was on drugs and was high as a kite twenty-four hours a day, and we're home eating hot dogs and tuna fish for supper each night to put him through school.

I worked as a secretary for ten years. I was making your standard secretarial salary. I worked really hard, though, and was promoted from my secretarial position to this one. And my husband did not take it well at all. He would never admit to it, but he didn't like it. Suddenly I'm going on business trips. And when he tries to call me at the office, I'm in meetings. His envy and jealousy really came through.

After my daughter was born I decided to go back to work. You try and rationalize: Well, it's going to be better for me, you think. But when I thought about it, I thought, She's going to be with the majority, not the minority. So it's not out of the norm. She knows exactly what I do. I tell her I'm going on a business trip, or to the office. I have a calculator at home, so she uses my calculator. She pretends she's going on a business trip, packs her bag, goes out the door. "Bye-bye," she says. "I'm going on a business trip."

I'm happy. She knows I like to work. She knows I have friends at work as well as at home. I know that I'm doing the right thing.

I'm very proud that I'm a working mother. It's an accomplishment and I think I do it very well. I'm able to give Michele things that I wouldn't be able to give her if I didn't work. I am able to support her. I'm not totally dependent upon my husband, and that makes me feel good. And I think she will look at me one day and say, "Hey, my mom got out and did something."

Elaine, 34, Dentist

I have to have an impact on my daughter, who is four, when I am home, because I'm with her only three hours a day. I talk to her a lot. I encourage her to be independent all the time. I keep telling her from time to time that she doesn't need me along, or anybody else. If she puts her clothes on backwards, I send her to school that way. It's more important to dress herself than to be wearing something the right way. It's the same when she's making her bed. I let her do it, and do not run in to fix it. I try to outline her responsibilities. Working encourages children to be more independent. They can't fall back on Mommy as much. The mother can't be tempted to do it for them because she isn't there.

Kate wants to be a dentist, like me. She has this T-shirt that reads, "I love my dentist. She's my mom." I think it's cute that she wants to do what I'm doing. I would encourage her to consider any profession. When I was her age, I wouldn't have considered working for a living, never mind having a career.

I see myself as the keeper of the family—the one who forms character and values. My daughter is aware that women have careers. It's something I think she gets through osmosis. So I am especially careful to encourage love of the family. She can get the achieving end of things quite easily, but it's not so easy to come by nurturing in this culture.

The children who are Kate's peers are definitely going to think that daddies do dishes and housework and take care of the children. Kate takes it totally for granted that both parents work and that both parents take care of her. There's nothing that's unique to either of us. Likewise, children will also think of women as doing all of the things that daddies do. Mothers are going out to work and contributing to the family income when they come home. Kate rejoices when I come home like children used to rejoice about Dad coming home. Of course, she rejoices when her dad comes home, too.

I'd like her not to grow up with rigid stereotypes. I want her to be nontraditional. I have bought her a dump truck, a football, a water pistol and a set of carpenter's tools. She was Wonder Woman at Halloween, and we talked about what a neat thing that was to be— to be a girl and have all that power.

Kate, 4 (Elaine's Daughter)

If I were a mommy, I'd give the children Popsicles, let them play outside and do other adult things. I'd be a doctor—the doctor that fixes teeth.

If I were a daddy, I'd do all the things mommies do.

Rebecca, 16, Student

My mother is my role model. She has a family, she has a house and she is a doctor. She's shown me it is possible to do all three, but I've also seen how hard it is, too. I've seen all the pluses and minuses up close. Nevertheless, I want to be a doctor, too, and to have a big family —four kids. I've known I wanted to be a heart surgeon since I was three years old. I never thought I would have to choose between being a heart surgeon and having a family, because my mother is someone who has both. I think having a family is just so special; and I think that having your own life and being a professional is special, too. I don't think women should have to choose between one or the other. And I don't think it's fair for society to say that you have to choose. I think women like my mother are sort of showing us that it's possible to do both.

I admire my father's intelligence, but it's my mother who is my role model. She's taught me so much about what it is to be a woman, and how different it is for me than it was for her when she was growing up. Many of my friends feel the same way. All of them want to have families and have some sort of career. Some of them, in fact, are thinking more about their professions than they are about families. My friends want to be artists, dancers, actors, businesswomen and doctors.

Linda, 15, Student

My mother works as a secretary to a lawyer. She works regular hours, nine to five. I'm expected to get dinner started when I come home from school. We always talk about what I'm supposed to do before she leaves for work in the morning, and since she works close by, I can always call her. I do sometimes call her if something is going wrong at school, or I have a problem. She always listens to me, but it's hard for her to talk at the office, with everyone listening.

Sometimes I'm lonely in the afternoons. I just broke up with my boyfriend. Me and my mother, we're really close. I can really talk to her, and sometimes, like lately, I wish she was here so that I could talk to her, although she really didn't approve of my having a boyfriend in the first place, but still. I have an older sister, but she works and doesn't get home until after my parents do usually. So I'm alone a lot, and it bothers me. But then I'm glad that my mother works, for her sake, and for my sake, too. I know she's making money to save so that I will be able to go to college, and I know that I wouldn't be able to go at all if she hadn't started working. She's talked to me a lot about her working, to make sure that I understand, and of course I understand. It's not that. I know it wasn't easy for her to go back to work at her age. And even though I help out, I know that she still has to work very hard around the house, too, when she gets home, and that she's tired a lot of the time. And I know that she has back trouble a lot, and it's hard for her to be sitting all day. So even though I'm sometimes lonely, I really respect her for what she's doing. She's really sacrificing for me, and I guess I'm really proud of her.

Rena, 41, High School Guidance Counselor

When I started working about twenty years ago, I was a teacher. Any woman I knew who thought of herself as a professional was either a teacher or a nurse or in one of the "helping professions." What's interesting is that so many of us who started out teaching are still in the education field, but we've become more ambitious within that field. I'm head of the guidance department, for example. One of my friends runs a graduate program at a nearby junior college. Another one is head of a special-needs school. It used to be that if you were a girl, you had to think in terms of a "giving profession." That's no longer the case today—and you see this not only in terms of the students but also in terms of the women who have been working in these "helping professions" for years.

A couple of months ago, I had to go to a conference in Ohio. I was away from home for four days. My husband and my kids came to get me at the airport. When I was getting off the plane, I had this black suit on and my briefcase, and my husband and my daughter and my son were there waiting for me, and this light went on in my head. This was a scene that ten years ago you would have seen in reverse. Mom and kids waiting for Dad to come home from a business trip. Now it was Dad and kids, who had been doing all the housework and cooking and cleaning at home for four days, coming to the airport to get Mom from a business trip.

My generation will always have the stereotypes. But our kids don't have them. Just last week we were driving along the street, and I saw this woman mail carrier. It registered. I thought to myself, Hey, look, there's a woman being a mailman. I said that to my kids. They said, "Huh?" It didn't even *register* on them that anything was amiss or different. They see a woman on a roof with a bunch of other roofers and they don't miss a beat. It's simply the way things are. But to me, it will always be different and remarkable. Times have changed and, frankly, I don't think they'll ever go back to the way it was in my day.

Pat, 31, Newspaper Advertising Sales

I would like my daughter, who is four, to grow up very prepared and very directed. I think it's important that she sees me as a working woman and that she understands what I do. I take her to accounts with me once a week. She has a comprehension of what it is that I do. I don't think she understands what her father does, however. He's in sales, too, but he doesn't feel comfortable taking her with him on calls. Somehow, in this culture, it's still more acceptable for the woman to bring her child along than it is for the man.

I think it's important, too, that she understand the economic reason why a mother works. I like her to know that both her father and I contribute to the economic welfare of the family. She understands that my working brings in income, and that's important for her to know. Hey, we need the money. That's a fact.

Her father and I share child-rearing and household tasks. Peter, for example, does all his own ironing each morning before work. She watches cartoons while I'm doing my exercises, and Peter's right there with her doing the ironing. She's going to grow up thinking that fathers do the ironing, I'm sure.

Barbara, 38, Administrator, Chamber of Commerce

I grew up in an Irish Catholic family near Boston. My father worked for the government, and my mother never worked. In fact, she almost never even left the house. There were three kids in my family—two girls and one boy. The boy was the youngest, and he's got a Ph.D. from Harvard in biochemical physics. We girls were encouraged to have families when we grew up, and my brother was encouraged to go to college and earn a good living. It was subtle, but we grew up definitely thinking the boy was the most important child in the family. As it happened, that was pretty poor planning. My sister is divorced now and has to make her own way. I've got four kids, ages seventeen, sixteen, fourteen and eleven, and my husband is handicapped and can't work. So I'm the sole support of the family.

I started off being a secretary. But once I realized I was going to work forever, I wanted to make sure that my job was going to be something worthwhile and that I was going to be able to make some decent money at it and be able to support my family. Sometimes I think: Wow, wouldn't it be great if I won the lottery, or something. But I think I would probably get very bored after a while not working. I like people, and I think I would miss that a lot, that contact.

I think I'm a good role model for my children because I work very hard, and they know this. They're also proud that I've been able to do what I've done. The older ones remember me at home scrubbing floors and being a housewife, and now they see me in a position of responsibility in the outside world. I know they understand that they wouldn't have what they have if I didn't work. I make $28,500 a year, and it's a struggle to make it on that, but if I didn't have that income, I don't know what we'd do. They see that I've had a lot of problems in my life, but that I've always tried to figure out a way to solve them. I've tried not to let these problems hurt them, and I think they respect me for that.

I think the fact that my husband is home all the time and I'm out working really has something to do with how my kids see each of us. My husband can't do very much. He can do some housework and he can drive a car, but that's about all. Not getting out and learning new things and not being with other people, like the traditional housewife, has altered his personality. He's concerned about things that I remember I used to be concerned about years ago. He gets all upset about when the guy is going to come to put the carpet down, or if the kids throw their baseball gloves and bats all over the living room. I'm saying, So okay, we'll pick them up later, but he gets all upset, like I remember I used to. I think sometimes the kids think, Gee, this person can't be very smart if he's spending all this time worrying about a baseball glove on a rug. In the old days, I think kids used to think their fathers were smarter than their mothers, because the fathers were out in the world and had other interests besides when the carpet was going to get laid. When I was growing up, I thought my father was smarter. In my family, it seems to be the other way around. I think in families where both parents worked, the kids would probably think both parents were equally smart and competent.

I think, for this generation, that their perceptions of both parents will be the same. I think it's wonderful for a boy to do the dishes as well as a girl, because why should a girl do the dishes all the time? I mean, it's ridiculous. It's good for boys not to have those inhibited feelings, like I'm a boy, I'm not supposed to do that, and vice versa. People should be able to do the same things. There's no reason why we can't.

Let me tell you a story. My daughter is thirteen, my son is eleven. They're both very good baseball players, but my daughter is a real star. Two years ago, they were both in the minor league in Little League. I don't know if you know much about that, but first you're in the minor league, and then you get to be in the major league. In our town, there had never been a girl in the major league, and the coach was on record as saying that as long as he was coach, he would never draft a girl to the major league. So my daughter and my son were in the minor league together. She was ten times better than he was. I mean, she had eight game balls for pitching and she could hit like you would not believe. She was the best hitter in the league. But my son got drafted and she didn't. I went crazy. I said to her, I'm not going to embarrass you if you don't want me to, and I'm not going to make a fool of you, but this is totally unfair and you have to understand that, and she said, I want you to do it. And I said, Are you going to feel pressured if I get you into the majors? And she said, No, I can handle it. So I got the coach on the phone for three hours. And I said, You are being totally unfair. My son is only nine years old, and he's nowhere as good as Leslie. If you don't take her, I'm going to expose the league. The next day he called me and apologized and he said that I was absolutely right, that he was being totally unfair, but that he had sworn his whole life that he would never take a girl on his baseball team. But he said he would do it. And she was fabulous. She made City All Stars. She was batting over 400, hitting home runs. She was the only girl in the majors. The kids really respected her. The kids were fine. It's the adults that were the problem.

Susan, 35, Day-care Director

My mother always worked as a stockbroker, so I always had a role model who was a working mother. She's eighty-one and she's still working.

Right after she had me, three days later, she was back in her office. I'm sure that's the reason I have instilled in my girls that I don't care what else they do, but they've got to have a profession. I've worked very hard at giving them that direction since the day they were born. I just felt so strongly about it. I've always worked, and when they were little, I know that, among their friends, I was looked upon as kind of a freak because all the mothers were home then, but now, I'd say, gradually over the course of time, now all their friends' mothers work.

Laurie, 17, Student

My mother has an interesting story. When she was growing up she wanted to go to college, and her father sat down with her and told her, "Listen, I'll send you to college, but it can only be a state school." My mother grew up in a fairly wealthy family, so money was not the problem. It was attitude. Her father said to her if she were a son, he would pay for the best school that the son could get into. But he told my mother, You have three choices: You can be a secretary, you can be a nurse or you can be a teacher. It was assumed that she would just get married and pregnant and her education would go out the window.

Now my mother works. She's a nursery school teacher. She likes her work, but I know she wishes she had done more. Always she drills into my head, the most important thing is to go to school, get a good education and go out and be my own person first. Live on my own, get my own apartment and be independent. She has a real fear of me going to college and finding someone and marrying him shortly after graduation. She really wants me to take about five years at least and just get to know myself.

She is definitely my role model, but I want a more competitive career. I plan to go into the business world and have a full-time executive position. I want my career to be the first thing, whereas for her, she's always had to fit her career around the family. She was expected to have a family first, and to get a part-time job if it could be arranged around the family.

I think working has given my mother a lot of confidence, though. Working is a place that she likes to be. She likes her job and that gives her a feeling of self-worth. I know I will have a career and a family, because she has shown me it is possible to do both. Sometimes I get anxious about it, though. You know, how can I work this out because you have to be independent to have a career, and yet I'm also a romantic and nobody loves kids like I do, and it does concern me how it's all going to work out. How can you do both without shortchanging your career or your family? I think a lot will depend on my position in the business world when I decide to get married. And it would depend on the stress of the job at the time I decide to have children.

One thing is for sure: I would never marry a man who wasn't willing to share household tasks with me. I think a man that expects not to do anything around the house would just turn me off right from the beginning. There are personality traits that go along with that kind of attitude: You are the woman and I am the man kind of thing. I'd want a man who treated a woman as an equal. It's not fair that everything should be the woman's responsibility.

My friends and I talk about this a lot. They want to be engineers, businesswomen, executives, doctors, lawyers. None of my friends ever talks about being a schoolteacher or a secretary or a nurse, like they did in my mother's day.

Nancy, 38, Doctor

My mother was a nurse, and went back to work when I was about eight or nine years old. I was an only child, so my parents had all their hopes pinned on me. I was encouraged to be a doctor from an early age. Nothing at home or in high school ever discouraged me. It was only when I got to college and was told very clearly by my male social contacts that this was really unacceptable, and that working wasn't going to fit in with my plan of having children and being married, that I had trouble with this idea.

As for my own daughter, who is four, both her parents are doctors. I'm not exactly sure what the effect on her is, but I have some ideas. I think it's extremely important that her mother is a working mother —the important element being that she feels herself to be equally competent to any male. And I think she does. She is someone who has a lot of feminine traits in that she is gentle and poised and that type of thing, but she is also quite assertive and really doesn't buckle under to anyone who comes into her territory or does something that she thinks is incorrect. I think she is growing up with the idea that both parents are worthwhile people and that they both have important things to contribute. I think she thinks of herself as a competent worthwhile person who is capable of achieving whatever she wants to achieve.

Jayne, 41, Architecture Critic

I have two daughters, thirteen and eleven. I think working mothers say things to their children that are very different from the things mothers who stay home say to their children. Children pick up on attitudes and characteristics subliminally just by noticing who you are and what you do, but I've always stressed with them that it's very important to be able to take care of yourself. In our family, there has always been the assumption that they will have careers, and we often talk about what different choices will mean in terms of options later in life.

It's interesting the assumptions that they grow up with. Recently one of my daughters came home from playing at her friend's house. She said to me, "Mom, did you know that Mrs. X makes dinner all by herself?" This was a surprise to her, since in our household her father and I both make dinner. She had just assumed it was a shared activity.

I've found, also, among my daughter's friends, that it's a status symbol to have a mother who works. More than that, the type of job also confers status in the same way that when I was growing up the type of job your father had conferred status.

My girls assume they will always work. Almost all of their friends have mothers who work, and the teachers at school, I've discovered, also reinforce this attitude. I'm pleased about this. I think self-esteem for a girl is terribly important, and a lot of self-esteem comes from one's work. I've found in my experience that women who have careers have greater self-esteem than women who stay home and don't have work. I also think one's expectations are important. If you grow up thinking you'll be a doctor, you won't be a nurse. You'll be a lawyer maybe, but you won't be a paralegal.

I think it's terribly risky and irresponsible to assume someone will take care of you. I mean, it's really impossible at times to be a working mother, but it's more impossible not to be.

Gretchen, 16, Student

My mother is the director of admissions at a private boarding school in Tennessee. When she started working, and we were kind of on our own, she always said to me that she wanted me to be able to support myself. I think from her I've really gotten an idea of how society is changing. When I was little, the societal structure was for the husband to support the family, but I feel really strongly that in our generation it will be accepted that both parents work. When I was little and living with both parents, and my mother wasn't working, I had the expectation that when I grew up I would get married and stay home and be a mother. But after my parents got divorced, I think it was my mom who introduced me to the idea that women are equal to men and women should work and they are just as good or better than men. Since I've been in school, I think the culture also has really influenced me in terms of the people that I have met and other families that I have seen. I think none of us is really going to end up in the traditional structure of Mom stays home and Dad works.

I think from my mom I've learned the importance of being a strong person, a strong woman especially, and how you shouldn't come to depend on your husband. You have to be your own person.

Zelma, 45, Taxi Driver

I've been a waitress, a cleaning woman, a maid in a hotel, a cook and a school crossing guard. I've always worked, even when my kids were little. I've been working since I was sixteen. The best job I ever had, though, was distributing leaflets for an advertising company, because the money was good and I could take the kids with me. They were good workers. We went door-to-door, starting right after school, and we could give out close to three thousand leaflets before nightfall. I'd give the kids two meals—one right after school and then one later at night, because they'd really work up an appetite. My two daughters are now seventeen and twenty-one. The seventeen-year-old lives at home with me. She works in a warehouse now. The twenty-one-year-old, she's on her own. She works with the airlines.

I feel it's good to be a working mother if you've got the right hours.

Now, the advertising was good because I had the girls with me, and being a school crossing guard was good because I could do that when they were in school. The other jobs, though, I worked at night. My husband walked in the door, and I'd walk out. But you have to be with the children. Otherwise you don't know what they're getting into or bringing home.

A working mother *can* make it. I didn't live rich, but I lived middle-class. I didn't want to live slum-like. I couldn't bring my children up in the slum. I always had nice clothing for the children to wear. I got us a house in the suburbs. I've never taken any public assistance of any kind. If God gives me the strength, I'm gonna work 'til the day I die.

The only bad thing though, the only thing that's hurt me, is that both of my girls wanted to work as soon as they got out of high school. Neither one of them went to college. If my working has encouraged them to go out to work too fast then that's no good. They just wanted to get out quick and earn the money.

Megan, 41, Bank Executive Vice President

I'm driven. I've always been driven. I was driven when I was a school-teacher, and I was driven when I stayed home for six years with my child when she was a baby. Then I went back to school and got my MBA, and I was driven to be successful. Actually, it was my husband's idea. He said, "If you're so driven, you might as well be driven toward money."

I'm very, very successful. I've always known that I was going to be very, very successful. I have a staff of forty men under me, and I make $100,000 a year. I think that's nothing when I think of other successful women—Barbara Walters, she makes a million. I would hope, in the next five years, to be making in the vicinity of $300,000. I equate success with money, absolutely.

I'm the boss of forty men. I don't think men have accepted women as bosses. They look at me as a mother, as a sex symbol. But I find men to be for my benefit—the best resource for my personal success. They're much more driven than women. They've been brought up for success, whereas, as a girl, I was never told to go for it. Women come into my office—I can see they're ambivalent. I understand that ambivalence. I feel it myself sometimes. My husband and I, we have this argument all the time. I get a couple of drinks in me, and I'll say, "But I thought I was going to be taken care of." And he'll say, "But you *don't want* anyone to take care of you." And he's right.

I'm up at 4:30 every morning. My husband and our daughter, Harriet, who is eleven now, get up at about 4:45. I do a half hour of exercise, see that my daughter is dressed, check out her homework, and help to plan her day. I'm very organized. I never leave anything to chance. We have breakfast together, but I'm never here for dinner. I leave the house at 6:30, and I never come home until 8:30 or later. I'm away traveling for business at least one week a month. My husband is the primary parent. He's a child psychologist, and he doesn't leave for work until Harriet is on the bus. He's home every night at five; he does all the cooking, and they eat together. He does all the caretaking things. Everyone in this family understands that I work longer hours than he does, I work harder hours than he does, and I have more stress.

I stayed home for the first six years of Harriet's life. I did this deliberately because I believed it was the right thing to do, and I still do, but I hated it. I think it's better for the whole family now that I'm working. I was miserable then. I'm happy now. I think that happiness energizes the rest of the family, and we're all better off.

I think all the effects of my working have been positive ones for Harriet. She's very independent. I'm sure that's a consequence of my being a working mother. I think that she is going to be very, very successful, because I've been so successful. She's different from other eleven-year-olds. Very mature. She knows the value of working. She has traveled and she has nice things, but she knows I can give her this because I've been very, very successful. Work brings money. Money buys nice things. My daughter knows I'm smart and creative and very successful. I bring my child at least four times a year to work to see where I sit, to see my secretary, to see the pressure that I'm involved in. To see that I'm not off having lunch, not out drinking martinis.

I said all the effects of my working have been positive ones for Harriet. But I'm very tough with everyone, including my child, and perhaps I've put too much pressure on her. I have extremely high standards. I feel bad about this. I'm working hard on this. I have a lot of ambition. So I tell my child, If you have a problem, you can just decide to do whatever you have to do, and it will get done. But not everyone has this threshold for success. Success means a tremendous amount to me. I will deal with it, but I will be very, very unhappy if she is not successful. Now, that's pressure, right? Is that fair to her?

She comes first. I come last. I can always have a job. I can't redo having a child. You know, I really don't have a child anymore. It's over. She's eleven now. She's not a child.

Carol, 28, Waitress

Number one, I work because I have to. My husband, God bless him, I love him, but if we had to live on what he made, we'd be in the streets. I mean, not really, but close. He works for a lawn and tree service company that his brother owns. My mom, she takes care of the kids. I have two—a boy, Carl, who is five, and my daughter, Elaine, who is two. We live upstairs from my mother, so it works out fine. I bring them down about eleven in the morning and my husband picks them up about 5:30 when he gets off from work. I work the lunch and dinner shifts. I could go home for about an hour in between, and sometimes I do, especially if they're sick, or if I have to take them to the doctor, or if my mom needs to go shopping—she doesn't drive—but usually I just do my own errands then.

Number two, I work because I want to. People say being a waitress is kind of a lower-class job, but I have to tell you that I really like this job. I'm good at it; I'm really fast. I have a lot of friends here. The customers know me and like me. I get really good tips. I can't think of another job where I could make this kind of money. I couldn't stand being a secretary, just sitting there all day in those cubicles, or working in a store. I get good exercise, too. You'd be surprised. I've never had a weight problem.

This doesn't mean I don't bitch. Sometimes I come home late, the house is a mess. The kids are fed and in bed, but the house looks like a bomb hit it. My husband, he's a great father. He plays with the kids, he reads to them. He can cook the simple things, get a meal on the table. He can give them a bath. He's toilet-trained my daughter already. But he doesn't do housework. He leaves it all for me, and sometimes I just can't cope with it. By the time I get home, the place is really wrecked. Dirty clothes and dishes everywhere. And he's sitting in front of the TV with a beer. I don't think it's fair, and we fight, but then

I look at some of my friends, and their husbands don't do anything, and I think, So be glad for what you've got, right?

The kids. They're okay. I think they're doing fine. My son is in nursery school in the afternoon, and he's doing very well there. They've been lucky, I think, to have my mom take care of them, instead of some babysitter that maybe didn't really care about them, or a day-care center. I'm not sure what I think about day-care centers. Anyway, I think I've been really lucky, because my mom doesn't charge us, or anything, and so the childcare is free. Otherwise, we'd really be in bad shape, because nearly all my earnings would have to go for childcare.

All my kids' friends' mothers work. It doesn't seem odd to them. When my husband and I first got married, he said, no way, he wasn't going to let any wife of his work. But then, there's the bills, there's reality, and what are you going to do? I said, when Carl was about eighteen months, I'm going back to work, and he said okay. And that's all there was to it. I don't see any bad effects on my kids not having me around all day. Frankly, I think they're better off. First they have me when I'm at my best, in the morning. Then they have my mom, who is terrific with kids, for six and a half hours (except when Carl is in nursery school). Then they have their dad, who really tries hard to be a good father. Then it starts all over again the next morning. I think the kids are doing great.

Ellen, 41, Education Researcher and Writer

I often see myself as a role model for my daughter, who is ten, and my son, who is fifteen. When my kids were afraid of new experiences, like walking about the city by themselves or going to a new friend's house to spend the night, I was able to say that I knew how they felt. I, too, often had to do things that were sometimes difficult for me, like giving a speech in a different city. I would tell them that I wasn't sure how people were going to respond to me, but that I thought it was important to take chances. I have to travel a lot in my work, and my kids know that I'm not thrilled about flying, but they also know that in order to live an interesting life you've got to be willing to take reasonable chances.

I am who I am. Even in my vulnerabilities, I'm a good role model. If I yell and scream, or they see I'm having a bad time at work, it's probably good for them because it helps them to accept their own imperfections. I also think that the skills that I have learned at work are useful in the family. I've taught them to try to figure out how to get what they want and to assess the effective ways of getting it. These are skills I learned in the workplace. I also learned how to be an authority at work, and this is useful at home. I learned at work that when you say no in a managerial situation, you really have to mean no.

On the other hand, I think that family skills can be parlayed into work skills. The two realms don't detract from each other; they enhance each other. I've really learned how to listen at work, and I've learned how to motivate people to work well, and to feel part of a team. Being a mother has helped me to do that. Work gives you a chance to see yourself as you never could. And so does parenting. You use both of them as learning processes. And my kids see this all the time.

When I first started working, it was unacceptable to work when your children were little. Now it's the opposite. My friends who have chosen to stay home are nervous. In a way, I think we're all nervous about the decisions we've made. You always think the reason your child cries is because of what you do. It's easy to pin the blame on any one fact, but I think all struggles are normal struggles. On balance, I think the work life is beneficial to a child. It has the potential of bringing new information and new experiences into the family. We often close our children out of the life of work, but I don't think that's helpful.

Jackie, 39, Administrator, University and Community Relations

When my daughter, Leigh, who is six now, asked me about my job, I was remembering how we described to her what her father did. He used to be in politics, but then he left it to become a venture capitalist. How do you explain venture capitalist to a six-year-old? So we said: He used to work at the State House, but now he is the boss of himself. I could see that the idea of boss, the whole notion of authority in the workplace, was very intriguing to her. She always asked about it and she was fascinated to learn that I'm a boss, too, and that I have people who work for me. Some of these people are older than I am and some of them are male. She's spent a lot of time in my office, and she knows everybody and where she can go to get Scotch tape, who's got this and who's got that. And she has asked me if I am the boss and who are the people who work for me and what do they do, and you can tell that she is sort of absorbing this notion that people can be bosses even though they are younger than other people and even though they may be a different sex than other people, and you can see she is sort of churning this around. I don't know that it comes out in any particular way, except that when she is playing with her dolls, she will line them all up and she'll give them instructions, and she plays office a lot. For Christmas, she wanted a typewriter and an ironing board, which is unbelievable to me, since I don't think she's ever once seen me ironing. But she loves the ironing board. When she's not ironing, she's playing office and dictating to the dolls. She seems to be comfortable with both images. I think when she's playing office, she's emulating her mother; the other seems to be more of an instinctual thing.

I'm actually a fourth-generation working mother. My great-grandmother was an immigrant from Lebanon. She worked in the garment industry. Her daughter, my grandmother Rose, was one of the most powerful role models for me. She was a very active, self-sufficient, independent woman. She was the business person in the family. My grandfather had no idea where the checkbook was or how to pay a bill. She made all the financial decisions. She invested money in the stock market, and she always had very strong political interests. My own mother was more typical of the 1950s and early 1960s. She worked in retail, but she did so only when I was in school. I never came home that she wasn't there. My mother felt it was important to be home for me, and my parents really gave me everything. The only thing they didn't give me, and it was through no fault of their own, was a broader sense of horizons. And the reason that they didn't give it to me was that they couldn't give it to me. They didn't know themselves. When I was growing up, I remember once saying I wanted to be a psychiatrist. But after a while, I became more sensitive to the sort of directions my parents thought were appropriate for me. They never said you should be a teacher, but it was sort of assumed that was what I should do. My father felt that was a wonderful job for a woman. I think he revered the teaching profession as a great achievement for a daughter to accomplish. I was the first person in my family ever to go to college. When I think about it, I think: My God, there were so many other careers. I mean, so many other things might have been possible, but they weren't for me.

That's not going to be the case with my daughter. She has a whole range of choices open to her that were not at all evident to us. I don't have fears about her having too many choices, and having pressure to achieve and seeing two achieving parents. I'm sure there will be some of that, but my instinct is that the progress that we have made can only help our children.

Claire, 17, Student

My mother has been married for thirty-four years, and she's never worked. I think it would have been good for her to go out and get a job, so that she would have something to come home and share with us, so her whole world wouldn't be just the family and my father. My mother is a role model for nurturing and caring—I would like to be the kind of mother to my children that she was to me. But I have had to look outside my family to find role models of working women. I want to be a graphic designer, and I know other mothers who have families but have gone after what they want in a career.

I do plan to marry and to have a family. And I would want the kind of man who encouraged me to have a career. I would like the kind of man who would enjoy a paternity leave when the children were young, and who might stay home with them. I would like one of us to be there when the children were very young, and it would be nice if my husband and I could share that.

Laura, 31, Nurse

My daughter, Lilly, who is five, knows that some mothers don't go out of the house to work, and that others, like me, do. I've tried to explain to her that it has to do with money. In our household, both parents have to contribute to the income. I tell her that you get a certain amount of money in a paycheck for the work that you do, that you deposit that check in the bank, and then you can write checks to pay bills and buy the things that you need. I've let her see the kind of work that I do, too. I'm a public-health nurse, so I visit sick people in their homes. I've let Lilly come with me and watch me take blood pressure and that kind of thing. She sits very quietly and watches everything I do.

My parents were absolutely traditional. The man was the head of the household and didn't do a thing for himself. The wife did everything. I never liked that. In the beginning of my marriage, I had to fight against these stereotypical roles. It's taken us all these years to work it out, but now we share everything. It's a definite departure from my parents.

We share child-rearing and housekeeping tasks equally. It depends on who has more free time. If I've been up late working, my husband gets up early with the children. If he's had a late shift, then I get up with them. He'll do dishes. He'll do laundry. He doesn't like vacuuming, though. I think that Lilly is growing up with the idea that we both work, we both bring in income, we both take care of the children and we both share household tasks. And I like that.

Sometimes our roles switch so fast, it's like a comedy routine on TV. If I've had the kids all day and my husband comes home, I'm a little short with the kids by then, and I say to my husband, "Go into the living room. Have a drink. Take the kids with you, and let me finish up the cooking all by myself in here." When I come home from work, and he's had them all day, he says, "Listen, go have a drink in the living room and take the kids with you. I need to be by myself so I can finish cooking dinner." I really think it's the task that defines the personality so much of the time.

Mary, 35, Editor

I've worked ever since my daughter, who is four now, was too little to remember. As far as she knows, I've always worked. In fact, among her very first words were "Mommy is an editor," and "Daddy is a writer." We also had a computer right from the start, and it was used by both her father and me. Another of her very earliest words was " 'puter." I'm not sure if that had to do with me as a role model, or my husband, but I think the fact that she saw me working at it made it more acceptable to her. We got her a little desk for her room, and she started referring to it as her 'puter.

About a year ago, I had to stay late at work, so David picked her up. He asked her, just for the hell of it, "Who works harder, mommies or daddies?" And she said, "Well, mommies, of course." Her immediate response was that mommies work harder, which we both thought was pretty funny, since there are many occasions on which David works harder than I do.

Combining working and mothering has been very difficult for me. And I think the fact that I didn't have a working-mother role model myself is the problem. It's been very hard for me to overcome the various pulls inside me that have said, "Well, maybe you're not supposed to do this kind of thing." Sometimes I feel as if I'm foundering every step of the way. What we're doing—trying to have careers and have families, too—we're doing in a vacuum. When I first went back to work after having Lauren, I kept thinking: Why isn't there anybody to tell me how to do it? I just felt so lost. I felt lonely and helpless and as if I was always having to pave the way. I was constantly having to break down barriers. There was no reassurance out there. There was no one saying to me: This is the right way to do it.

My mother did occasionally work when I was growing up, but she never stuck to anything. She never had what you would call a commitment to a career. In fact, as soon as she became successful at something, she would quit. In that way, she was a terrible role model for me because it's made it very difficult for me to follow through in my ambitions. If I'd had a mother who was committed both to her work and to her family, I'm sure I would experience less of the conflict that I feel now. Ever since Lauren was born, the pull of domesticity has been very hard for me to reject completely. And whenever things get tough at work, I think: Gee, why don't I just throw it all over and go home and be a housewife. I mean, I've never said it with more than just a fraction of my brain, but the pull is there. I somehow always feel that I would be more confident if I was at home because I had a super role model of an at-home mother. This is true especially when something happens at work to lower my self-esteem.

When I was in the seventh grade, I had this fabulous science teacher. My father is a doctor and my brother is a doctor. Well, I got really interested in science because of this teacher, and I remember so well one day I came home and announced that I was going to be a doctor, and my mother just laughed. It was devastating to me. It happened when I was thirteen years old, and I've never forgotten it. It's unthinkable that I would ever do anything like that to Lauren. There would never be anything that she wanted to be that I would discourage her from trying. When I was growing up, whenever anyone asked me what

I was going to be, I always said *teacher*. The only women I knew who worked were teachers. You ask Lauren what she wants to be when she grows up, and she'll give you a list of nineteen different things. Teacher and mother are on the list, but so are doctor, editor and writer.

In her class at her day-care center, all her classmates have working mothers. One is going to medical school, and there are several lawyers. One of the first things that they did was have each of the children bring in pictures of their mothers in their work environment. It was interesting that they focused on the mothers working, and not the fathers. They talked a lot about our jobs to the children, and sometimes the kids took class trips to see the mothers at work. I found this so interesting, because when I was growing up, if you took a class trip to see the parent's work environment, it was always to Dad's work. I remember when I was a kid feeling sorry for the children whose mothers worked. Now it's completely the other way around.

I think my daughter's world is going to be completely different from ours. I think they will be much better off in that a lot of the issues that troubled me will be resolved for them. Working and mothering will be more acceptable. Society is still fighting that idea. It still looks down on working mothers. That won't be the case for our children. There is still a terrible stigma attached to surrogate parenting, and there is, in this country, an inability to make any kind of investment in childcare or maternity leave. I think the changes that are taking place—the fact that we work and our children see us work—will have a tremendous impact. It's going to make all the difference in the world—especially to girl children. I feel this so strongly in my own personal life. As I said earlier, if I had had a mother who worked, my life would be so much easier now. I would have some idea how to go about doing this thing that we're all doing.

I think our children are just going to be so much luckier than we were. I feel as if we really suffered. I would be shocked if I saw Lauren raising her daughter twenty years from now and she was going through the same struggles. I mean, they may have their own struggles. But I hope to God it's not this.

4

Mother: The New Role Model

A bit of folkloric wisdom posits that "we do not see the lens through which we see." This is particularly true of the controversy surrounding the effects of a working mother on her children. I have been impressed, in my reading of the recent popular press on this issue, by the need of some authors to legitimize the personal choices they have made. To what extent do we perceive to be true what we want to be true? A number of examples have surfaced recently from women seeking to legitimize their exit from the work force and their return to the home. Because I recognize in myself the same desire to legitimize my own choices—or to have my choices validated for me—I feel I have to be especially alert to the ways in which these desires might sway my thinking and interpretation of the data. As I began researching this book, a number of my colleagues as well as several psychologists I interviewed said that I'd have to deal with the issue of myself as a working mother before I could write the book. To that end, I have occasionally included myself and my family in these pages.

It has also been said that "you can prove anything you want to with statistics." In several of the chapters of this book, I present an array of academic studies. The academicians I cite are well-respected, and their work is regarded as first-rate. It is important to keep in mind, however, that academic studies are not infallible. Some look at a small part of the whole; others are deductive in nature, seeking to give evidence to support a pre-existing theory. Although there may be flaws in the studies which are not readily visible to the layman's eye, I have confidence in the research I cite—particularly so since many of the findings in the studies are echoed in my interviews with mothers and children and with child psychologists.

It is my hope that this book will stimulate questions beyond the ones I have asked. And it should be said at the outset that all the answers are not yet known. For example, the answers are different for different genders, economic classes and races. Unfortunately, however, most of the articles, books and television documentaries about the working mother have tended to focus on the top 5 to 10 percent of the working-mother population (in terms of income and professional levels). Because of this, I have tried to include a wider sampling of both working-class and middle-class mothers. Yet it is important to point out that some of the information learned in various studies about working mothers will not hold true for women who fall below the poverty line. For them, lack of adequate income and the struggle to obtain it are such strong variables that it is often very difficult to assess other factors. This fact, I found, occasionally holds true for working-class mothers as well. (I also discovered, during my interviews for the book, that the lines that divide working class from middle class and from upper middle class are often blurred in this country—especially so if one attempts to assign class by profession and work history. If a woman raised in an upper-middle-class home is now a mail carrier by choice, to what class does she belong for research purposes? If another woman, raised in a working-class home and presently married to a construction worker, is now a schoolteacher, to what class does she belong for research purposes? Occasionally, in the case of the latter, her childhood origins and the orientation of her husband may outweigh the influences of her middle-class job. Conversely, her self-definition as having a middle-class career may be a far more powerful influence than her husband's or parents' beliefs. Because a woman's self-perceptions, however, are the most important ingredient in how her work life affects her children, it would seem that self-definition would be the most important indicator of class for future researchers.)

As is true for women in the underclass, some of the information in this book will apply to black women and some of it will not. On the one hand, I have been struck, in my interviews with black middle-class working mothers, by how important their own working mothers were to them in shaping their values about working and mothering and combining the two endeavors. As one black working mother in Boston pointed out to me, she now finds it easier to combine working and mothering than her white counterparts because she, like many of her black contemporaries, had a working mother. She says she feels she suffers less from guilt and conflict than her colleagues and is more confident about her sexual role. On the other hand, *because* so many black adult women today had working-class or underclass working mothers when they were young children, they fall outside the norm for much of the historical discussion in Chapter 2.

In this book, general theories and trends, ascertained from interviews and from research, will be presented. But there is no one general truth that can ever be correct for all mothers and children. The variables and permutations are endless. Not only is every mother a unique individual, with a very personal constellation of attitudes, habits, beliefs and history, but so is every child one of a kind. No two families are ever exactly alike, no two work situations are identical, no two sets of childcare arrangements are perfectly symmetrical. You can have an ambitious, superachieving working mother who raises a girl whose primary passion is to get married and have babies. Likewise, you can have an at-home nurturing mother who raises a female CEO. And in the same way that there is no one general truth for all working mothers and their children, there is no one best profile for a child. This book, therefore, is not a prescription. Rather, it is hoped, it will be a catalyst to stimulate a re-evaluation of the attitudes about the effects of a working mother on her children.

HOW IS THE MOTHER A ROLE MODEL?

The term "role model" is a difficult and awkward phrase—one of those unlovable combinations of words that gets the job done, in that it accurately conveys the thing meant, but smacks of laboratories, experimental trials and sociological constructs. As a concept, it defines a relationship between what might loosely be called a superior and an inferior, or a teacher and an apprentice; but where it fails is in its ability to convey any warmth or passion—the underpinnings of the mother-child bond. The term, for example, doesn't even begin to suggest the idiosyncratic love, playfulness or even exasperation that passes between one individual mother and her child, and by which the child comes to define her mother. Nevertheless, it is a term with which we are stuck, both because of its legitimacy in the various fields of scientific research that employ it and because it does accurately describe an important aspect of the parent-child relationship. It's not so much that the term is incorrect that tends to grate; it's that it falls short of conveying the rich panoply of passions that make this bond such a powerful one.

Long before there were researchers and sociological terms, however, mothers knew that they were role models. For centuries, others before us have accepted as a given the fact that a mother teaches a child, influences that child's behavior, and helps to shape that child's beliefs and values. How that is done, however, is a matter of controversy.

Regardless of whether one believes that a child acquires his or her sex-role identity through imitation, biologically internalized motivations or cognitive researches, the various theories agree that most of this effort takes place in early childhood and that the mother first, followed by the father (if one is present), is the most important "shaper" and "influencer." The work the child does during his or her early years is part of a socialization process to fit the child for the adult world in which he lives. In the past, as we will see in Chapter 5, this process has tended to prepare girls for nurturing roles as wives and mothers and boys for active roles as breadwinners. Today, however, that sexual division of labor is changing. Mothers (and fathers) are socializing children of both sexes to possess characteristics that will help them in the work force as well as in parenting.

All adults are models for children—some more potent than others. The most powerful model for a child, however, is the same-sex parent, even though reinforcement can come from either parent or from the society at large. Thus, in a traditional nuclear family, a boy may be socialized to imitate his father by liking trucks, disliking dolls, excelling at baseball or by not crying when hurt, and may be rewarded for this male-appropriate behavior by both the mother and the father, either verbally or perhaps by something as subtle as a relaxed attitude toward the child's play. A daughter, on the other hand, gets her notion of appropriate sex-role behavior from observing her mother. Her ideas about what's correct for her will stem, at least initially—before society and peers become an increasingly powerful influence—from the range of behavior the mother models. If that includes insulating the attic, bathing a baby, leaving the house each morning with a briefcase and being assertive in her relationship with her husband, then the daughter's range of appropriate behavior will include them, too. Likewise, if the mother's behavior includes depression, suicide or child abuse, the daughter's repertoire will also include the potential for these. If this behavior is then reinforced by the parents and by the society outside of the nuclear family, the daughter will grow into adulthood with it as part of her *range of possibilities.* Observing a kind of behavior does not guarantee that the child will adopt it—a child can observe yet choose not to imitate—but it does make the behavior a more likely possibility in the scheme of things.

Theories of child development differ in important respects, but most clearly show that the mother is the primary role model for a daughter and an important reinforcer of sex-appropriate attitudes for a son. According to Dr. Lawrence Balter of New York University, "For girls during the preschool years, there is a heightened identification with the mother. If the mother is actively involved in a predominantly male arena, the girl will incorporate this into her own personality. Little boys, though they identify with their fathers, will nevertheless see in their mothers a potential they might otherwise not have noticed in women. This may contribute to the mental image of what's appropriate for women, and the boy may be sensitized to the fact that women can occupy any number of different roles."

That the mother is an influential role model for her child is believed by most researchers to be true, and some have set out to examine the power of this modeling. In a study conducted in 1981, researchers found that daughters mirrored their mothers' attitudes about work in every respect, except that 98 percent of them expected that they would always work with minimal time off in order to raise children.[1]

Dr. J. Brooks-Gunn of the Educational Testing Service recently conducted a study which also demonstrates the power of modeling. She evaluated 132 mothers as being either "masculine," "feminine" or "androgynous," according to a list of sex-role characteristics developed by Sandra Bem of Cornell University. "Androgynous" mothers, who, according to Dr. Brooks-Gunn, share personality characteristics with working women, scored high in both masculine and feminine traits. For example, they were self-reliant as well as tender, affectionate as well as assertive. "Feminine" mothers scored high only in feminine traits. Dr. Brooks-Gunn then watched the androgynous and feminine mothers at play with their own children. (The masculine sample was judged to be too small to be significant.) She discovered that feminine mothers promoted feminine behavior in their girls, and that androgynous mothers promoted self-reliance and independent behavior in their daughters.

The power of modeling was also demonstrated during a study conducted at Yale University's Child Study Center. Researchers there found a relationship between the quality of interaction between the mother and child and a child's personality. Researchers observed both mothers and children in play situations. Children who had mothers who were "in charge" and prohibitive were aggressive and assertive in play situations. Children with flexible mothers were somewhat more sociable and tended to watch one another more carefully.

That the mother is a powerful role model is clear, but some critics of the working mother have suggested that her influence as a role model wanes in direct proportion to the number of hours she is absent from the home. Is the impact of a working mother on a child diluted by the presence of a surrogate caretaker (or multiple caretakers, as in the case of a day-care center)? Is it possible that a mother who has only three or four hours a day to spend with her child can be as potent a model for her child as the at-home mother who is with the child all of his or her waking hours?

Lois Hoffman, in her review of the literature on the effects of maternal employment on the young child, published in 1984 in *The Minnesota Symposia on Child Psychology*, offered some interesting findings: "Employed mothers spend less time with their preschool children, but the time spent with them is more likely to be direct or intense interaction." She also discovered that "either because of intrinsic motivation or conscious effort, employed mothers, and particularly the more educated, compensate to some extent for their absence." In conclusion, she found that "there is no evidence for diminished quality of interaction between employed mothers and their young children and some evidence for the opposite pattern."

Sandra Scarr, in a review of maternal time-use studies in her book

Mother Care, Other Care also had some intriguing observations: "It is popularly assumed that mothers at home spend a great deal of time in direct interaction with their children, playing educational games and improving their children's minds. . . . [But] in middle- and working-class families, the child of a mother at home full-time spends only five percent of her waking hours in direct interaction with her mother. . . .

"Time-use studies . . . show that employed women spend as much time as nonworking women in *direct* interaction with their children. Employed mothers spend as much time as those at home reading to and playing with their young children, although they do not, of course, spend as much time simply in the same room or house with the children."

The amount of time a working mother spends with her child seems to me to be at the very heart of the maelstrom of feelings that surround the issue of working mothers and children. A recent *Redbook* survey of one thousand respondents (40 percent of whom worked outside the home) highlighted the anxieties that many working mothers feel simply because they don't have enough hours in the day with their children. Although 66 percent of the working mothers felt that "quality time" could compensate for a mother's absence, others wrote of "missing something by being gone from seven in the morning until six at night," and of being "haunted" by their children's faces.

I'm not sure that "quality time" is a very useful phrase to employ when assessing what happens when a mother and child spend time together. By referring to it, one assumes that all *direct* hours are "better" than all *indirect* hours. While it is almost certainly true that reading to a child or teaching that child how to paint a fence is a better way to interact with a son or daughter than putting him or her in front of a TV while you vacuum the rug, there are many moments of indirect interaction that seem to me to have just as much "quality" as those spent one-on-one.

I know, from my own experience, that I like being in the same room with my child, even if I am cooking or paying bills. When the atmosphere is relaxed, my daughter goes about her business in tandem with mine, and I think she feels a sense of comfort at having me nearby to help her find a Lego piece or set up a paintbox should the urge to paint strike her. Yet it is also true that she has the same sense of comfort if it is her father in the room, or her grandmother or a neighbor she has gotten to know well. This sense of nurturing or comfort—of having a loving adult nearby to *take care of you*—is at least as important, I believe, as being read to or taught something and should not be devalued by not coming under the umbrella of "quality time."

The question that remains to be answered, however, is how important is it that it be the mother who provides those long hours of nurturing and comfort—that indirect interaction that nevertheless gives a child a sense of security? The question is a particularly difficult one to answer because the solution seems to rely heavily on the personality and needs of each individual child and mother, and on the culture in which these mothers and children live. I know one at-home mother of a seven-year-old boy, to give one unusual example, who recently discovered, via a child psychologist, that her son was emotionally "at risk" because he needed *more* time and attention from his mother. The mother had certainly been giving her child more hours per day than any working mother; but the child's own personality, different from the norm, required exceptional amounts of maternal maintenance.

Some working mothers speak of terrible anxieties at being away from their children, and the need to intensify their mothering when they are at home. Elaine, the dentist, for example, said that because she is with her daughter for only a few hours a day, she feels a special responsibility to "have an impact on my daughter."

Yet Carol, the waitress, felt that her children were better off for having three primary nurturers—herself, her mother and her husband. She believed her children were getting the best of each adult, and that they were doing "fine" because of this. In other cultures I have observed—the Kikuyu society in Kenya, for instance—children learn early on that nurturing comes from a variety of female adults and semi-adults (older girl children). In that society, the "working" mothers often form a kind of informal collective within their villages and settlements, whereby all adult females are responsible for all children, and these responsibilities vary according to the schedules and tasks of the individual mothers.

What is missing in our culture is a feeling of comfort at allowing children to have multiple nurturers, stemming not only from the traditional upbringing, with its rigid set of expectations, in which most mothers today were raised, but also from a lack of suitable surrogate nurturers and an inflexibility in the workplace. Good quality childcare, as I will discuss in Chapter 9, is difficult to obtain for many working mothers and has become something of a national scandal. The workplace, in large part, remains inflexible, denying part-time work, job-sharing, flextime schedules or at-home work to most working mothers. Without adequate childcare or the opportunity to discover for oneself the optimum number of hours per day a child needs with the mother, anxiety, guilt and discomfort may take precedence over any good feelings the mother has about her role.

A mother who is deeply troubled may not be an effective role model, but for those families in which the mother is not so distraught, an argument can be made that children today see the working mother as a kind of super role model with enhanced powers. The concept of power is extremely important to a young child. "One of the most significant forces for the child in the early years is the notion of power," says Dr. Sylvia Feinberg, chairman of the Eliot Pearson Department of Child Study at Tufts University. "Who's got it, and in what circumstances?"

In the past, the mother had the power in the home, and the father had the power in the world outside. It was common, in fact, for girls in previous generations to take their fathers for role models if they planned to become achievers outside the home. Today, in the homes of working mothers, children perceive mothers as having power in both arenas. Mothers are often perceived, in fact, as having more power than fathers.[2]

Working mothers still perform work that deeply affects the child's well-being: cooking, feeding the family, bathing the child, nurturing other children. For a very young child, ultimate power resides in the home. But as that child matures and gains a clearer understanding of what the mother does outside the home, becoming intrigued by the "coming and going" nature of the mother's work, he or she will associate this work with power in the same way that previous generations of children assigned power to their fathers. The child may understand that the mother gets money outside the home (economic power), makes things happen in the outside world (produces goods or services) and may even have an important position in the workplace. This mother may then be perceived as having more cumulative power (power both inside and outside the home), and perhaps being a more powerful influence than either the at-home mother or the father. In an important study of over ninety teenagers in two-career families, conducted by Patricia Knaub at the University of Nebraska, she asked the following question: "Thinking back to your childhood and up through your teenage years, which of your parents seems to have been the more influential, on the whole, in shaping your attitudes and your general outlook on life? Decide between your mother and father, even if the difference was slight." The mother was indicated by 72.7 percent of the sample (80 percent of the females and 63.1 percent of the males), whereas 27.6 percent (20 percent of females and 36.9 percent of the males) said it was their father who was more influential.

It may also be that the instability of marriage and the demise of the extended family have combined to make the contemporary mother an even more powerful role model. In the past, when many families were large and contained accessible grandmothers and aunts and cousins, a woman's mothering was often shared by extended family members. Power in the home was split among a number of women and men, and occasionally it was not the mother at all who had the power in the house but rather the eldest female in the household, sometimes the grandmother.

With the loss of these extended families, and the rise of the isolated nuclear family, power, in a child's eyes, was concentrated between two people (instead of among three or four)—his parents. But today, with more than half of all marriages ending in divorce, and with the prediction that by 1990 half of all families may be headed by single parents, 90 percent of whom will be women, more and more children are seeing power concentrated in one individual—the mother. In most single-parent families, she not only controls power in the home, but she is often the sole breadwinner. This kind of funneling down of the American family to its most essential components—mother and child—has had the effect of intensifying power in the person of the working mother.

It is extremely important to point out, however, that the way in which a mother perceives that power is more important than the power itself. The attitude of the working mother toward her own work life and sexual role may be the single most important factor in shaping the child's perceptions. If a mother is oppressed in the home by her husband or by her economic situation, and in the workplace by the nature of her job or by her supervisors, the ideas that she will convey to her child about the value of working—*and the effects of that mother's employment on her child*—will be considerably different from the mother who is happy and comfortable in her home life, who is proud of her accomplishments in the workplace and who is pleased with the way she is combining the two. Mothers who feel ambivalent about working and mothering may convey negative messages to their children. Job satisfaction, self-esteem in the workplace, self-definition as a worker, her husband's attitude toward her employment as well as the extent to which he shares household and child-rearing tasks, her confidence in her childcare arrangements, and her economic situation will all affect a working mother's attitudes toward her employment. *It is not the working itself that has such a powerful effect on the child, but what the mother conveys to that child about her own satisfaction or dissatisfaction with her life as a working mother.*

As noted earlier, jobs that inspire alienation rather than some measure of fulfillment are not a fertile environment for the development of self-esteem—a crucial prerequisite for extolling the value of work, whether in words or by actions. In an ideal society all jobs would be filled by people who enjoyed them, or they would have built-in incentives, variation and opportunities for advancement that made them at least tolerable. In reality, however, many jobs in America, both corporate and noncorporate, are demoralizing, if not actually demeaning. There are certainly women (and men) who leave their homes daily to perform tasks in which they can find no value (other than to their employer), and they return home disgruntled and feeling in some way abused by their day's work. Nightly complaints about work assignments, workload, work environment, fellow workers, employees, or even commuting are commonplace in many homes; and when both parents are employed, the chance of children experiencing such dissatisfaction is obviously twice as great. Given the case that most women who find themselves in jobs or careers that depress them must continue to work out of necessity, it is clear that the mere fact of a mother working does not automatically result in her children growing up with an appetite for success or self-expression in the workplace. As hard as a mother might try to hide her frustrations, it is inevitably impossible to lie to a child about something as primary as work.

This book is in no way a call to women to adjust their lives and aspirations so as to feel at home in jobs with which they can make no personal connection or in which they can find no meaning. On the contrary, it is an affirmation of the benefits to children as well as to their mothers of *meaningful* work—work that results in a feeling of accomplishment. Without reference to any studies or statistics, common sense dictates that a mother who conveys a sense of self-esteem and accomplishment to her children functions as a better barometer of life's possibilities than a mother filled with nostalgia for what she might have been or what she might have done.

5

The Effects on Daughters

When I was a child, I could not glimpse a plane flying overhead without wondering if my father was in the cockpit. I was in awe of the way a Constellation could leave the ground and head into the clouds with nothing under it but air, the way a DC-3 could find its way to Boston all the way from London in one long lonely night. I was vaguely aware of the vectors and currents of flight, but they refused to sink in and become comprehensible, in the same way that when I was an adult I could not understand the biology of a random sperm meeting a random egg and becoming my daughter.

Sometimes when I was sitting in the front yard, lolling on the grass or waiting for a friend with that lack of urgency that is childhood's gift, my father would emerge from the house, in his uniform, on his way to work. He would kiss my mother good-bye, and she would stay behind. But he went off to work. He often said to me that he was merely a glorified bus driver, but when he was in his black-and-gold uniform I didn't believe him. He would be headed for another flight: to Tampa, to Atlanta, to Detroit, to New York. I would imagine the gleaming plane and the passengers waiting for him, and how he would, in an hour's time, lift the plane off the ground and into the air.

When I was a child, I wanted to be a pilot. Because this desire was preposterous, I kept it to myself, but I often imagined myself at the controls and loved the delirious feeling of flight. My father taught flying at a local airport in his spare time and sometimes, because he had access to the planes, he would take me flying with him. I would sit next to him in the tiny interior of a Piper Cub, listening as he talked to ground control. Then we would be bumping along the runway, gathering speed. In an instant we would be aloft, above the trees—a tiny capsule floating effortlessly over my house, my school, my town. Sometimes, for my benefit, my father would perform tricks with the plane. Nosing steeply up and making a loop in the cloudless sky, he would then right the plane as my stomach pressed up against my throat. It was as if we were a feather caught in an updraft—now turning, now banking, now cruising in an invisible figure eight. We would come in low over the trees and I would think we would brush the tops, but just in time my father would execute a graceful arc, soaring in a slow roll out toward the horizon.

I believe that if I had been a son, I would know how to fly today. There is, of course, no way to prove this; but it is a feeling that I have. Had I been a son, I am quite sure that my childhood would have been very different than it was. For since birth, my parents—and indeed all who came in contact with me (friends, teachers and other adults)— would have been encouraging certain characteristics and expectations and would have been discouraging others. For example, had I been a son and had I wanted to be a pilot, I would have said so; I wouldn't have been too embarrassed to admit it. In my room at home, there would have been model airplanes and not Barbie dolls. On the flights with my father, I would have been encouraged to take the controls, rather than getting a free ride. Someone, one day, might have lifted the hood of a car and invited me to poke around the engine. I might have had more practice solving practical problems and might have been better in math and science than I was. It is even possible I'd have learned to be more comfortable with my own authority as I grew older, and perhaps I would have had greater self-esteem. Without question, I would have grown up with the certainty that I would one day have a career.

It is difficult to say whether I would have been happier or more fulfilled as a pilot, but that is not the point. The point is this: Because

I was a daughter and not a son, an entire range of possibilities was closed to me. It was assumed that I would one day marry and have a family, and that these roles were incompatible with wanting to learn to fly.

For years, parents have treated girl children differently from boy children. This different treatment has had the effect of teaching girls that they are second-best, dependent and passive individuals.

In the past, among some African and Indian cultures, girl babies were killed at birth or sold as slaves. Although we do not murder our daughters in this country, the birth of a girl child often causes emotional distress in a family immediately after a birth; but such is not likely to be the case, researchers have found, with a son.[1]

In almost all cultures, boys have been preferred to girls. In 1970, a group of unmarried college students were queried as to their preference for a boy or a girl. Ninety percent of the males and 78 percent of the females said a boy.[2] This preference for boy children—and the sense of distress or failure when a girl arrives instead—may give daughters, from day one, a diminished sense of their own worth.

Sex-role stereotyping begins at birth. On one occasion, thirty parents were interviewed twenty-four hours after the birth of their first baby. Although the babies themselves clearly had no obvious male or female traits, the parents of girls rated their babies as softer and smaller and described them as prettier and cuter and more beautiful than the parents of boy babies.[3] When adults were shown videotapes of two seventeen-month-old babies playing (a boy and a girl), similar preconceptions arose. If the adults were told the child was a boy—regardless of whether or not this was the case—the adults, and the males in particular, said the child was independent, active and alert. If the child was labeled as a girl, the adults characterized the child as cuddly and delicate.[4]

Parents' preconceptions begin to translate into parental behavior in the very first weeks of the infant's life. Researchers Susan Goldberg and Michael Lewis (in a study cited by J. Brooks-Gunn and Wendy Schempp Matthews in *He and She*) noticed that for the first six months of infancy, mothers exhibited physically closer behavior toward boys than toward girls. But at the age of six months, this behavior reversed itself. As the boys matured, they were encouraged to explore and were discouraged from dependent "clinginess." Mothers of girl babies, conversely, began to touch their daughters more, subtly encouraging dependence. It may be, speculated the researchers, that mothers are closer to sons at birth because sons require more physical attention (maintenance) to quiet them, but then as their bodies mature, mothers push them toward independent behavior and exploration.

Stereotyping continues through the toddler and preschool years when a child is forming and confirming his or her sex-role identity— that "constellation of qualities an individual understands to characterize males and females in his or her culture."[5] Although the society surrounding the child contributes, as we shall see in a moment, the primary molders and shapers are the child's parents. In study after study of preschool children from traditional families, researchers find the same results: Parents encourage boys to roughhouse, act aggressively, explore, take risks and be independent; girls, on the other hand, may sing, dance, play with dolls and engage in passive "quiet" activities such as reading and coloring. Mothers of kindergarten children have been shown to be more tolerant of aggression from boys than from girls,[6] and to restrict and supervise girls more than boys. Parents have also admitted to allowing boys freer access to a wider area of the community and to allowing boys earlier than girls to use scissors, cross the street, tie their own shoes, play away from home without first telling the parents and take a bus ride.[7] Even in families in which the parents professed to encourage their girls to play with trucks and other "boyish" toys—in a self-described effort to lessen sex-stereotyping—researchers found when observing parent-child interaction that these same parents were much more tolerant of requests for "help" from their daughters than they were from their sons, thus subtly encouraging dependency in girls and independent behavior for boys.[8]

But we don't need studies to convince us that parents have treated girls and boys differently from one another or that sex-role stereotyping can begin at a very early age. Take a look, for example, at the rooms of toddlers and preschoolers, which are often accurate indicators of sex-stereotyping within a household. Although relatives and friends give children toys as gifts, it is the parents who really fill the child's room. In traditional families, the rooms of boys almost always contain active "doing"-type toys, such as action figures, trucks, cars, boats, sports equipment and military paraphernalia, and the rooms of girls often contain dolls, stuffed animals, books, tea sets and "quiet activity" toys, such as sewing cards and coloring books. Yet girls, according to one study of eighteen-month-olds, play with trucks, when given access to them, as much as do boys. "It is interesting to note that one of the differences between boys and girls that shows up consistently in tests is that boys are better in visual-spatial ability, which involves estimating distances and size of figures. Does what shows up on the tests reflect the absence of vehicles and other time-and-movement toys in girls' rooms, rather than any inborn psychological difference? Apparently so. [Researchers] gave young girls and boys practice on visual-spatial tasks —making designs with blocks. The girls' ability improved, but the boys' ability stayed the same. This seems to indicate that the reason the girls had not done as well as the boys was that they hadn't had as much practice. These sorts of skills are crucial to any field in which mathematics and mechanics play a part—architecture, stage design, physics, engineering and economics, among others."[9]

Unfortunately, as children mature, stereotypical attitudes may become more deeply entrenched. Boys raised in traditional families were asked their opinions about what both men and women needed to know in order to function in the world. The boys said that men needed to be strong, to make decisions, to protect women and children in emergencies, to do rough work, to get money to support their families and to have a good business head. In addition they were described as being the boss, having authority as to the disposal of money and getting the first choice of the most comfortable chair in the house. When asked to describe women, the boys said that they were indecisive, afraid of many things, got tired a lot, needed someone to help them, stayed home most of the time, were not as strong as men, didn't like adventure, didn't know what to do in an emergency and were not very intelligent. In a subsequent study of girls' opinions of men and women, the girls said that men were competent, logical and active, and that females were gentle, neat and affectionate.[10]

Parents continue to foster stereotypical attitudes even when their children are teenagers. Researcher Lois Hoffman asked parents what kind of an adult they hoped their child would turn out to be. Twice as many parents wanted their sons, rather than their daughters, to be ambitious and hardworking. Fathers were more likely to want their sons

be career-oriented than their daughters and were more disapproving
a son who had failed to acquire high achievement goals. Expectations
for daughters, on the other hand, ran the gamut from hoping they
would be kind and loving to having a good marriage.[11] (I recall that
there was even a moral imperative to this stereotyping. More than
once, in my own childhood, I heard that women should not take jobs
away from men because men had to support families and women did
not.) In fact, no matter where one turns in the literature, one finds the
same conclusions: Parents in the past expected that their sons would
one day have careers and that their daughters would not.

Although the parents begin the process of sex-role stereotyping, the
culture surrounding the child—toy manufacturers, the media and
schools—carries on the dismaying message: Girls are not only less
active than boys, but their capabilities and options are limited. Brooks-
Gunn and Matthews, authors of *He and She*, cite in their book a
particularly revealing study conducted in the early 1970s by the members of NOW chapters in the national capital area and Montgomery
County, Maryland. The members surveyed eight hundred toys—felt to
be appropriate for children of both genders—on the shelves of a large
chain of children's toy stores. "Among the preschool toys, they found
almost twice as many boys on the covers of the toys as girls. Those girls
who were depicted on the boxes and toy covers were twice as likely to
be passively watching than actively playing with the toy. Of the cars,
trucks and trains, only two percent of the illustrated packages depicted
girls. On the packages of science and educational toys, illustrations of
boys outnumber girls sixteen to one. When boys and girls are shown
together, the chances are fourteen to one that the girls will be looking
on. . . . The implicit message on the covers is that complicated, enrich-
ing, creative and career-serving play material is for boys. Girls get to
stay on the sidelines. The theme of boys doing and girls just being is
a recurring one."

This theme is prevalent in children's media, too. In shows designed
for children, male roles exceed female roles by two to one. And the
males are portrayed as aggressive and as constructive, while females
remain passive.[12] On a recent Saturday morning, sitting in front of the
television to "research" the matter (the most interesting type of work
her mother has done to date, thinks my daughter), Katherine and I
observed that even on a contemporary cartoon show one associates with

more progressive thinking, sex-role stereotyping was rampant. Males were portrayed as active, courageous and daring, taunting dragons to "come out here," while females were portrayed as helpless, needing to be saved, passive and patient. Instead of taunting dragons, female characters were waiting, helpless, on balconies to be saved, spouting lines such as "How romantic," "I'm in love," and "Let me go." ("Let me go" is especially interesting. Notice that it's not "I'm going to get myself out of this jam," but rather a plea to someone stronger to release her.)

In tandem with the sex-role stereotyping of the shows themselves are the commercial messages from advertisers. One researcher noted that boys in ads were shown outdoors and actively involved with a toy, perhaps learning about a technical or athletic field, while girls were shown at home in their bedrooms, engaged in a repetitive behavior such as dressing and undressing a doll.[13]

Teachers and school materials, too, have often been unwitting abettors of sex-role stereotyping in the classroom. Researchers have discovered that teachers expect boys to be more rowdy and inattentive than girls in the classroom. Therefore, when they are criticized, the problem is lack of attention, not lack of ability. Girls, on the other hand, are seen as well-behaved and always doing their best. If they fail, the problem is not something other than their own ability—inattention—but rather something very central to their selfhood—they failed because they could not do the work.[14]

Even school books, those tools children use to learn about the world around them, are full of stereotypical attitudes. In a study of 2,760 stories in 134 elementary-school readers, boy-centered stories outnumbered girl-centered stories three to one. Stories about men outnumbered those about women three to one, and male biographies outnumbered female biographies six to one. In these stories, male characters had 147 different jobs, including architect, computer operator, news reporter and principal. Female characters had only twenty-six occupations, chief among them mother. Other occupations suitable for females included dressmaker, cleaning woman and fat lady.[15]

The idea of being second-best, dependent or passive rather than first-rate, independent and active threads its way through a girl's life. It affects her emotional and physical health, her cognitive development, her vocational choices, her achievements and her relationships with others.

Girls who are encouraged to adopt a role model or a mode of behavior devalued by society run the risk of devaluing themselves. Contemporary American society, unfortunately, does not value its at-home mothers. Some child-care experts, some husbands and some mothers themselves have recently extolled the virtues of the mother who sacrifices all to stay home with her children, but one has only to glance at how the at-home mother has been treated in the media or to talk with at-home mothers to realize that hers is neither a respected nor a coveted role for a woman today. "I often feel uncomfortable in social situations," says Dale, thirty-seven, an at-home mother. "It's a feeling of having to justify my existence. People ask me what I do, and I'm embarrassed to say I'm staying home with my children. You get the idea your life isn't as stimulating as it should be. Although I think I'm doing the right thing for my children, I definitely feel inferior when I'm in a social situation with mothers who work."

Interestingly, being a housewife/mother has *never* been a highly respected role in our society, even when it was the norm. Housewives in the 1950s—when almost all mothers stayed at home—complained that they felt devalued and that they suffered from a lack of self-esteem. Studies from the 1950s on middle-aged women confirmed this: Statistics showed them to be a particularly distressed group, vulnerable to depression and feelings of uselessness.[16] In my interviews with working mothers, they often recalled that their own at-home mothers didn't seem particularly fulfilled. "It just seems that in the past the cost to the woman was too much. . . ." "I had a very strong feeling that [my mother] was very lonely. . . ." "My mother never worked. In fact she almost never even left the house."

If, as we have seen, an important aspect of acquiring a sex-role identity and becoming an adult is to identify with the parent of the same sex, identifying with a parent who has been labeled by society as second-class is clearly a problem for daughters. If, in the home, the girl child sees that the father's work is more respected than the mother's, that he has more economic power, that he appears to be more competent, achievement-oriented and independent, and that his life is more interesting, being expected to adopt a traditional female role may produce feelings of anxiety and conflict in a daughter. As the child matures, these feelings may resolve themselves either by taking on the father as a role model (but not without concerns about one's femininity), by looking outside the family for role models or by resigning oneself to a dependent and restrictive future.

For children, identification with traditional parental roles in our society results in a less positive self-image for girls than for boys. Girls who identify with a parent who appears to be less competent and less powerful than the other parent may develop a relatively low sense of self-esteem and may mature with a tendency toward depression. One researcher found, in a survey of two hundred children aged eight to fifteen, that as girls grew older they valued the opposite sex more and began to devalue their own sex. Boys, too, perceived the number of desirable traits in girls diminishing as they grew older. The nearer both boys and girls got to adulthood, the more devalued the image of the female appeared to them.[17]

In the *Lifeprints* study referred to earlier, the authors found that both satisfactory love relationships and a fulfilling work life were essential to the emotional health of many of the women they surveyed. Central to this finding was the suggestion that traditional indications of a woman's happiness—the state of her love life, her age and whether or not she was a mother—were poor predictors of a woman's sense of pride and power and her sense of mastery. In fact, the authors began to suspect that being a housewife was hazardous to a woman's emotional health. "It's hard to derive self-esteem from a role that society doesn't think much of; it's hard to feel in control of a job where the standards are so unclear," the authors wrote. They also pointed out that in one official Labor Department ranking of jobs according to the complexity of tasks required, homemakers got the same ranking as parking-lot attendants.

In addition to giving girls conflicting messages about adulthood, early sex-role stereotyping interferes with the development of a girl's autonomy. Autonomy is the ability to think and make decisions for oneself, to *choose* how to be or feel. It is, say many child specialists, probably the most treasured attribute a parent can help a child to attain. But the development of autonomy may be difficult for a girl whose same-sex parent does not possess it herself, or whose self-image is one characterized by low self-esteem, dependency and deference to others. Continual messages that daughters "are" rather than "do" and that they will eventually attach themselves to the lives of "doers" (males) may cripple their ability to make judgments and to believe they can stand on their own. The end result of this handicap may be that the girl matures with the idea, as Phyllis, the librarian, put it, that "for years I always felt that I was just nothing. . . . When I was a child I was taught to look for happiness in a man."

One can see, also, how sex-role stereotyping might lead to fewer opportunities for physical exercise in girls than in boys. Encouraged to be "passive" rather than active, girls in traditional households play indoors more than do boys, thus promoting less physically strenuous activity. This early form of physical "crippling" in turn leads to less participation in team sports because skills necessary to feel competent in such sports—throwing, catching and hitting a ball, for example— have not been practiced or perfected.

Girls raised in homes in which traditional stereotypical attitudes were taught and reinforced *expected* to do less well in school than boys. This sense of lowered expectations begins as early as kindergarten, but becomes particularly pronounced during the adolescent years and on into college. Despite the fact that girls in school actually did quite well when grades alone were considered, girls' feelings of incompetence as a result of cultural stereotypes persisted. Although researchers have found no difference in abilities or intelligence in girls and boys in the nursery and preschool years, they have found that girls consistently had less confidence in their abilities than did boys.

As children matured during the elementary school years, teachers noticed that girls began to pull ahead in verbal ability, boys in mathematical skills. For years it was thought that female children had innately superior verbal skills and that boys, by their very nature, had superior spatial and mathematical abilities. Others suspected, however, that *nurture* and not *nature* was the key to this divergence in intelligence. Girls, for example, frequently excelled in reading and spelling because these activities were perceived to be feminine. Encouraged to pursue passive activities since toddlerhood (looking at books, coloring, sitting at a desk or table with paper and pencils), girls often began these quiet activities earlier than did boys, and by the time they reached school age together, these tasks had already been branded as female in nature. When researcher Judith Schickedanz looked at third-grade boys, she found that boys who perceived reading to be a masculine activity did better at this skill than boys who perceived it to be a feminine activity.[18] Conversely, boys excelled in mathematical and visual-spatial abilities because these activities were perceived to be masculine. Not only, as we have seen, did boys have more access than girls to toys that fostered these abilities, but parents began to value mathematical skills more for sons than for daughters from an early age. After the elementary school years, as children entered adolescence, this divergence became especially noticeable, and many experts feel that it stemmed from the fact that both parents and teachers anticipated that boys would need math skills vocationally and that girls would not.

Across the board, with few exceptions, girls had much lower career aspirations than boys. In the past, girls automatically began narrowing their range of possibilities—even at a very early age—and by the teenage years, when vocational aspirations began to translate into occupational choices, girls listed far fewer jobs as available to them than did boys. Of the occupations they chose, almost all of them were in the "helping professions," and the majority chose teacher, nurse or secretary. This pattern was a result of cultural stereotypes which dictated that a woman would eventually marry and therefore didn't need a career; that it was seemly for a woman to go into one of the helping professions since deference and subservience to others was part of the female character; and that a girl shouldn't be too rigid in her plans for the future because she would, of course, eventually attach her life to that of a man who would determine her fate. Even when a few brave girls attempted to pursue careers which required years of forethought and schooling, they often designed their futures so that they could accommodate a husband and children. (Boys virtually never planned for this accommodation.) Nancy, the doctor, recalled that when she thought about her future, she planned to be a pediatrician not only because it was a field that a woman could be comfortable in (it dealt with children), but also because she could have her office in her house and could have her own children near her.

Once vocational choices were made, girls, as a whole, had low expectations for success. Girls, as we have seen, were given less encouragement than boys to explore, to take risks or to be independent. "As a result," says Lois Hoffman, "[a girl] does not develop skills in coping with her environment, nor confidence in her ability to do so. She continues to be dependent on adults for solving her problems. . . ."[19]

One of the effects of sex-stereotyping at an early age is that girls, with less confidence in themselves, have an excuse to withdraw from a task should it prove frustrating or difficult for any reason. Recall the words of Mary, the editor: "My mother did occasionally work when I was growing up, but she never stuck to anything. She never had what you would call a commitment to a career. In fact, as soon as she became successful at something, she would quit. In that way, she was a terrible role model for me because it's made it very difficult for me to follow through in my ambitions. If I'd had a mother who was committed both to her work and to her family, I'm sure I would experience less of the conflict that I feel now. . . . This is true especially when something happens at work to lower my self-esteem."

Because they were not expected to succeed, girls in adolescence, and later when they became women, often suffered terrible anxieties when approaching the threshold of success. Time after time, women would deliberately drop out, drop back or sabotage their own success in a chosen field. This "fear of success" syndrome, first identified by Matina Horner, president of Radcliffe College, and later elaborated upon by social scientists, had several components:

(1) Having fewer expectations for success to begin with, the surprise of success was alienating and guilt-provoking for many women.

(2) Success, a masculine attribute, was not seen as consistent with femininity. Indeed, the cultural stereotype of the successful woman was one whose sexuality, and certainly her femininity, were suspect. (Nancy, the doctor, recalled: "Nothing at home or in high school ever discouraged me [from wanting to be a doctor]. It was only when I got to college and was told very clearly by my male social contacts that this was really unacceptable, and that working wasn't going to fit in with my plan of having children and being married, that I had trouble with this idea.").

(3) Adolescent girls, and later women, consistently failed to credit themselves with success, although they were particularly good at blaming themselves for failure. Success, if it came at all, was never viewed

as richly deserved for hard work; rather, it was a product of luck. Therefore success was suspect and could be taken away as easily as it had been given.

If success could not be tolerated in oneself, it could certainly be tolerated in the man the woman attached herself to. Indeed, keeping your options open, waiting for Prince Charming and living vicariously through his achievements was sanctioned as the proper role for a female. Girls who noticed, as they were growing up, that women appeared to have less self-esteem than men, that women were economically and emotionally dependent on men, and that men seemed to have the ticket to the outside world might be forgiven if they decided to hitch their future to a star. Particularly sad was the fact that girls who had been encouraged to achieve in school, and who had done so, suddenly found in adolescence that they were expected to stifle their ambitions and instead pay attention to boys. Some of the brightest minds of an entire generation whiled away hundreds of hours waiting for the telephone to ring so boys could ask them out. Even in this arena, girls could not be active or assertive. The girl's role was to sit and wait to be chosen, ideally by Mr. Right, who would sweep her off her feet. The phrase is particularly apt: She would no longer be able to stand on her own.

The catalogue of the damage done to girls growing up with traditional cultural stereotypes is dismaying, but it should be pointed out that this was not the *fault* of the mothers. They were not poor mothers in any way, nor were they to blame for the inhibitions and restrictions imposed upon them and which they then passed on to their children. To , the contrary, these mothers were as good or as bad as any generation of mothers. As a whole, they tended to be quite nurturing and self-sacrificing. One fact that is seldom pointed out is that many of these mothers put both their daughters and sons through college at quite a cost to themselves. Some historians believe that the first stirrings of the working-mother boom began when mothers of teenagers realized they had to enter the work force in order to enhance the family income enough to send their children to college.

These mothers, like the current generation of working mothers, were victims of cultural stereotypes, handed down from mother to daughter, that were intended to preserve the status quo. Unfortunately, however, that status quo had the effect of undermining the quality of life for half the population. But the chain is broken, and that social legacy is disintegrating.

THE DAUGHTERS OF WORKING MOTHERS

Logically, one would expect working mothers to treat their daughters differently than do at-home mothers. First, the mother's time with the daughter is more limited than that of a traditional mother's, and so she may feel that when she is with the child, she must use that time not only for experiencing her daughter but also for instilling certain attitudes and values. "I have to have an impact on my daughter, who is four, when I am home, because I'm with her only three hours a day," said Elaine, the dentist. "I talk to her a lot. I encourage her to be independent." This sense of needing to have an impact may be intensified by the realization that the child, for many hours a day, is under the influence of another individual or set of individuals who may have values different from those of the mother.

Second, achieving self-esteem, autonomy and a feeling of mastery did not come easily to many of the women of the current generation of working mothers. If a woman has struggled to achieve these attributes, she may have a keener appreciation of them and, as a result, might consciously try to pass on these characteristics to her daughter. "I think I'm a positive role model for my daughter in that I'm letting her know that a woman just doesn't get taken care of in life," said Sue, the typesetter. "She really has to go out on her own and make her own life. She has to make her own happiness. She shouldn't depend on anybody to take charge of her. When I was growing up, I was raised to believe that you're going to meet Prince Charming and be swept away, and it's going to be okay just because you're in love. And you know, that's not the way it is, and it's very hard when you find that out. I don't want my daughter to grow up under that illusion."

Third, a working-mother model behaves, by necessity, in ways that are different from the at-home mother. Going and coming to and from work; discussing one's triumphs and frustrations with one's spouse; sharing, of necessity, child-rearing tasks; and expressing certain attitudes about economic independence and assertiveness in the workplace to other adults cannot fail to impinge on a child's consciousness. "I think working mothers say things to their children that are very different from the things mothers who stay home say to their children," said Jayne, the architecture critic. "Children pick up on attitudes and characteristics subliminally just by noticing who you are and what you do."

And fourth, working mothers instill independence and autonomy in their daughters to a greater degree than do at-home mothers for the simple reason that the mothers aren't *there* for the daughters, in a physical sense, as much as at-home mothers can be. "I remember from the time my daughter, Elizabeth, was a very young child encouraging a certain amount of independence in her," recalled Celeste, the interior designer. "I did this both because I'd never had it as a child and wished I had, and also because I had just started working and I simply didn't have the time to hover over her." (Although the concept of not being physically *there* all the time for one's child may seem particularly anxiety- or guilt-provoking, the research is quite clear on this point: Distal behavior on the part of the mother—that is, behavior that is less physically and emotionally close—encourages a higher achievement-orientation in daughters. One can argue, of course, that the trade-off is too great, that a mother would prefer to experience her daughter as intimately as possible and that this intimacy is more valuable than the potential in her daughter for high achievement.)

The fostering of independence and autonomy has been among the clearest of the research findings on the effects of working mothers on daughters. In a survey published by Jeanne Bodin and Bonnie Mitelman in their book *Mothers Who Work*, the majority of mothers polled said that their children were more independent and responsible as a result of having a working mother. Earlier, in a study by Dr. Brooks-Gunn, we saw how androgynous mothers (mothers who describe themselves as possessing both masculine and feminine characteristics—that is, they are both nurturing and assertive, both affectionate and achievement-oriented) treated their daughters differently than did feminine mothers. (Feminine mothers are those who define themselves as possessing only traditional feminine characteristics.) Androgynous mothers, who researchers say share personality characteristics with working mothers, encouraged their daughters in play situations to be more independent and competent than the feminine mothers did. "This seems to agree with other data suggesting that maternal employment has a positive effect on girls," says Dr. Brooks-Gunn. "Girls whose mothers work have higher self-esteem and career aspirations than girls whose mothers don't work."

In her definitive review of the literature on the effects of maternal employment on children, Lois Hoffman had similar conclusions: "The employed mother provides a model that is associated with competence and accorded higher status in the family. The children of employed mothers received more independence training, a pattern that is particularly valuable for daughters since they often receive too little in the traditional nonemployed-mother family. Other aspects of the employed-mother family—the involvement of the father, the greater participation of children in household responsibilities, and the more egalitarian sex-role attitudes—have all been linked to greater self-confidence and competence in girls." Hoffman also found that this fostering of self-reliance seemed to have a direct correlation with a mother's satisfaction with her work. When working mothers were happy with their decision to work, they were more likely to encourage their daughters to be independent.[20]

At-home mothers, on the other hand, may unconsciously allow their children to become overly dependent on them because these mothers see their primary role as "mother" and may need to be needed. Indeed, many mothers who embrace this way of being are often compensating for not being needed in the world by anyone save their husbands and children, and often only in a service or "servant" role. "Mother-daughter relationships in which the mother is supported by a network of women kin and friends, and has meaningful work and self-esteem, produce daughters with capacities for nurturance and a *strong sense of self.* [Italics mine.] Mother-daughter relationships in which the mother has no other adult support or meaningful work and remains ambivalently attached to her own mother produce ambivalent attachment and inability to separate in daughters," writes Nancy Chodorow in *The Reproduction of Mothering*. (Again, it is important to remember one of the caveats stated earlier in this book. It is certainly possible for at-home mothers to produce autonomous daughters, and conversely, to find working mothers with an excessive need to be needed. *In general,* however, the findings discussed above are consistent throughout the literature to date.)

Like mother, like daughter. Researchers have found that daughters mirror their working mothers' attitudes, particularly about appropriate sex roles. The more nonstereotypical the mother's attitudes about the roles of men and women, the more nonstereotypical the daughter's attitudes will be.[21] More specifically, the presence of a working mother in the home results in fewer differences in perceptions of male and female roles by children. And if the mother's work is regarded as successful by the children, this will lead to more egalitarian sex-role ideologies as they mature.[22]

Throughout the research, the link between mother and daughter is quite direct. Remember the studies that asked both boys and girls to list the things that men and women needed to know in order to function in the world? If you ask the daughters of working mothers those same questions, the answers are quite different from the answers of daughters raised in traditional families: Interestingly, daughters of working mothers don't just see women as having a wider range of behavior; they see women *and* men engaging in more cross-sex activities. In their responses they indicate that *each* sex is less limited than the traditional model, and they tend to describe both males and females as possessing a wider variety of traits.[23]

As we have seen, girls acquire their sex-role identity by imitating their mothers. If the mother appears to have a role in the world similar to the father's (breadwinner as well as nurturer, for example), then this will broaden the daughter's concept of what is appropriate for women. Clearly, the parental division of labor and the parental division of child-rearing contribute to this concept. This only holds true, however, if the mother is content with her own sex-role identity; if she is conflicted about her sexuality and uncomfortable or guilt-ridden about her role as a working mother, then the daughter might be expected to be aware of this discomfort and come away with conflicting messages about working and mothering.

The easing of sex-role stereotypes appears to begin unconsciously right from birth and shows up as early as nursery school. One study discovered that working mothers played with their babies in a manner formerly seen mostly in fathers: The mothers handled their infants in a physically robust manner, suggesting that sex differences in parenting style may be a function of work roles.[24] Another study noticed that mothers who had more egalitarian sex-role ideologies encouraged their daughters to play more and to be more active than did mothers with traditional ideas about sex roles.[25] Nursery schoolteachers' comments on how girls' play has changed as a result of the presence of the working mother appear to confirm this. "Ten years ago, girls would not have been playing 'going off to work,'" says Dr. Nancy Close, a lecturer in child development and a day-care consultant at the Yale Child Study Center. "Today, however, they are packing up briefcases to go to the office just like Mom." Dr. Close has also noted changes in dramatic play among girls. "Girls are now taking on more of the superhero roles. They are playing at being Superman and Wonder Woman. Girls demonstrate more power than they would have in play situations ten years ago—and frankly, it's very nice to see."

Some of this interaction is due, of course, to the fact that society is more approving of cross-sex behavior for girls than it is for boys. Mothers who are perfectly comfortable encouraging their daughters to be independent and assertive, wear pants and play with trucks, admit to being nervous if they observe their sons playing with dolls and tea sets. As I will explore in Chapter 7, working mothers have been slower to ease sex stereotypes for boys than they have for girls.

For girls, however, the benefits of a more egalitarian sex-role ideology are impressive. Not only, as one would expect, do girls then have higher expectations for achievement, greater self-esteem and more ambitious vocational choices; they also have higher achievement scores. "Cross-sex behavior is associated with higher cognitive functioning and achievement motivation in middle childhood," writes Dr. Brooks-Gunn in her paper "The Relationship of Maternal Beliefs About Sex-Typing to Maternal and Young Children's Behavior." But she also discovered, in the study described in Chapter 4 of 132 mothers, that daughters of mothers who professed more egalitarian sex-role ideologies had higher intelligence scores at twenty-four months of age than daughters of mothers with traditional sex-role ideologies—and this was true even when the intelligence scores of both groups of mothers were the same. These results appear to correlate with other studies of young children. One investigation of children in publicly funded New York City day-care centers discovered that children had higher I.Q. scores at eighteen months and at three years of age than did a comparable home-raised sample.[26]

These higher I.Q. scores for the daughters of working mothers are partially the result, say experts, of easing sex stereotypes, but they may also have other origins. Studies of working mothers with young children indicate that these mothers are more verbally attentive to their daughters than at-home mothers are, and that infants of working mothers, even as young as five months, show higher rates of exploration and accompanying verbalization.[27] Discouraging clinginess and, conversely, demanding independent and mature behavior have also been associated with higher intelligence scores and higher levels of achievement in school. In a study conducted by the National Assessment of Educational Progress, 100,000 daughters *and* sons of working mothers in grades four, eight and eleven were found to have significantly higher reading scores than their classmates. Researchers engaged in the study speculated that working mothers tend to be better educated than at-home mothers and that children of working mothers attend nursery school at an earlier age than do the children of at-home mothers.

Like mother, like daughter. The employment status of the mother directly affects a daughter's perception of her vocational choices. Researchers have found that the experience of having a mother who works strengthens a daughter's interest and commitment to a career.[28] Women attending college have a stronger career orientation if their own mothers worked, for example,[29] and women who report that they have successfully combined career and family life also say that they had greater maternal encouragement than did their colleagues who failed to establish their priorities at an early age.[30] In addition, the more supportive the mother is of the right to work, the more supportive is her daughter.[31] Although a working mother can sometimes put too many demands on a daughter to succeed, most working mothers appear to encourage and support their daughters rather than provide an atmosphere of excessive pressure. "The daughters of working mothers have a larger set of expectations about what they can do," says Dr. Sylvia Feinberg. "Their sphere of what can be done is unquestionably broader."

Psychologists at Yale University's Child Study Center agree. "I think there *is* something new among girls," says Dr. Phyllis Cohen. "I think that girls have intuitively a greater selection of roles." Adds her colleague, Dr. Kirsten Dahl, "Girls are aware of more possibilities. They no longer imagine they will only have children. Girls during the grade-school years used to talk about stereotypical jobs—teachers, nurses and the like. Now girls talk more freely about other possibilities."

Susan Weissman, director of the Park Center day-care centers in New York City, has had a firsthand opportunity to observe how preschool girls begin to learn about the world of work from their mothers. "I can see that these girls all believe that they are going to be something when they grow up. They seem to have the confidence that they can do just what they want to do, that the world is really wide open to them. Recently we had the children make a book about what they wanted to be when they grew up. And every girl epitomized the life that her mother was living—although to the level of the child's cognitive ability. One of the mothers owns a chain of ice-cream stores, and her little girl said she was going to grow up and scoop ice cream. Another said that she wanted to grow up and write checks and pay bills—her mother has her own business. Another said she was going to write a book—her mother is a writer. They see themselves as working; working is just part of the given—like first you're a teenager and then you work. Not one of them expected to be 'just' a mother, and not one of them said they were going to be what their fathers were. They all took on the mothers' roles."

Rena Merkin, director of the guidance department at Reading High School in Reading, Massachusetts, has firsthand knowledge of how girls translate those early ideas about what women can do into vocational choices. "Girls today fully expect to work the greater part of their lifetime. I have five hundred sophomore girls in my careers course. Out of that five hundred, only one girl came up to me and said, 'I really don't want to work; I really want to get married and have children and stay home.' Twenty years ago, if I'd been teaching the same course, at least four hundred of them would have said they planned to stay home."

Merkin has also observed that career choices have changed radically. "Twenty years ago, of the careers that the girls chose, I'd say that two-thirds of them would have been teachers. Today out of 1,500 reports on careers [each student writes three reports], I won't get two dozen on teachers. Instead, the girls want to be lawyers and engineers. They do reports on carpentry and medicine. They don't think twice about it. Out of the top twenty kids in the senior class today, twelve are girls. Out of my top five students, four are girls. One is looking at a liberal arts curriculum, but the rest of them are going into mathematics, engineering or one of the sciences. They no longer see a distinction that boys should do math and girls should do English and social studies. About four years ago, I had hundreds of girls doing reports on being a flight attendant. Now reports on flight attendants are way down—but I'm getting a lot of reports on women pilots. And another thing: Four years ago, if a girl wrote a report on being a pilot, she'd write,

'*He* does such and such.' Now, when I get a report, the girl will write of a pilot, 'When *she* does such and such.' These changes are very recent—I'd say in the last four or five years."

Merkin believes these changes have come about primarily because the mothers of these girls are working. "Two-thirds of the mothers of these girls are working mothers. And it's not just that the mothers are working—they're involved in careers. When I was little, mothers went to work if you needed money, and they took jobs as clerks or stenographers. Now mothers aren't working just to make money; they are working for self-fulfillment. Their children—my students—have the expectation, because of this, that they will work forever. The day of the stay-at-home mom is over. And these girls figure that if they're going to work, they might as well do something they like. There's nothing that's not open to them."

As Weissman and Merkin noted, one of the most positive things that working mothers convey to their daughters is a sense of the value of working. Other professionals who observe children have noticed this attribute as well. According to Dr. Lawrence Balter, "Because both parents work, children are more likely to see the importance of having a field of endeavor, of contributing to the economic welfare of the family. Regardless of whether the child is a girl or a boy, the working-mother model enlarges the child's scope."

That girls today will grow up committed to work seems fairly certain, but will they be happier because they have work outside the home? Certainly combining working and mothering in today's society is difficult and often stressful, as this book will explore in Chapter 8, but most evidence seems to indicate that paid work for women may be a boon to emotional health. A study conducted in 1977 showed that women had twice the incidence of symptoms of psychological disorders that men had. The only group in the study that had as low a rate of psychiatric problems as men were employed women—particularly women whose occupational status was high.[32] In the *Lifeprints* study, cited earlier, the authors found in their sample that the best preventative against depression was fostering a sense of mastery—something that was most often accomplished in the world of work outside the home. Self-esteem and a feeling of being in control of one's life tended to ward off depression. An earlier study, cited in *Lifeprints*, conducted by psychologist Judith Birnbaum at the University of Michigan, compared groups of homemakers with professional women and discovered that the professional women had a higher sense of self-esteem and were more satisfied with their lives than the women at home. Surprisingly, the homemakers felt less competent even at childcare skills than the professional women.[33]

Interestingly, this heightened sense of well-being of women in the work force appears to carry over into their mothering as well. A strong work commitment has a positive impact on the emotional health of the mothers of preschoolers, one study found,[34] and research conducted in 1983 discovered that the employed mothers of eighteen-month-olds displayed significantly more positive emotional behavior toward their children than did nonemployed mothers.[35]

This is not surprising, since feeling better about oneself often translates into better relationships with others. But the observed positive attitudes that working mothers display toward their children might also have something to do with time—or, more precisely, the lack thereof. It is harder to feel frustrated or bored with young children if you spend less time with them. In my interviews with working mothers, I have been impressed by the sense of specialness they assign to the hours they get to spend with their children. When children are around all day, one is less likely to regard time spent with them as precious.

The children, too, appear to have a heightened appreciation of their mothers. Both sons and daughters of working mothers tend to name their mothers as the more influential parent in the household, but girls, in particular, have a high regard for their working mothers, and, as a consequence of this, for their own sex in general. According to Lois Hoffman in her review of the literature of the effects of working mothers on children, to which I have referred earlier, "Daughters of working mothers . . . admire their mothers more." Adolescent daughters in particular are more likely than daughters of at-home mothers to name their mothers as the persons they most admire. "It's my mother who is my role model," said Rebecca, the student. "She's taught me so much about what it is to be a woman, and how different it is for me than it was for her when she was growing up."

I read in the paper today that the first ever all-female crew piloted a commercial passenger plane. The flight was aboard an Indian Airlines Fokker Friendship aircraft, and the flight, after "an easy takeoff, had a comfortable cruise and an absolutely safe landing in Calcutta." Saudamini Deshmukh and Nivedita Bhasin were the pilots.

6

Mothers and Sons: Voices

*O*verheard outside the vice principal's office at Reading High School, Reading, Massachusetts:

First boy: "Let's go to the skating rink after school. Your mother can drive us."

Second boy: "No, she can't. She works."

First boy: "Oh, really? My mother doesn't work."

Third boy: "You're kidding. I thought *all* mothers worked."

Chris, 31, Secretary

I've been working since my son was three months old. He's ten now. He's never known anything different. I think my son will grow up expecting that his wife will work. It's just a given. All the mothers work. All my friends work. Kids today just think that's the way it is.

When I was growing up, and you knew a mother who worked, everybody was going, "Oh, those kids are going to turn out terrible." Of course, that hasn't happened. A lot of those kids have become very independent—a lot stronger than we were. Frankly, I think it's a lot

It's so much healthier than sitting home with Mommy because Mommy feels guilty that she's leaving you.

The ideas my son has about life are different from the ideas I had growing up. I have three brothers—one older than me and two younger. When I was in high school, my oldest brother was in college, and I had the two younger brothers coming right up after me. We don't come from a lot of money. My father was determined to put my brothers through school, but when it came to me he said I should just take the business course and go to secretarial school because I'd probably get married and have children, but it would be good to have the typing and shorthand to fall back on. My father's priority was to get my brothers through. Two are doctors now, and one is a corporate VP. I'm a secretary.

My brothers were taught that when they grew up they were going to marry women and have to take care of them. And that's exactly what happened. I'm not teaching my son that.

Rena, 41, High School Guidance Counselor

I have a ninth-grade son. I said to him once, "Doug, give me two words —one to describe men and one to describe women." For men he said "bureaucratic," and for women he said "aggressive."

I asked him why he picked the word aggressive for women. And he answered, "Well, who took on Brown University when they insulted the school? And who goes out of their way to . . ." He was referring to times when I'd gone to battle for the high school. His reasoning and his perceptions were good, although before we had that conversation, the last thing I'd ever have called myself is aggressive.

And then another day we were riding in the car talking about people's strengths and weaknesses, and I said, "Okay, what do you see as my weaknesses and what do you see as my strengths?" And he said, "Your greatest strength is that you run a good show, Mom, whether it's at home or at school. You're an organized manager." He saw me organized both as a mother and as a professional person, and I thought that was very interesting.

I think my working has had an effect on my son. He's more independent than other boys and he sees women in general, not just me, as more well-rounded people. I think he fully expects to marry a woman who works and I think he'll share the household tasks. I still make dinners and lunches at home, because my husband and I are still struggling with the old expectations, but I don't think my son's wife will do that. He sees family life as a working family life. You all do your work, and then you all share the household responsibilities.

Tee, 36, Investment Adviser

My son, Lincoln, is three. One of the most important effects on him of my working is the extent to which he has developed a diverse number of trusting relationships. This seems to me to be the biggest single difference between him and other children who are with their mothers full-time.

Another effect I've noticed is that his perception of what men and women do seems not as dichotomized as it is in other households. His dad, for example, is a terrific cook, and because of this, Lincoln seems to gravitate to kitchen implements for toys. On the other hand, Lincoln associates me with athletics. I'm the more athletic member of the family, and he says things like he wants running shorts like Mama's. In terms of who takes care of him, I think he clearly sees us as interchangeable.

One of the most fundamental things I want to give my son is a genuine respect for women, and not only for women who are achieving in traditionally male arenas, but a respect for a fuller complement of skills. I would like him to grow up with a fundamental respect for women as well as for men.

Sylvia, 47, Child Psychologist

I have three sons—in their teens and early twenties. They accept the fact, not just because of me, but because of all the other women who have come into their lives, that women do work. I think it would be unusual if any of them ended up with a woman who stayed home permanently. I believe my working has certainly enlarged their construction of what is possible.

My sons expect an intelligent woman to be productive, but I don't think any of them would be disappointed if their wives wanted to stay home for a time with an infant. They believe that childbearing and infancy demand something qualitatively unique from a woman: No matter how much men participate, it still demands more from a woman. Women have to negotiate both worlds—the outside world of work and the intimate world of the infant. I think my sons' understanding of the complexities in women's lives is greater because they have seen me and other women working.

Pat, 31, Advertising Saleswoman

Peter and I had all these discussions when my son, Michael, was six weeks old about whether or not I should go back to work. Peter looks at me and says, "If you want to work, fine," almost as though he and the culture and even myself are giving me their blessing, giving me permission. But will anyone need "permission" when Michael is a grown man? Everybody will be working then, and he'll have known that his mother worked since he was six weeks old. I don't even think it will register with them that, hey, it's okay for a woman to work. They'll just be doing it, and that will be the way it is.

Barbara, 38, Administrator, Chamber of Commerce

I was asking my son during the last election whom he would vote for for President, and he said, in a flash, Geraldine Ferraro. He said there was no question about it. She was much more appealing, she was smarter, and he thought she had a lot of guts. It wasn't even relevant to him that she was a woman. He's not encumbered with that. He's not burdened with the old ideas that women can't do that sort of thing. It never even enters his mind, I mean, that a woman couldn't be president of a company. He keeps telling me, "How come you don't run the Chamber of Commerce?" He just thinks if you've got the talent, you should get the job. He never thinks in terms of men and women.

Around the house, he's not burdened with the old ideas that women should houseclean and men shouldn't. He does the dishes, vacuums, cleans up. I try to think if it's the culture that's made this big difference in him or me as a role model. And I think it might be me.

Sean, 17, Student

I would expect to marry a woman who had a career, because the girls I hang around with are oriented that way. I would say it would be fair to split household tasks. My mother works, and we all share the household chores. It's work that's got to be done, and she can't do it because she's not going to be around all the time, and my stepfather can't do it, because he's not going to be around all the time, so I've got to pick up the slack. You know, we all do our own part.

Kent, 17, Student

When my mother started working, it created tensions between her and my father. It created tension with my father because my mother started saying that she was the only one who cared about the children and was trying to go to all the games and everything, and she said that he had to start sharing going to the games with her. But instead, my father got really involved in his job, and started coming home really late at night, and so my mother got mad and said that if he wasn't going to do it, well, she wasn't going to do it either. And so it left my brother and me independent. I could handle it because I was older, but my brother was only twelve. And I think he's going to end up being just a little bit out of control.

Jo, 32, Real Estate Associate

In our house, I work and my husband works. We both do everything. We both help out with the chores. We both prepare meals and we both take care of my son, who is four. My son has never said, "That's Daddy's job," or "That's Mommy's job."

I think my son will grow up with the idea of equality in a marriage because I can see the living proof in my husband. He had a working mother—she was a teacher. In his family, both parents worked, and both parents took care of him and did household chores. I think that's why it's so easy for him today to share that work with me. A lot of my friends, their husbands don't do *anything*.

Nancy, 39, Doctor

I can see with my son that I have trouble breaking the stereotypes, because his father doesn't do any work around the house at all. It's something I work on all the time with my son, who is seven now. I try to encourage the children to have chores around the house that they interchange with each other, so they don't become stereotyped. One week my daughter will set the table, while my son cleans up. The next week, my son will set the table. They both have to strip their beds and bring the laundry down. I plan to continue to do these types of things because I want them both to be confident about being able to do all kinds of chores in the house, and for my son not to regard them as women's work, as his father does. I would rather that my son see these chores as just things that have to be done around the home to contribute to how a home is run.

Neil, 17, Student

My mother is the town treasurer. I like the fact that she works, because it gives her something important to do. She feels she's being constructive, and she's adding to the family income. With a working mother, I feel that I have more freedom to make my own decisions than I would if my mother were at home all the time.

Both a career and a family have extreme value, and no one should miss out on either one. They are essential parts of living life and contributing to society.

Jill, 35, Home Economics Teacher

I have two sons, nine and four. They are both very aware of the fact that I work. My younger son, in fact, goes around telling people that his mother works. I think it helps him define who he is.

I think that my sons see my working in a positive light. My older son is aware that my working makes his life harder in some ways—I can't be class mother, for example. But he's very proud of me and of what I am doing.

I hope that my sons will have a more flexible view of what males and females do. I think my working will change their ideas about childcare and housework. My husband works late, so I often do the evening chores, but in the mornings, he makes the bed, does the wash and cooks the breakfast. All in all, I'd say the positive aspects for my sons of growing up in a dual-career family far outweigh the negative aspects.

Roberta, 43, Fundraiser

I'm divorced now, but in my marriage my husband and I both worked. But I did all the household chores. My husband wouldn't do any housework. If he got home before I did, he just sat there and waited until I got home. This was very upsetting to me. I'm raising my sons very differently. They have to take care of their own clothes, their own ironing, and everybody has a week of dishes. Everybody has to cook for the whole week or one day a week, however they choose to do it. But everybody has to be involved in the household. There is no such thing as sitting down in my house to wait for Mother to come home to make dinner.

Maryanne, 40, Administrator

I can't see household chores as a job anymore. This is 1985, and everybody has a little space and we all have to clean it. Isn't that the attitude now? I've tried hard to make my sons at least capable of taking care of themselves. I've made them understand that no one else is responsible for providing for them. You have to provide for yourself. My husband tries, but he still has a sexist attitude about housework. It's subconscious. I mean, he'll empty and load the dishwasher, and that kind of thing, but whenever he does it, I see all of his old attitudes sprouting out of his shoulders. He does the work because he knows it's the proper thing to do, but I don't think he's convinced.

My sons, on the other hand, will be more sensitive. I think that they'll have enough of a handle on themselves that they will be more secure about that kind of thing. I think they'll be more secure people in general.

Phyllis, 45, Psychologist

I have two sons—one is eighteen and the other is just a toddler. The little one likes to play with cookbooks and kitchen tools. He's seen his father take up cooking, and he knows his mother works. The older boy is not comfortable in the kitchen, because when he was a child, his father didn't cook and his mother didn't work. He was brought up in a more traditional way. You can see all the changes and influences of the working mother just in one family.

Dale, 35, Housewife

Although I am not a working mother, I think it is extremely important to let my son know that women work. I think by the time my son gets old enough and gets into the job market, there will be more and more women going back to work, including his mother eventually, and women working will be more accepted. So I think it's important for him to realize that's the way it's going to be, and for him to try to come to terms with equal rights for women in the home and in the job market.

7

The Effects on Sons

A three-year-old boy, whose mother is a businesswoman, is asked to identify twenty items on the Stanford-Binet Vocabulary Test, one of which is a picture of a sport coat. "That's Mommy's dress," he says with total confidence.

A preschool boy, whose mother is a physician and whose father is a lawyer, sets up a "pretend" office in his room, at which he plays at being a lawyer and sees "clients." As his mother observes this play, she says to her son, "Do you ever imagine that your office is a doctor's office, and that the 'clients' are 'patients'?" The boy is shocked by this suggestion. "Being a doctor is for girls to do!" he exclaims indignantly. "I'm a boy!"

An eight-year-old boy, whose mother is a lawyer and whose father is in the construction business, is asked by another eight-year-old what he wants to be when he grows up. "I want to build things," he says, "just like my father." "But don't you want to be a lawyer?" asks the friend. "That's a really good job."

"Nah," says the boy. "That's women's work."

Comparing the effects of a working mother on a son as opposed to the effects on a daughter is a little like looking into a pond rather than into a mirror. With the mirror (daughter), the reflection stays put. You can see it clearly and think about it and make descriptive statements about it. With the pond (son), the image is more illusive and ephemeral; a sudden breeze or a dropped stone will cause it to ripple or perhaps disappear altogether. The image, imprinted as it is on a fluid medium, appears to shift and change.

Such is the case with the relationship between a working mother and a son. A mother is a primary role model for a daughter. She is not for a son. Her effectiveness as a role model is therefore more oblique than it is for a daughter and harder to pin down.

During a child's early years, a girl's identity becomes inextricably bound up with that of her mother. A boy, on the other hand, learns to differentiate himself from his mother in order to establish his maleness. Although the mother may be a keen shaper of the boy's attitudes and values, and may help to form his understanding of women in the world, she is unlikely to be the model from whom the child learns to be a boy and then a man.

The benefits to a boy of having a working mother are also harder to see and quantify than the benefits to a girl. Many of the attributes that accrue to a daughter of a working mother—increased independence, greater self-esteem, the widening of career options and an enhanced confidence in one's abilities—are characteristics that are not necessarily striking in boys. Either these characteristics have already been conferred upon boys by virtue of having competent achieving male role models or they are regarded by the growing boy and the culture around him as male in nature.

An understanding of a working mother's influence on a son is further confused by the research. One detects, in the studies, a certain lack of confidence in the findings. While the results of the investigations regarding the impact of the working mother on girls are fairly clear and consistent, those on sons of working mothers are often inconclusive. If you talk to the boys themselves as well as to their mothers, the effects appear to be positive. The results of academic studies are mixed, however, with more positive results reported the more recent the study. And the issue is further complicated by class. Occasionally the effects on boys from middle-class homes are reported to be different from boys from working-class homes. (Such a class distinction is barely noticeable among girls of working mothers.) In order to make sense of this mild chaos, I will first take a look at the positive effects on boys, then at the negative ones. Later I will examine why some research finds no effects at all—or what are called neutral effects.

POSITIVE EFFECTS

Like girls, boys in a home of dual-career parents perceive themselves as having a wider range of possibilities in their future. The reasons for this perception appear to be similar in fundamental ways to those of girls. Because the working-mother role model allows boys as well as girls to value women more highly, women's work—traditionally devalued by males—loses its untouchable status, therefore permitting sons to explore the nurturing and domestic sides of their personalities. Another reason has to do with the fact that as is the case with daughters in two-career families, boys often experience both their mothers and fathers as people who go off to work and then come home to take care of them. As I will explore later in Chapter 10, "The New Working Father," the presence of the working mother in the majority of American homes has instigated an evolution in the concept of fatherhood: Fathers now participate in child-rearing—as a nurturer as well as a moral guide—more than ever before. Fathers wrestle with Pampers, walk the floors at night with newborns and pick young children up from day-care centers on the way to the supermarket for milk and Cheerios for the next day's breakfast. In some families, such as in the home of Mayra, the financial comptroller, or Elaine, the dentist, or Laura, the nurse, husband and wife appear to be virtually interchangeable as far as domestic tasks are concerned, with no one household chore the exclusive province of either sex. If we think of the range of adult possibilities a child has available to him as a continuum—with the stereotypical workaholic who puts in sixty-to-eighty-hour weeks and arrives home when the children are asleep on one end, and the traditional stay-at-home housewife/mother on the other—one can see how dual-career parents (as a result of the presence of the working mother) enlarge a child's individual range on that continuum, whether or not that child is a girl or a boy. The son is able more fully to develop his nurturing instincts and to show physical and emotional care and love, *like Dad.* Not surprisingly, researchers have discovered that sons of working mothers see men as warmer and more expressive than sons of at-home mothers.[1] When male college students were questioned about their attitudes toward sex roles, researchers found that the sons of working mothers perceived fewer differences between men and women than did the students whose mothers did not work.[2]

"No one, even in more traditional families, is totally masculine or feminine," says Dr. Kirsten Dahl of Yale University's Child Study Center. "We all have within us these two forces. The children of this generation may not see feminine and masculine traits as being so irreconcilable." Dr. Diane Ehrensaft, a psychologist at the Wright Institute in Berkeley, California, agrees that having two working parents enlarges a child's perceptions of sex roles. "In cases where both parents define themselves as 'primary,' and parenting responsibilities are equally assumed, the children develop a broader sense of self. The roles they choose in life won't be dictated by their sex."[3]

These nascent evolving attitudes on the part of sons of working mothers have been observed as early as nursery school. Mary Anne Weinberger, a nursery school teacher at Sonshine Community Center in New City, New York, has been intrigued by the way boys in her classes—all of whom have working mothers—perceive sex roles: "Boys play in the kitchen more than they used to. Some of them will even take on feminine personas. They'll say, 'I'll be the grandma.'" Weinberger recalls that one little boy liked the kitchen so much that she had all she could do to get him out of it when other activities beckoned. On the other hand, she says, "Right in the middle of this play, they'll often revert to boyish behavior. They'll pick up the mops and start using them as guns.

"It's unclear," she adds, "whether the boys in the kitchen are being like Mom because it's now perceived as okay to take on some feminine behavior, or if they're being like Dad because more dads today are exhibiting nurturing behavior. What I hope is happening is that children are getting a feeling, not of who can achieve something in terms of sex, but of who has the capability and the desire to achieve something."

As one might expect, sons of working mothers also appear to have a greater respect for their own mothers and for women in general than do sons of at-home mothers. This has two potential effects. First, the boy may become more sensitized to the needs of women as he matures. And second, because he does not devalue women and women's roles, he may feel more comfortable adopting formerly (and exclusively) feminine behavior. "I saw my mother and therefore other women as my equal" and "I had two intelligent people to raise me and help me through life" were two of the comments by teenage sons of working mothers elicited in an important study of dual-career families. In this study, Patricia Kain Knaub of the University of Nebraska set out to discover the attitudes that both sons and daughters who had grown up in dual-career families had about that lifestyle. She found that both boys and girls said they would follow in their parents' footsteps, that 84.9 percent said they were proud of their mother's success, and that 72.7 percent considered their mothers the more influential parent. "What I think is so interesting," says Dr. Knaub, "is that the boys, too, liked the lifestyle. They weren't saying that, hey, Dad got a bad deal. They were making it very clear that they were going to model themselves after their parents. They expected that they would have a lifestyle that would involve a career for both themselves and their spouse, as well as their children."

Having more respect for women leads to more egalitarian attitudes toward women and toward an easing of rigid thinking about male and female sex roles. In one study of seventy-five high school boys—half of whom had working mothers and half of whom didn't—those boys whose mothers worked had significantly stronger ideas that men could do chores around the house and share the child-rearing. Working mothers themselves seem to support the idea that this is true for their own sons. "I've been working since my son was three months old. He's ten now. He's never known anything different. I think my son will grow up expecting that his wife will work. It's just a given," said Chris, the secretary. "I'm positive that my working will make Michael accept women in a much clearer way. It will give him a greater sense of equality between men and women," said Pat, the advertising saleswoman. "[My son isn't] burdened with the old ideas that women can't do that sort of thing. It never even enters his mind that a woman couldn't be president of a company," said Barbara, the administrator. "Both a career and a family have extreme value, and no one should miss out on either one," said Neil, the student.

"High school boys now expect their wives to work," adds Rena Merkin, the guidance counselor. "I think, on the whole, the boys are definitely going to be willing to take active roles in household management and parenting, and expect their wives to have professional careers. I think they see it as a sharing thing."

A concrete benefit to the son of a working mother appears to be better social adjustment. This finding shows up in several studies. Lois Hoffman reports in her review of the literature of the effects of working mothers on children that both sons and daughters of employed mothers appear to be better adjusted socially.[4] In one study of working-class families, both sons and daughters of working mothers showed a better adjustment in school and higher intelligence scores than children of at-home mothers. This was especially true if the mother's attitude toward her job was a positive one.[5]

Dr. Kyle Pruett, in an intriguing study he conducted at Yale University's Child Study Center, found that both sons and daughters of working mothers seem to be more outgoing, more socially flexible and smarter in certain tests. Dr. Pruett, a clinical professor of psychiatry, spent six years observing the children of seventeen role-reversed families—that is, families in which the father stayed home full-time and was the primary parent, while the mother worked full-time. Although these families were by no means typical, they provided an opportunity to see, perhaps more clearly than in other families, just how young children were affected by full-time working mothers.

The children in Dr. Pruett's study tended to be more socially active and to perform better on adaptive-skill tests than babies in traditional families where the father worked and the mother stayed home. "We found that the babies were not only okay—they were interestingly okay," says Dr. Pruett. "A typical eight-month-old is startled when a stranger enters the room. He perceives the stranger as a noxious stimulant. Our babies noticed when strangers came into the room, but approached this stranger actively. This was not the indiscriminate friendliness we observe in disturbed children, but rather seemed to be an approach to the world that suggested they were curious about what such people could offer them. They also did a little better than other children in adaptive tests. If you place three red cubes in front of a baby, you present him with a problem. The baby has two hands and a mouth to try to cope with them. Our babies tended to stick with the problem longer."

Dr. Pruett believes that one explanation for these positive attributes in the children he studied is that the babies have two "stimulating" parents, whereas children in traditional family settings have only one. Even in role-reversed families, fathers tend to handle children differently from mothers—they jostle them, bounce them, tease them. Mothers, by contrast, usually handle babies more gently. But children also regard the coming-and-going parent (in this case, the mother) with more curiosity. "There is a mystery about the absent parent," says Dr. Pruett. "Where does she go? What does she do?"

In the dual-career family, both parents, by this criterion, may be nurturing as well as "stimulating." Dr. Pruett thinks it is better for the child if both parents exhibit cuddling and stimulating behavior, so that the child sees a whole range of response. In this way, a boy, as well as a girl, is able to fully develop his own nurturing as well as achieving instincts.

And one provocative sidelight: Dr. Pruett discovered that when the fathers in his study were trying to figure out how to be parents, they reached back to how their mothers did it. This observation prompts one to ask if the children of these role-reversed parents will, when they are adults, reach back to their fathers for nurturing skills and to their mothers for organizational, achievement and breadwinning skills. It also prompts one to ask if children in families in which both parents are nurturers as well as achievers will look to both parents for parenting and breadwinning.

NEGATIVE EFFECTS

The research on the negative effects of the working mother on sons is untidy, and no one has made better sense of the contradictory findings than Lois Hoffman in her definitive review of the literature, to which I have referred earlier. Hoffman assessed all the studies available to her at the time (1984) and attempted to summarize the results. She found that while sons of working mothers do show better social and personal adjustment than do sons of at-home mothers, there was a recurring finding that middle-class sons of working mothers demonstrated lower academic performance in grade school and sometimes lower I.Q. scores than sons of traditional mothers. This result, surprisingly, does not seem to be true for working-class boys; in fact, if any academic differences do show up for working-class boys, they tend to favor the sons of working mothers. But she did find that working-class sons of employed mothers appear to have increased strain in their relationships with their fathers. This finding, said Hoffman, did not show up among middle-class sons. "The pattern for boys in the blue-collar class was seen as reflecting the fact that here maternal employment, though very prevalent, is still not seen as socially desirable or normative and may be viewed as a failure on the part of the father," concluded Hoffman. "In fact, the mother often enters the labor force at a point of financial need. It might be expected, if this interpretation is correct, that as the acceptability of maternal employment, and awareness of its prevalence, extends to the blue-collar class, the father-son strain may disappear."

As for the pattern of lower academic performance and lower I.Q. scores among middle-class sons of working mothers, Hoffman reported one possible reason: While greater independence brings girls up to optimum level, it may push boys over the edge. American parents encourage independence in sons more than in daughters. Hoffman writes, "If maternal employment increases independence-training for both sons and daughters, as indeed the data indicate, it might have a positive effect on daughters, but may involve a push toward independence in sons that is too early or too much."

Another reason may lie in the fact that boys in the homes of dual-career families lose their age-old exalted position and may even have to take a backseat to girls. As was pointed out in an earlier chapter, the preference for boy children and the favoring of boy children in traditional families is ubiquitous. But because employed mothers are less likely to hold traditional sex-role attitudes, reported Hoffman, they are less likely to demonstrate this preference and favoring. In addition, she speculated, because boys are more active and less compliant than girls at an early age, they may present a strain that working mothers have less time to deal with than at-home mothers. For these reasons, boys in dual-wage and dual-career families may come in for more psychological "hard knocks" than do the sons of at-home mothers.

There is some speculation that sons of dual-wage parents may have a harder time establishing a sex-role identity than either the sons of middle-class dual-career parents or sons in the homes of at-home mothers. In a paper entitled "Developmental Comparisons Between Ten-Year-Old Children with Employed and Unemployed Mothers," appearing in the journal *Child Development* (1978), an article which also examines the literature to date on the effects of working mothers on sons, the authors, Dolores Gold and David Andres, report that working-class sons of employed mothers may have more difficulty daughters in the development of sex-role identity. Girls come by sex-role identity by imitating their mothers, while boys must acquire their identity by differentiating themselves from their mothers. "Consequently, the greater role similarity between mothers and fathers when mothers are employed should broaden the daughters' conception of their own identity but should cause problems for sons in establishing a separate masculine identity," report Gold and Andres. "Difficulties in development of an adequate sex-role identity have been linked to cognitive and emotional adjustment problems in males."

Gold and Andres therefore predicted, for purposes of further investigation, that sons of employed mothers should have poorer cognitive performance and more adjustment problems than sons of nonemployed mothers, but they found only partial support for this hypothesis: Adjustment difficulties did not appear to be true for middle-class sons of working mothers, but did show up among working-class sons. "Working-class boys have some adjustment difficulties. These boys are described more negatively by fathers, are more shy and nervous, differentiate more between sex roles, have poorer school relations, dislike school more and report poorer grades."

This finding, of course, could be expected to be neutralized as the working-class working mother becomes not only the norm but also more acceptable among the husbands and fathers of the working class, as is indeed happening today. Labor union officials report that attitudes among working-class men toward their wives, childcare and housework have changed dramatically in the last five years. Working-class men not only support their wives emotionally in their jobs or careers (and even brag about their wives at the factories and on the job), but also, because shift work is prevalent among working-class men, take on a large, if not equal, share of the childcare and housework. "We had a workshop on work and family at a factory in New Jersey," said one labor-union organizer. "And one by one, shyly at first, but later with more confidence as they saw how many other men were doing the same thing, they began to admit just how much childcare and housework they actually did during an average week. The difference between them and the yuppies was that they were doing just as much as, or more than, middle-class men—they just weren't talking about it."

NEUTRAL EFFECTS

Some of the research promotes the idea that boys benefit from the presence of a working mother. Another segment of the research suggests that there may be some negative effects, especially among the working class. But a third segment seems to find no effects whatsoever.

In an earlier chapter, I referred to a revealing study conducted by Dr. J. Brooks-Gunn at the Educational Testing Service. She discovered that androgynous mothers promoted competence and independence in their daughters, but that feminine mothers did not. But she also found something else very interesting: Although androgynous and feminine mothers encouraged different behavior for daughters, they appeared to be identical when it came to sons. Both sets of mothers promoted independence and self-reliance in sons, but neither encouraged nurturing behavior in their boys. In essence, there appeared to be no differences at all in how traditional mothers and nontraditional mothers treated their sons, nor did they seem to treat them any differently than boys have always been treated. Dr. Brooks-Gunn found this very surprising.

"The data suggest—and not just my data, but other good data as well —that there aren't any particularly strong or consistent effects on the sons of working mothers. There aren't many negative effects, but there aren't many positive effects, either. It just seems to be a neutral situation."

Dr. Brooks-Gunn was asked why she thought this was so. "It is considered by many to be all right to socialize your daughter to be competent as well as nurturing, to contemplate having a job as well as being a mother and a wife. Few people have any trouble with that anymore. Parents talk about sending their daughters off to college with the same pride as they do their sons. But for some reason, many parents in this culture still have difficulty encouraging their sons to be intimate and nurturing. They pay lip service to it—they'll say, 'I want my son to be a good father,' but they aren't really treating their sons very differently than they ever did. I think the old stereotypes die hard."

Dr. Brooks-Gunn thinks the reason for this behavior may lie in the fact that there seems to be more urgency to socialize daughters for a future that will include the necessity to be able to support oneself. "People realize that in this economy you'd better have a skill with which you can support yourself, and with the high divorce rate, there is a good chance a daughter might end up a single parent. I don't think there's a similar urgency to socialize males to be nurturing fathers."

Dr. Brooks-Gunn, in her paper entitled "The Relationship of Maternal Beliefs About Sex-Typing to Maternal and Young Children's Behavior," prepared for the International Conference on Infant Study in 1984, summed up the relevant research in this manner. "Boys do not show a wider range of interests, attitudes and preferences when their mothers are working. This disappointing fact may be due in part to the salience of the same-sex model: Mothers' behavior may have less of an effect on boys' perceptions than fathers' behavior. . . . An alternative explanation has to do with the mother's actual behavior. If parents place more restrictions on cross-sex behavior for boys than girls, one might expect that changes in parents' roles and attitudes would not translate into less rigid treatment of boys. Finally, perhaps maternal employment allows children to see women as goal-directed, competent, and independent (Hoffman and Nye, 1974; Huston-Stein and Higgins-Trenk, 1978). However, if men are not participating in the home equally or interacting with children in specific ways then children may not see them as particularly nurturing or empathic."

Dr. Brooks-Gunn concludes that her findings may be somewhat alarming in terms of what it may mean for the future: "I foresee a future of androgynous women and traditional men. A wide range of behaviors will be acceptable for women, but a much narrower range will be acceptable for men. What will this mean for relationships between men and women, and for marriage and the family?"

That American society sanctions cross-sex behavior for girls considerably more than it does for boys—and may therefore be the underlying reason why working mothers appear to have less of an impact on sons than they do on daughters—has been noted by other experts who work with children, too. Dr. Lawrence Balter of New York University thinks the reason may be an irrational fear of homosexuality on the part of the parents. "It is seen as adding to a girl's repertoire to teach her to use tools or allow her to play with trucks and motorbikes, but we still have trouble being comfortable when we see little boys playing with tea sets and dolls. Recently, in a parenting group in a New York nursery school, this very issue was the topic of discussion. While the majority of the parents felt that it was fine for their little girls to strive toward 'masculine' endeavors, they were hesitant and reserved when it came to wanting their sons to strive toward 'feminine' activities. Trucks for girls were fine. Tea sets for boys were a bit of a problem. One of the mothers pointed out that some men do grow up to become chefs and waiters, but it still bothered the majority to think that their sons would want to play at serving tea. As the discussion progressed, some of these mothers confessed that they feared their sons might become homosexual. What was interesting was that no one felt that if their girls played with trucks, they would become homosexual. But why? Why would it work for one sex and not for the other?

"Society thinks it's a disservice to a boy to make him more like a girl, whereas it's a credit to a girl if she's able to share in masculine activities. Some have suggested a political motivation for these feelings. Because our society tends to value masculine activity more than feminine activity, we think we are adding to a girl's development to have her take on masculine roles. Conversely, we think we are taking valuable time away from the boy's natural masculine endeavors if he pursues so-called feminine play.

"This doesn't necessarily explain, however, why parents immediately hop to the thought of homosexuality when they see little boys playing with dolls. Where does the sexual connection come in?"

Dr. Balter explains further: "One point of view is that in the unconscious mind a homosexual male is missing some essential male ingredient. Some people may think of a homosexual as symbolically missing a penis and therefore like a woman. Although this is obviously not true and is a prejudice, this primitive idea is a potent one lodged in our unconscious. When adults look at a boy playing with teacups, they may unconsciously think that something has been subtracted from him and that he has become a 'girl-like' boy."

Dr. Balter thinks that parents can successfully socialize boys to be more nurturing by the way in which they explain tea sets or dolls or trucks to children. "Why can't a boy do a nurturing activity, but pretend to be a father instead of a mother? Then the boy can identify with the father and still play out a number of 'nurturing' roles. It will be clear to him that he's going to grow up to be a man—like Daddy —and that fathers do lots of things, many of which are loving and caring and giving."[6]

CONCLUSION

The pond ripples. Nancy Chodorow, whose book *The Reproduction of Mothering* examines the psychology and sociology of gender, believes that the manner in which women mother is responsible for the promotion of nurturing behavior in girls and its repression in boys. "Women, as mothers, produce daughters with mothering capacities and the desire to mother. These capacities and needs are built into and grow out of the mother-daughter relationship itself," she writes. "By contrast, women as mothers (and men as not-mothers) produce sons whose nurturant capacities and needs have been systematically curtailed and repressed. This prepares men for their less affective later family role, and for primary participation in the impersonal extra-familial world of work and public life. . . . A boy represses those qualities he takes to be feminine inside himself, and rejects and devalues women and whatever he considers to be feminine in the social world."

Chodorow was writing about the traditional family. Although this scheme was undoubtedly true in the past, and may even still be true in many traditional families today, the presence of the working mother in a majority of homes and the subsequent increase in the number of nurturing fathers in those same homes is subtly, if slowly, changing the way boys think about themselves, women and their own futures. Working mothers give sons the potential for greater respect for women and help to foster less stereotypically rigid notions about sex roles. Many sons now say they expect to marry women who work, and they tentatively make egalitarian pronouncements about who will do the chores. And if working mothers themselves do not always promote nurturing behavior in their sons (although one theory suggests that they do), they are, by their very presence, stimulating more fathers to model, for their sons, this affiliative behavior, thus widening a son's repertoire. The population of fathers who exhibit no nurturing behavior in the home is shrinking. Even men who recently possessed and coveted diehard traditional beliefs—working-class men—are giving their sons an opportunity to see this nurturing behavior firsthand.

Although excessive independence may arise as a difficulty for the middle-class sons of working mothers, as these mothers become more prevalent and more accepted within all classes the strain on working-class sons should disappear. The reported difficulty boys have in establishing their sex-role identities may ease also as the working-class working mother becomes the norm.

In this chapter much contradictory evidence has been presented, and it may be years before we understand fully the impact of the working mother and the dual-career and dual-wage family on a son. Until we do, we can look to the many boys and young men who appear already to have expanded their range of possibilities and to have done away with the old rigid stereotypes. One of my favorite examples emerges in a story Mary Anne Weinberger tells about a little nine-year-old friend of hers named Andrew. She asked him one day what jobs he thought mothers could do. "Mothers can be lawyers, cops and presidents," he said. Then he added as an afterthought: "Fathers can be lawyers, cops and presidents, too."

8

Stresses and Strains

A three-year-old girl, whose mother is a professional—described by colleagues and friends as being so well-organized that she is something of a superwoman—announces one morning that she wants to be a father when she grows up. "Why?" asks an adult friend. The girl has no trouble answering. "Because mommies work too hard," she says.

———————

— Katherine, time to wake up now. It's a school day and Mommy has to get to work.
— No, you can't stay in bed. It's a school day, and we have to get going.
— Come on, honey. Time to get going now.
— Seriously, now, we don't have much time.
— No, please don't get the Legos out now. We have to eat.
— Katherine, I told you to get dressed. How come you only have one sock on? *Now*, Katherine.
— Look. Hurry up. I'm serious now. If you don't get dressed, I'll have to do it for you.
— You've got two minutes to get dressed. I'm counting.

— I don't know where your Care Bear undies are. There isn't time to look for them. Put these on.
— Look, it isn't necessary to cry. These undies are perfectly fine. School is starting now, and you're going to be late, and I'm going to be late for my appointment.
— Eat your Cheerios.
— Katherine, *please* eat your Cheerios.
— No, I don't know where your favorite spoon is. It's in the dishwasher.
— Come on, I'm leaving. Where are your boots?
— What do you mean, you didn't bring your boots home from school?
— If you don't have your jacket on in one minute, I'm leaving without you.
— Isn't this fun?

(From a typical morning in the household of the author and her daughter.)

Trying to be a good working mother in this decade, in this society, is like trying to put a square peg into a round hole. It often doesn't fit right. It doesn't always feel right. Sometimes it produces tension, strain and stress. For most of us, this is not what we imagined we'd be doing with our lives, and it is hard to put those expectations aside. Worse, it is even harder for spouses to relinquish their expectations for the perfect wife and mother, or for bosses to relax rigid attitudes about the fully committed worker. One boy, the teenage son of dual-career parents, put it this way: "The greatest problems in our family stemmed from the fact that my parents were raised with 1940s values and were trying to integrate them into modern roles. This caused them a lot of heartache."[1]

All transition groups experience the stress of trying to fit into a society that was not designed for them and may even feel fundamentally threatened by them—and this has been the case for working mothers. In the absence of adequate day-care (there are nine times as many children who potentially need day-care as there are slots available nationwide), good role models, accommodating employers or experienced professionals from whom to seek advice, many women today feel like lost wanderers in an alien landscape. "Am I doing the right thing?" they worry constantly.

They wonder if the rewards of their career or job are worth the necessary eight- to fourteen-hour-a-day separation from their babies. They worry, as they steal time for their family, that they are putting their careers in jeopardy. They try to come to terms with the fear of being merely a "support player" in the lives of their children—and they are concerned about whether it is harmful to leave them in the care of surrogate parents. Finally, they struggle to reconcile what sometimes appear to them to be the antithetical skills and emotions needed to nurture and appreciate an infant on the one hand and to succeed at a job on the other. Both mothers and workers, without vital support systems, they may feel inadequate and unfulfilled in either role—a situation that plays into the working mother's greatest liability: guilt.

"When a child is presented to you, it's this little bundle that has all these physical attributes," says Jackie, the administrator. "And then it comes with this package. You can't see it, but it's there. It's the guilt. There isn't a working mother who has ever existed who is guilt-free. I mean it just comes with the territory. It's with you all the time. I'm happy working, and I think my daughter is happy having me as a working parent. But does that mean I am guilt-free? Absolutely not."

The high stress of trying to carve out a new way of being a family in a society that has thus far proven resistant to widespread change is among the most difficult problems working mothers have had to cope with. During a transitional period, when there are no institutionalized answers, families must create ad hoc, patchwork solutions, each one unique and idiosyncratic, reflecting the geographical location, personality, class and income level of the working mother and her spouse, if there is one. But such solutions—dependent as they are on the good will and reliability of individual bosses or surrogate caretakers, can come apart, exacerbating the stress on the working mother. "Statistically, psychologists are seeing a steep rise in the number of women caught in the two-career pressure cooker," says Dr. Martin V. Cohen, a clinical psychologist in private practice and on the faculty of New York Hospital–Cornell Medical Center. "It's the biggest cultural problem women in their thirties have today," adds Laurice Glover, a lay psychoanalyst in private practice who is also on the faculty of Einstein Medical College in New York.

As women race from role to role, trying to ration their limited inner resources, certain needs have become clear. They have discovered that they need understanding, sharing partners as well as sympathetic, facilitating employers. They want better day-care facilities, and they want to feel confident that surrogate care will not harm their children. Most important, they need some fundamental recognition from society of the enormous burden and responsibility they have taken upon themselves in a culture that has encouraged women to pursue careers, yet still expects them almost single-handedly to raise the next generation. "I think that society ought to view working women as part of their responsibility and accept the family obligations of working mothers," says Margaret, a magazine editor and the mother of two small children. "Anatomy dictates that it is a woman who must carry the baby. Given the way society works, why not account for these legitimate differences?

"We need to shift attitudes," she adds. "If people are interested in the continuation of the species, they'd better thank women. They'd also better recognize that these women have rights to a work life, too. We need a new ideology. We need to take a nonthreatening look at the workplace and the home."

While a new ideology is possible for the next generation (our children), the current generation of working mothers finds itself battling old ideas. Some give up the struggle—and their jobs or careers. The vast majority, however, do not want to—or cannot—give up working. Thus the bind. "The opportunity to work is very important," says Dr. Carol Galligan, a psychologist and psychoanalyst in clinical practice in New York and the director of the Women's Institute, an association of practicing women psychologists and psychoanalysts. "One of the ways you find yourself as a person is through productivity and subsequent feedback. Men have this opportunity available to them as a matter of course. But women need it just as much. It's difficult to go through life without this self-knowledge.

"Child-rearing, on the other hand, is terribly important, too," she continues, explaining that having a child is a healthy experience that can sometimes heal emotional wounds from one's own childhood. "I hate to see women lose this opportunity. But it isn't enough in the long haul. You need both. It isn't a matter of either/or—but *how?*"

Dr. Galligan admits that, in our still-traditional society, the "how" is, at the moment, difficult to achieve—and that the search for the "how" can impose an extraordinary psychological overload. She describes in detail the stress on some working mothers and its manifestations: "You feel that you're always running, that the machine is always in high gear. Time is the enemy, and you learn early on you have to pare down. You give up candles that match the tablecloth, for instance, and you realize that you look forward to Christmas with inner dread because you can't handle the extra work. Holidays or changing seasons become an insult to the system.

"You live by lists, and you're constantly preoccupied," she adds. "There's no such thing as time away for pleasure. All the time you can take, you've already taken for work. It's a strain on a marriage and on a woman's system. She finds herself unable to think straight. You often hear her saying, in conversation, 'I can't think of the right word,' or 'My memory is faulty.' "

Dr. Cohen, the clinical psychologist, describes the stress on women as having three sources: "The first is guilt. Most women have grown up in nondual-career families and have unrealistic ideas of what a mother should be. Inevitably, she has a sense of guilt over not doing enough—of not being as good a wife and mother as *her* mother was. Second, the woman has additional anxiety over her career. New to the marketplace, she may not yet be comfortable about career advancement or office politics and needs to learn to cope with pressures that men have typically felt. Third, there is the additional stress of the husband's unresolved fantasies of what a wife and mother should be like. If the wife is working and taking care of the kids, she may not be as sexually available as he would like, and this creates a strain.

"If the wife has taken on both roles fully [referring to those of mother and worker], she has nearly superhuman pressures. In addition, she has to work out something for which there is very little precedence."

The daily lives of many working mothers seem to echo the remarks of Drs. Galligan and Cohen. For couples in which both members work full-time (or more), the weekend is not enough to accomplish all the household and family tasks. Saturday becomes a kind of two-career purgatory, spent miserably at the laundromat or grocery store. And because women are usually responsible for running the house, free time for them becomes a rare and extremely precious commodity.

In the study by Patricia Kain Knaub referred to earlier, in which she surveyed the attitudes of the children of dual-career families, she asked the following question: "What are the problems associated with growing up in a family where both your mother and father had careers?" Time-related issues were the most common response (35 percent). This concern was expressed in comments from the children: "Sometimes your parents have previous commitments so they cannot fill yours—in school such as coming to sports events and awards ceremonies." "They are very tired sometimes—too exhausted to discuss problems." "There was not enough time for my parents to spend time alone together."

The simple physics of three jobs (hers, his and the homemaker/parent) trying to squeeze into the traditional American mode of family life is destined to cause a time crunch. The American family, and the society in which it functions, are still designed to best accommodate a parent who works full-time and a parent who is home full-time. And it is astonishing, despite the overwhelming evidence that most American families are no longer constituted that way, how hard we work to maintain that traditional shape. Women with full-time jobs feel compelled to keep houses as clean as their mother's, to prepare large evening meals, to entertain on weekends and to bake brownies for bake sales or make cakes in the shape of bunnies and trains for birthday parties—just as their mothers did. Husbands are often disgruntled or baffled by the lack of time working mothers have to perform chores, the lack of energy they have for sex or the lack of interest they have in their husband's office problems. And schools, maddeningly, continue to schedule conferences, school plays and sports events during school hours when neither parent is free to attend. Extracurricular events, such as music or dance lessons, are most often scheduled during afternoon after-school hours. Jackie, the administrator, worries that her daughter will miss out on after-school enrichment activities as a result of her not being there. "I don't have a lot of time, and I haven't been very good about making opportunities for her to play with other kids or do all the things that I could do if I did have more time. I worry that when she gets a little bit older and is ready for dancing or music lessons that she may get short-changed because I'm not going to have the time to plan those kinds of things."

Some child specialists see a trend, because of the absence of the working mother during after-school hours, toward poorer cognitive development on the part of the child, as well as a shrinking of the number of a child's peer relationships. If the mother is not there in the afternoon, they reason, she cannot help with homework. Nor can she drive her child to a friend's house to play or allow her child to entertain friends at home. Gone, say some observers, are the good old days when kids played for hours after school, came in for milk and cookies and a hug from Mom, and then went out to play again. Now children of working mothers must have their after-school hours rigidly scheduled with surrogate-mother supervision in the form of babysitters or an after-school enrichment program. (One disadvantage would seem to cancel the other, however. If the child spends time in an after-school enrichment program, his cognitive development may be enhanced, not hindered. It is also possible, of course, that children will make fast friends in these programs.)

Worse is the problem of latchkey children—children who come home to empty houses because there are no after-school enrichment programs available to them. Not every family has a grandparent or a neighbor to whom the child can go, resulting in more than a million latchkey children in this country. Although these children, in a variety of studies, have not been found to suffer any cognitive or developmental damage as a result of coming home to an empty house, no one can deny that an empty house feels lonely. "Not always having your mom there when you need her can be hard," said Cherche, a student. "Sometimes when I'm home, my mom has to go to work or she has to go to a workshop or she's traveling. She's not there when I need her. I know that's what she has to do, but it's hard to give up your mom, I guess. I have friends who have moms who don't work, and they are always at home and they make chocolate-chip cookies and have Kool-Aid around the house, but my mom sometimes says, 'Make your own dinner.' "

Latchkey children are also unsupervised children. Megan, the bank vice president, worried about her "adventurous" eleven-year-old and provided extra care for her after-school hours. Kent, the seventeen-year-old student, was concerned for his twelve-year-old brother, whom he feared might end up "just a little bit out of control."

Although time-use studies of working mothers versus at-home mothers often reveal that both sets of mothers spend the same amount of time in direct interaction with their children (this tends to be particularly true the more educated the working mother is), it appears that a lack of time to spend either with one's children or with one's spouse —or to accomplish all the tasks in any given day—may lead to tension and stress. This stress is naturally exacerbated if the working mother tries to be both a traditional and a nontraditional mother simultaneously—one of the biggest problems of this transitional group. With one foot in the past, they feel the old hankering to be a whiz in the kitchen, even as they take on the challenge of the operating room, the boardroom or the courtroom. "Colleagues of my husband's will be coming over to dinner on a Saturday night. I feel it's my responsibility to fix a nice gourmet dinner, and so I spend a lot of the day preparing and cleaning," said Nancy, the doctor. "Meanwhile I've been taking care of the kids, probably taking them to a museum or the park, and then I come back and I haven't given myself enough time to finish preparing the dinner or get myself ready. Michael's been out playing squash or over to his office, and hasn't done anything, and I come unglued. I feel crazy and angry. Actually when those kinds of situations arise, frequently it's because I've expected too much of myself, and that's another problem—that old silly supermother thing. It just doesn't work. No one can do it all, whatever that means. At least I know I'm one of those who can't do it all."

Occasionally the stress becomes nearly intolerable: "It was my day off," said Debbie, a thirty-three-year-old nurse. "But I had to get up at 7 A.M. with my son. I put him in the high chair. As I reached into the fridge to get him some juice, I knocked over a cup of milk on the shelf, and it spilled over everything. It was the last straw. I threw the cup into the sink and slammed the refrigerator door. I started crying. I felt incredibly angry—my day off, and I had to clean the fridge! I picked up a chair and threw it. My husband came in to see what was going on. He'd never seen me this upset. By that time, I was on my knees, taking everything off the bottom shelf and throwing it into the sink. My husband told me to get out of the room, that he'd take care of it. I went into the bedroom and just lay on the bed and sobbed. It was just too much. I'd had it."

Stress that results from the combination of an excess of pressure on the one hand and a lack of time in which to employ traditional modes of relaxation on the other often leads to marital distress—which in turn can affect children negatively. "My husband and I fight constantly about my having to work late," said Mary, the editor. "We tend to have our biggest fights about my working late when I get home and my daughter is fast asleep, but she does see us argue about time, and that's a very big issue. You know: Who's going to take care of her? Who's going to give her a bath? Who's going to put her to bed? You come home from work, you've had a long hard day and you're tired. I love playing with her and I love being with her, but to have to tackle all those routines when you've been working is too much. Putting her to bed used to be a joy for me. But now she's having sleep problems. It can take an hour and a half or two hours to put her to bed. It drives me crazy. I don't have the time, the energy, for that. You want to go to bed yourself. You want to relax. So sometimes if I'm tired, I will say to my husband: You do it tonight. And he'll say he's tired, too. And so we fight. We don't make much of an effort not to fight in front of her. Neither of us is the kind of person who can table an emotion. We tend to say what we are thinking. And she's now a high-strung little girl, not hyper, but definitely anxious. And I think that's a reflection of living in a house where there is more rather than less stress."

Part of this marital distress is caused by simple physics; another portion is caused by the desire to be supermother. Yet another contributing factor may be the large number of marriages between nontraditional women and traditional men.

One of the legacies of the women's movement is that it has expanded opportunities for women. It has given them a wider variety of choices than ever before. Women now may choose to test their skills and abilities in formerly male-dominated arenas, as well as to seek joy in nurturing their children and in caring for their homes. The end result is that women have been encouraged to expand their reach—encompassing, to the extent that their abilities and desires allow, both the nurturing and the breadwinning ends of the continuum.

But men have not expanded their reach to a similar degree. Because there was no men's movement to correspond to the women's movement, and because cross-sex behavior for men has not been as widely sanctioned by society as it has for women, men have been slower to embrace change. To be sure, many working fathers have had to take on a larger nurturing role as a result of having a working mother for a wife, and a few of these men have made profound fundamental changes in their sex-role ideology. There are now men, as we will see in Chapter 10, who work fewer hours in a week in exchange for more parenting chores, who believe in egalitarian marriages and who have sacrificed possible career advancement because they felt as equally responsible to their children as did their wives. But this is not the case for the majority of fathers in this country. Working fathers still do far less housework than do working mothers. And they tend to be, in the early years of the child's life, the secondary parent. More to the point, even fewer men have been willing to compromise their job security or career advancement in order to share equally in family life.

The result of this unequal range—or differing sets of attitudes and expectations—is that a dual-career couple may include a traditional man and an androgynous woman. In such marriages, power struggles, misunderstandings and marital stress may develop. On the surface, the power struggles may seem to revolve around chores and schedules—or as Mary put it, "who does what" when both parents are depleted and tired. Without established routines or without a sharing attitude toward the necessary tasks, parents may fight about cooking, cleaning, laundry, shopping, giving children baths, reading to them and putting them to bed. This marital stress, and the ensuing battles, not only cause tension between the parents that the child is bound to be aware of, but may cause anxious feelings within the child. If neither parent wants to read to him, what does that mean?

Often, the fights and battles about chores mask a deeper conflict, however. A man raised with traditional expectations, but who is trying to grow into a nontraditional marriage, may still have deep-seated longings for things as they used to be. A contemporary working father may silently long for a "wife" after a long day on the job to keep his house clean and to take care of his children. (Houses *are* getting dirtier. A *Good Housekeeping* survey recently reported that 68 percent of the women interviewed said their standards had fallen a great deal as a result of entering the workplace.) Such a husband may resent having to cook and clean after eight hours at the office, and may want to play with the child, like a traditional father, rather than wash the child's hair and find his Superman p.j.'s in the laundry. He may long for a "wife" who will attend to his sexual needs when the child is in bed—a wife who won't be too tired to seduce him. And he may feel fundamentally threatened by the prospect of having to share the center stage with another breadwinner—one who may even make more money than he, thus further confounding his inherited notions of male superiority. Won't his job take precedence at three in the morning, he wonders, when the child has a fever and both parents know that one of them won't be going to work the next day? Won't he come first, he worries, when he wants to make a career move to another city? Won't he still be the "man" of the house, just like his father was?

Marital stress disrupts a child's equilibrium because it threatens his security. Who will take care of me? the child frets. And such distress also robs the child of two calm, contented parents who are ready and willing to give the child the attention he craves and needs after having been away from his parents all or most of the day. In addition, children have a strong sense of family. One of their earliest cognitive researches involves discovering who all the members of their family are (and they will often endearingly add the family dog and goldfish to this intimate group with as much passion as they add siblings). Young children place strong emphasis on the family unit in their play and in their speech, and may act out in disruptive ways when that unit is threatened—as is apparent among some children of newly divorced parents.

But stress is also bad for kids because it leads to parental exhaustion—and exhaustion in turn can lead to neglect, indifference or a poorer quality of childcare on the part of the parent. It's unfortunate that in most dual-wage or dual-career families, parents and children share that portion of the day when their resources are most depleted. Charna Levine, an assistant professor in the Eliot Pearson Department of Child Study at Tufts University, worries about two busy and harassed parents. "I think children can be really neglected—if not physically, then emotionally. I have a picture in my mind of a mother picking up a child at 5:30 one day. This little bedraggled thing with her hat drooping off her head was carrying her lunchbox and hanging on to her mother's hand. Each of them was so fatigued as they were walking to the car. I knew that that mother was going to go home and cook dinner and bathe the child and try to be loving and giving—but each of them was so pooped."

Levine's colleague, Dr. Sylvia Feinberg, chairman of the department, believes that stress and exhaustion can make a working mother a poor role model. "A woman who feels exhausted, harassed, torn and guilt-ridden obviously is not going to model good things about work regardless of how much she earns and what her economic or status rewards are."

Some children, like the three-year-old girl at the beginning of this chapter who wanted to grow up to be a father, attribute parental exhaustion to the fact that "mommies work too hard." Older children sometimes see in their mothers signs of the workaholic—a syndrome we used to attribute only to absentee fathers. "I like the fact that my mother works. I know she enjoys it, and it makes her feel useful, but I don't like how much she works sometimes," said Elizabeth, the student. "I think she works too hard, too often, and I think she puts too much of herself into it. Sometimes it scares me, because everything revolves around her work—even her social life. She gets very tired. She works six days a week. She'll go in at seven in the morning and sometimes I'll call her at ten at night, and she's still there. She only eats when she has time. She buys

Doritos for lunch. When she's sick, she doesn't rest. She just complains about how much work she is missing. She can never let go. I plan to work when I grow up, but not like that. I want to have time to work and then time to be at home without the work."

Cherche, also a student, sometimes wonders if she is losing her mother to her work. "It's really hard and you don't know where you stand. I feel like I'm competing with her work. I never know if it's okay to ask her for something because she might still be thinking of her work. A lot of times I will want to say, hey, look what happened to me, or I need some help because I'm really having a problem, but she is so tied up with work that I don't feel that I can depend on her. I'll call her up at work and I'll say, guess what, I got this award or something, and she'll be, like, that's great, but not really excited. She's preoccupied with her work. She's got lists, and that wasn't on the list at the moment. Later, it will be on the list, and she'll get excited for me, but my attitude is, hey, what took you so long? Sometimes I feel like a client who has to make an appointment."

A workaholic mother, or a mother who is heavily invested in the world of work, may, ironically, narrow the range of options for her daughter. Such a mother may pressure a child to invest heavily in the world outside the home at the expense of the family. And some experts say that they are concerned that children may be overwhelmed by having to live up to the standards of two achieving parents. "Sometimes I feel that my mother would be disappointed if I became a housewife," said one sixteen-year-old. "I don't want to be a housewife, but I think if I did, I would have a hard time telling her that."

Elaine, the dentist, had similar fears for her two daughters. "I worry about Kate and Christine feeling they have to live up to two successful parents," she said. Dr. Nancy Close of the Yale Child Study Center, is also concerned. "On the positive side, a working mother offers a child more options in life and helps the child learn to be flexible. But if a child has to be too flexible, she may not be able to cope. An achieving mother also presents a girl with strong competition and with having to live up to the parents' expectations. It doesn't make growing up any easier."

Megan, the bank vice president, was worried about the effects of her own obsessive need for success on her child. "That's pressure, right?" said Megan.

Other child specialists wonder about the effects of too much stimulation on the child in the dual-career family as a result of the guilt both parents feel at having been away from the child for so long. "When I was bringing up my kids on the weekends, we left them with babysitters and we went off to things with adults ourselves," says Levine of Tufts University. "Now, no matter where we go with working parents, the kids are there all the time. That makes for more stimulation over all."

Dr. Feinberg of Tufts recalls a former student—the child of two working parents—who longed for less intense parenting. "She was at the day-care center all week—but on Saturday she went to every god-damn museum in town and on Sunday she picked every apple in the country. She had every organized experience available. What she was implying was that she would have given anything to have an open weekend with nothing to do but hang around."

It seems likely, as we have seen in previous chapters, that the working mother will inspire important changes in the next generation of children. But can so much be gained in one direction without losses in another? Some child specialists are concerned that the demands of the working world may cause mothers to lose their nurturing ability—the ability, especially in the early years, to cue into a child's needs, to give consistent and constant loving care, to provide not just food but the ability to be relaxed so that the child can relax, and to give the child a sense of security that he or she can absorb through the skin. According to Dr. Michael Bulmash, a clinical psychologist in Stamford, Connecticut, "Women have become increasingly uncomfortable in the role of nurturer. The pressure on women to succeed in male terms and the concurrent pressure to become discomfited by the traditional role of mother have created a generation of mothers who are losing their natural ability to pick up on cues and signals from their children."

Observers have noted that one of the more unfortunate legacies of the women's movement was to diminish the status of housewife and mother. In a race to embrace a wider variety of roles, old ways of being were cast aside. Women, so long resigned to lives without choice, were eager to tackle other endeavors that made use of more talents than nurturing. In the early years of any movement, revolution is necessary to achieve new goals. In this particular revolution, motherhood, as one's sole occupation, came in for sharp attack. In an effort to flee the bonds of motherhood, motherhood itself had to be devalued. Women whose investments increasingly took them away from the home began to place less and less emphasis on the home environment. "Women are in conflict today," says Dr. Feinberg, "because they were led to believe, either by themselves or by others, that bearing children was not real success."

Feminists and nonfeminists alike have long been arguing that what is needed in this country is a new appreciation of motherhood. To be a positive role model for a child, one must convey feelings of self-worth and satisfaction with one's choices. If motherhood were a highly valued profession—one which carried with it prestige, respect and even financial gain—then the differences between the at-home mother model and the working-mother model might be fewer. Daughters of both types of mothers would grow up without the handicaps of low self-esteem, lack of confidence and a limited range of options. Sons of both types of mothers would inherit, as Tee, the investment adviser, put it, "a genuine respect for women, and not only for women who are achieving in traditionally male arenas, but a respect for a fuller complement of skills."

Ultimately, the women's movement was about choice. But we seem to have forgotten that in our haste to savor the fruits of economic independence and more prestigious work. We have failed to make motherhood an attractive "choice" in society's catalogue of respected professions. It is not respected in the workplace, as working mothers discover when they need to take time off to care for young children; it is not respected in society at large, as working mothers discover when they try to find adequate childcare for their infants; and it is not respected among peers, as at-home mothers discover when they are called upon to account for themselves in social groups. To "just be a mother" in this decade, in this country, is perceived as having failed in some fundamental way.

But these perceptions are not entirely responsible for the "lost cues and signals" of the current generation of mothers. Many forces have coincidentally conspired to turn new mothers into spectators with performance anxieties.

My daughter is five now, and for all of her life, I have been trying to learn how to be a mother. I pay attention to what the experts say; I compare notes with other mothers and fathers. I have a childcare library three feet long. I have had to learn to be a parent in the only way I know how—not by instinct, but by the book; not as second nature, but as a career.

I am not alone. A whole generation of women like me has taken on parenting with professional zeal. Fresh from parenting courses, with our childcare compendiums tucked under our arms, we carefully pick and choose our way through a forest of theories, no longer certain, as our own parents seemed to be, that spanking is right or that thumb-sucking is wrong. Students in a field that is both baffling and joyous, we cram for the most important course of our lives.

We have turned to professionalism because we have little choice. We no longer live in extended families and most of us did not grow up having much experience with babies. Like many of my generation, I was not exposed to the intimacies of child-rearing. I had never changed a diaper, given a bath or fed a baby a bottle until I had my own child. When I discovered I was pregnant, I assumed that child-rearing, like childbearing, would wondrously reveal itself when the time came. But then I had a baby and I realized I didn't have the faintest idea what to do with her. I had waited too long to have a child; I had pursued my career instead. Scared, I did what most of the women I know have done: I fell back on the lessons my school and work experiences had taught me. If you're lost, you ask directions. If you don't know the answer, you look it up.

"The old myth of raising a child by instinct has disintegrated as our culture has become less certain of its values," says T. Berry Brazelton, M.D., the author of the popular childcare books *On Becoming a Family* and *Infants and Mothers*. "How can we raise children by the principle of 'do what feels right' if we don't know where we're headed? With the breakdown of the extended family and the disintegration of our cultural values, today's parents are working in a vacuum. We have lost the kind of instinct that is directed by a culture or by an extended family, and unfortunately, there's nothing to replace it yet."[2]

Dr. Benjamin Spock, author of the all-time best-selling parents' bible, *Baby and Child Care,* agreed with this perception during an interview I conducted with him in 1984.[3] "To read and go to lectures is a necessary evil. Anybody who starts a new career, like child-rearing, is insecure and finds it necessary to consult people already in it. In a more natural society, there are parents and relatives to consult, but if the relatives are hundreds, or even thousands, of miles away, you have to look to pediatricians, books, magazines and lectures for advice. There's nothing wrong in consulting books, but the sad thing is that the parents of this generation feel so ignorant—and guilty because they feel ignorant. They've been led to believe that only the professionals know the correct answers, which isn't true."

Perhaps it isn't true that only the professionals know the answers, but Charna Levine has been surprised at the fundamental ignorance of many educated women on basic childcare issues. "During the 1960s and 1970s, when everyone was examining the roles of women and the place of childcare, I thought that there was some thread of continuity about child-rearing that was lost. I'm surprised at the number of educated women who really don't know a lot of fundamental things about childcare that I knew as a teenager and from being part of a group of women. I have seen highly educated parents making terrible decisions about their young children, and I have been amazed at parents' inability to set limits. There seems to be an enormous reluctance to say *no* — perhaps the parents feel too guilty to deny the children anything, or perhaps they simply don't know when or how to set limits. They are out of touch with their children because they are missing out on the common body of information that gets transmitted when women are together in child-rearing."

"Today a baby is a novel, extraordinary, unique creature among upper-middle-class women," adds Dr. Feinberg. "What was commonplace and routine has turned into the most unique thing. It's like rediscovering the wheel. If you are an intellectual creature at thirty-eight, and you analyze, you are going to bring that way of approaching tasks toward parenting."

The loss of confidence in nurturing among the current generation of working mothers is no small matter. Childcare experts emphasize that how a mother nurtures her child is far more important than how a mother conveys the world of work to her child—particularly during the early years. "What's going on at a distance is nowhere near as important as what's going on at home," says Dr. Feinberg. "To a child, being able to give birth and run the nursery is more important than whether you can be a doctor or a lawyer. The fact that Mom is responsible for half of IBM doesn't hold a candle to the fact that Mommy can have another baby. When you are three, having babies is the whole world. Who cares about IBM when you are three? That's abstract. It's not comprehensible. It has steel desks and chairs. Who needs it? It doesn't compare with a stroller or nipples or diapers.

"Three-year-olds are too busy trying to figure out the kitchen and the living room and the bedroom," she adds. "That's where life begins. Until you can understand what goes on in your own home, you cannot understand what happens in the work world. Children need from women self-confidence, assurance and a sense of having your act together. If you can manage the nursery, then you are going to be able to manage IBM—if somebody lets you know that there is a connection between the two. If there is no connection between the two, then you are going to confine your confidence to the home."

Yet experience in the workplace, ironically, may help women at home. "As women work and go out and find contests in the workplace, many of them will feel more confident and more secure, and it may help the way they operate domestically as well," says Dr. Feinberg. "The more experiences you have with success, the larger the sphere."

Dr. Sam Ritvo, a professor of psychiatry at Yale, believes that many mothers are much better mothers in the time they have with their children if they also have time for their own development, their own interests and their own careers. "Society needs them in these roles. Their own families need them in these roles. A working mother has a positive impact, but only when it's carried out with adequate understanding and meeting the basic needs of the children." But Dr. Ritvo believes it is important for a mother to put the emphasis on nurturing rather than on achieving. "A child today can get the achieving model and the nurturing model from one person, which is very different from previous generations," says Dr. Ritvo. "But it's important that the mother be a good nurturer first and foremost. In other words, if the mother is a good achiever and not a very good nurturer, this has a much bigger impact on the young child than if the mother is a good nurturer and not a very good achiever. On the other hand, a super-duper model who is good at both achieving and nurturing could have a significant impact on a young child in terms of helping that child to adapt in a flexible way."

Another ingredient in the success or failure of the mother as achiever and nurturer is her attitude toward these roles: "If the mother is in conflict about her role," says Dr. Ritvo, "this could create difficulties. If the mother is unhappy about her function in life—and I'm not talking about who does the dishes, but rather about her feelings about her femininity or her sexual role—this will be communicated to the child."

Some mothers are concerned that they are role models for achievement, but not for nurturing. "What I worry about is the flip side of an independent lifestyle such as mine," said Celeste, the interior designer. "I worry that my daughter will devalue relationships or devalue a singular relationship with a man, because I don't put a lot of store in it. I don't need anybody else for income, for security or identity. She probably has an image of me as someone totally self-sufficient. I am a workaholic. I do always put my work first. My work pans out better than my relationships do—perhaps because I put my work first. I would be a negative role model if she internalized that."

Elaine, the dentist, has also thought about her own balance between nurturing and achieving and how this is communicated to her daughter. "I see myself as the keeper of the family," said Elaine. "At night, before Kate goes to bed, we have little talks. I tell her how important it is to love the family and to care about each other. I almost feel that I have to work harder to instill in her a love of family than a love of career. I think she gets the career part almost by osmosis. But the nurturing part is much harder to come by in today's society."

Although nurturing should take precedence in the family setting, Dr. Ritvo emphasizes that much of this nurturing can be taken on by the father—it needn't be the mother's province alone. This sharing of the nurturing responsibility—between spouses, among women, among surrogate caretakers—is an essential factor, as I shall explore in later chapters, in alleviating dual-career or dual-wage family stress.

Even a woman who has successfully achieved a good balance between achieving and nurturing, or who knows that her child is being well cared for, may find, on any given day, that it is difficult to make the transition between these two modes of behavior, resulting in a period of discomfort when the mother and child first come together. Moving abruptly from the office to the home can be a wrench for many women. The skills needed to succeed in one environment—running a meeting, making a presentation, sitting for long hours at a computer, being a boss, taking orders, being a social creature—may not necessarily easily translate into another environment, where what is most needed is a good hug and a wrestle on the floor. Leaving work at the office is essential if a mother is to give a child the full attention he needs when she is there, but many mothers find such an arbitrary dichotomy unnatural. Many men have traditionally brought their office problems home with them—often in hopes that a wife might prove an efficacious sounding board—but there seems to be little room for mothers of young children to do the same. Either because of guilt, lack of time, or because some husbands show little inclination to be sounding boards themselves, many working mothers describe a period of awkward transition from worker to mother.

Split selves, the mothers leave the office persona in the car or the bus, and begin to gear up—or gear down—for motherhood. "I would take a long slow drive in the car from the office to the apartment," recalled Mary, the editor. "In the car, I could feel myself changing. I would try to put my problems at work away, and I would try to relax so that I would be in good shape when I got home for my daughter."

The devaluation of motherhood, the disintegration of the extended family, the dearth of homogeneous communities and the necessity of having to learn mothering "by the book" is not confined to working mothers alone. At-home mothers speak of isolation and the inability to ask their mothers about child-rearing. Nor do working mothers have a corner on the guilt market. "I have a short temper and I yell," said Karen, the at-home mother of a seven-year-old boy and a five-year-old girl. "I don't like people who yell, but I yell. I hate myself when I do it, and I'm afraid that they see me as this screaming meemie all the time instead of this calm person who takes everything in stride and knows how to handle a situation. I seem to lose it a lot with them. It could be tied into my frustrations at being home with them all the time. Maybe I would be better off if I were out of the house on a part-time basis, so I wouldn't have to deal with them all the time.

"I also worry that I don't build them up as often as I should. Instilling confidence in children and giving them a good self-image is very important, and when you don't take the time to explain things to them or you are impatient, then I think you're hurting their self-image somewhere down the line. And a lot of the time I just don't have the patience to let them be independent. It's much easier for me to just cook the meal and get it over with than to have them scraping the carrot peels all over the kitchen floor, making a mess. I don't feel that I take the time to encourage them to do all these kinds of things. I'm very busy trying to get them involved in things just to get them out of my hair—so I have a lot of guilt about that, too."

Any woman who is unhappy about the choices that she has made, or about the choices that have been imposed upon her, will have difficulty being a positive role model for a child. Job dissatisfaction—whether that job be as an at-home mother or as a clerical worker—conveys itself to a child. Guilt, frustration and anxiety are contagious in a family, and as hard as a mother might try, it is difficult to hide those feelings from a small child. If at-home motherhood and housewifery have been devalued in our society, the at-home mother may experience conflict about her role within herself and have a particularly difficult time conveying positive feelings about what she does to her child. Even more stressful is the situation of the mother who works because she has to but who does not feel appreciated or valued at her job. Such a woman may feel that she is handling two second-class roles: She is not the highly successful career woman she reads about in the magazines; nor is she much appreciated—by society—for all the work she does in the home. All that work, all those chores, all those hours—and for what? she might rightly ask herself. Disappointment, a sense of worthlessness and low self-esteem may characterize her interaction with her children.

This isn't to say that we should lie to our children about how we feel about our work. Although a woman who does not value herself may not be a very good role model for her child, children can absorb valuable lessons about the world of work from observing even disgruntled or harassed parents. Likewise, they can learn from our mistakes. They are not blind or uncritical. Elizabeth, the student, could say, without confusion, that she wanted to be a working mother, but she didn't want to become a workaholic, as she feared her own mother had done.

Stresses and strains in the nontraditional American family exist. It is not a fact that can be glossed over. In some families, where the stress is severe, or where the mother suffers from excessive guilt, the mother may be a poor role model for a child. Being alert to this distress can, however, lead to fundamental changes in the way the nontraditional family operates and in external changes in society at large. And it is important to keep in mind that, despite these stresses, most working mothers continue to feel that they are good role models for their children, as we have seen in previous chapters.

Part of the burden of being a transitional group is that the mistakes have to be made and endured without benefit of role models. But *our* children will have role models. As those role models, we will have paved the way. We will have been responsible for instilling in them attitudes and expectations that will make mothering and working easier for them. From the distance of a generation, they will see more clearly than we do. They will discard ideas and actions that have proven to be unworkable, and they will take from us ways of being which have proved valuable. Said Ellen, the educational researcher: "Even in my vulnerabilities, I'm a good role model."

9

A More Positive Outlook

*I*n Patricia Knaub's 1982 study of dual-career families, she sought to determine what couples thought about their lives. Were they all, as some had suggested, unhappy because of excessive strain and stress? Were these families coming apart at the seams as a result of not having enough time together? How did they perceive their strengths and weaknesses? In what areas were they successful, and in what areas were they failing?

Knaub surveyed 103 dual-career couples around the country. To her surprise, she discovered that the vast majority of the couples perceived their families as being happy, united and strong. Both husbands and wives, independently of each other, gave their families high scores on a number of standard measurements of family strength: positive communication patterns, ability to manage conflict and expression of respect—as well as commitment, appreciation, concern and support. These families, she found, compensated for lack of time together by being efficient and planning activities for themselves, for their spouses and for the whole family. Emotional turmoil, as a result of competing demands for time between career and family, was reported to be low. "It would appear as if the couples were aware of the extensive time demands and coped by attempting to use time efficiently, purposefully scheduling events with their spouses and children, and, although they said they would like to spend more time if they could do so, they were not suffering from internal conflict because of their multiple role responsibilities," said Knaub.

"Clearly, satisfaction with the dual-career lifestyle was high," the researcher concluded. Although both husbands and wives worked long hours, "they expressed satisfaction with their current work, their career choices and felt that they were achieving their career goals. No doubt such satisfaction spills over into other aspects of their lives."

This feeling of well-being appeared to be particularly true for the women. "Interestingly, both wives and husbands perceived the dual-career lifestyle as especially beneficial to wives. Perhaps the perception remains that the multiple role dimension of the dual-career experience is viewed as more salient to wives than husbands. Or, the value of work, in addition to the benefits of marriage and family, may be seen as a newly acquired benefit to women whereas the benefits of all three roles have traditionally been assumed for men. In other words, both husbands and wives seemed to be assuming that the lifestyle allows wives to have something extra—it is, therefore, an advantage for her. Husbands, however, did not seem to be negative about the benefits the lifestyle provided their wives. Rather, they reported being proud of their wives' ambitions and successes, saying that the lifestyle allowed her needs to be met better than any other."

All well and good, thought Knaub. But what about the children? Did they, too, perceive the dual-career family as a positive one in which to grow up? To find out, Knaub interviewed the children in the 103 families. Not all of the sons and daughters were able to participate, but in the end, she had a sample of ninety-three children from diverse geographical areas. The children ranged in age from twelve to twenty-nine years of age.

Again, across the board, the parents received high marks. Ninety percent of the children were either satisfied or highly satisfied with the dual-career lifestyle. The children "perceived their lifestyle as positive; they didn't feel that they had been cheated. They didn't feel neglected by their parents." In the study, two-thirds of the group said they intended to combine marriage, career and parenthood, as their parents were doing. Eighty-five percent said they were proud of their mother's success, and 73 percent of the children said they considered their mothers the more influential parent. When asked to list the benefits of living in a dual-career family, the children mentioned financial security, self-sufficiency, having two intelligent people to raise them and seeing the parents as equal. Fifty-four percent mentioned having positive role models as a benefit to living in such a family.

"For the most part the children were highly supportive of their families' dual-career lifestyle," said Knaub. "Recognizing the value of having two parents provide positive role models for the world of work as well as in nurturance roles, the perception that the lifestyle encourages the development of their independence, and awareness of the obvious financial advantages all speak to a positive definition of the lifestyle. The kids felt it was a good way to live. They said they felt their parents were busy, but when they really needed them, they were there for them. They didn't have a sense that they had been deprived in any way, and I gave them ample opportunity to say that."

The results of Knaub's study are encouraging. Despite the stresses and strains of being a working mother in the 1980s, despite the awkward fit of being a part of a transitional group in a still-traditional society, the working mother appears to be a positive role model for her children—a perception that was confirmed in my own interviews with mothers and children. Not only did the majority of the children I interviewed say their mothers were positive role models, but the mothers themselves were quick to echo similar perceptions. In fact, as the interviews progressed, an interesting pattern emerged. I asked each mother in what way she was a positive role model for her child, and in what way she was a negative role model. In most cases, the mothers spoke easily, quickly and comfortably about the many ways in which they were positive role models. In general, the mothers were halting, uncertain and sometimes totally unresponsive to the negatively oriented question. "Let me think a minute." "Could you repeat the question?" "Give me some hints and maybe I'll be able to think of something." These were the most common responses. Often I had to suggest ways in which I thought *I* was a negative role model for my daughter (instilling "hurry-up sickness" usually came to mind) before they could respond. (I don't know the reason for this. One is tempted to conclude that the mothers just didn't think of themselves as negative influences on their children, but perhaps there was an underlying reason, not apparent to me, as to why the responses were so uniform. Possibly it was the need to see as correct decisions in which they had heavily invested.)

As we have seen in previous chapters, the working mother is an especially viable role model if she takes genuine pleasure and excitement in what she does and if that sense of joy and gratification in her work is communicated to her children. The child is then able to internalize the good feelings the mother gives off and can associate them with well-being. As a result, the child may be the recipient of certain benefits: better social adjustment, a higher I.Q., a more expansive sex-role ideology, greater self-esteem, greater confidence in one's abilities, a more positive view of women, better educational progress, more vocational options and a potential for greater economic independence. In addition, mothers speak of instilling in their children *the value of work,* of modeling for their children *a more humane approach to the workplace,* and finally, of being, for their children, a model of *emotional self-sufficiency.* "I am a positive role model for my daughter because I work," said Celeste, the interior designer. "Work is very important for anyone, regardless of their sex. Anyone who doesn't work in some way, shape or form atrophies. A woman has to have an identity that belongs to her, and her alone. The best way to get that is to do something constructive. She has to get out in the world.

"My daughter has seen me in the past work for a large corporation. She's watched me in a management position. She has observed me dealing with a corporate situation from a more humanistic point of view. I've demonstrated for her a more feminine way of dealing with problems in the corporate arena.

"Also, she's seen that I have responsibility for my own life. And I'm not just talking about food, clothing and shelter. I'm talking about responsibility for my emotional life as well."

Various research studies suggest that better emotional health is often a by-product of entering the work force. In the *Lifeprints* study referred to in earlier chapters, the authors discovered that the busiest women in their sample—employed married women with children—had a high sense of well-being, a high sense of mastery and a heightened sense of pleasure. The authors also found that having multiple roles did not necessarily lead to "role strain" or excess stress. In fact, going to work often alleviated much of the emotional stress in a woman's life. "The workplace can sometimes seem like a health spa compared to life at home," the authors concluded. "We also found that the number of roles a woman occupied told us very little about her level of role strain. Women with three roles had only slightly higher role strain scores than women with only one role. The real issue turns out to be how a woman manages the roles and the resources she commands. . . . A working woman who feels she has to be 'superwife' and whip up three-course dinners after work or keep the kitchen floor gleaming with a new coat of wax may feel role strain, while more relaxed women may not. . . ."

Other studies have confirmed that working women may have better emotional health. In a study I referred to in an earlier chapter, researchers found that the percentage of women with psychiatric symptomology was twice that of men. The only group of women who scored as low (or who were as emotionally healthy) as men were employed women whose occupational status was high.[1] A Boston University study of 133 women found that married career women with children reported feeling the least depressed or ill in response to stress.[2] Thomas Berndt in his paper "Peer Relationships in Children of Working Parents: A Theoretical Analysis and Some Conclusions" (*Children of Working Parents: Experiences and Outcomes,* Washington, D.C.: National Academy Press, 1983), also notes that "There is . . . some evidence that satisfaction with life is greater for working mothers than for nonworking mothers . . . perhaps because working women have a more positive opinion of their own competence." According to a *Newsweek* poll, conducted by the Gallup organization, 75 percent of working mothers say they would work even if they didn't need the money.

When mothers are feeling good about their lives, they communicate this satisfaction to their children, who, in turn, internalize these positive feelings. These affirmative feelings often then find expression in young children in the pride they take in their mothers' work. Children today tend to brag about what their mothers do in the same way that we, as kids, used to brag about what our fathers did, often inflating the job or the career beyond what it really is. "I've seen children who appear quite proud of their mothers," said Dr. Nancy Close of the Yale Child Study Center. "'My mother's a doctor,' a four-year-old will say. I'm not so sure she knew what that entailed. The pride came from the mother. Children often respond to a mother's experience of the situation."

As we saw earlier, working mothers can be valuable and viable role models for both sons and daughters. Usually this happens without conscious effort. But occasionally it may be unclear exactly how a mother's choices and behavior affect a young child. Because working mothers today are often conflicted about the decisions they have made, they are not always certain if they "are doing the right thing." This uncertainty may cause them to hedge their bets, to hide their work from their children, to play down their competence in the face of a threatened spouse, to devalue themselves, to succumb to the stress of trying to be supermother, or, conversely, to eschew their nurturing responsibilities and become workaholics. "You need both working and mothering," said Dr. Carol Galligan. "It isn't a matter of either/or— but *how?*"

In my reporting, I asked mothers, psychologists, researchers and child specialists to take a look at the *how* and to try to isolate some of the more important components, which follow:

- *Be positive about your choices.*   Experts say that a key ingredient to being a positive role model is taking responsibility for the choices that you have made and conveying to young children good feelings about those choices. Conflict over whether or not one has made the right choice—that is, whether to work or not when children are at home or are very young—leads to guilt, anxiety and stress. Children— small creatures with exceptionally long antennae—become readily aware of this distress and emotional discord and, as a result, may not feel comfortable with a working mother. If the mother is not secure in her choice, then the child cannot be expected to feel secure, either. "Children can handle anything if the mother has her act together," said Dr. Feinberg.

Most experts agree that what affects a child is not whether the mother works or not, but how she feels about her roles. A working mother who comes home every night miserable, who fights with her husband over chores, and who grumbles every weekend at the endless amount of work to be done at the office and at home will not provide a positive role model of a working mother for her child. According to Lois Hoffman, "If employment provides satisfaction and increases the mother's morale, the quality of her interaction with the child should be enhanced. If, on the other hand, the dual role of mother and employer involves strain, her interaction will be adversely affected. Similarly, if the full-time homemaker would prefer to be employed, her resentment and discontent may be expressed in her interaction with the child. . . . Studies with infants, as well as with older children, have consistently demonstrated that the mother's satisfaction with her employment status relates positively to the quality of mother-child interaction and to various indices of the child's adjustment and abilities."[3]

In her study, Patricia Knaub found a direct correlation between clarity about one's choices and family strength: Women who had made firm choices were among those who rated their families as stronger and happier. Concluded Knaub: "The most important thing that parents can do is to not approach their working with guilt. I've found over and over again that dual-career families often try to create a lifestyle as nearly like the traditional one as possible because they are feeling guilty. They don't really enlist the kids as often as they could and should in creating a new family structure. But if the parents were to say to the children, 'This is a really good way to live,' a kid will believe it. If Mom and Dad believe it, then they will believe it, too. And that eliminates much of the tension and the guilt."

Because so many of us who are working mothers today belong to a transition group of working women, we often have one foot stuck in the past, while we tentatively explore the future with the other. Our only model for family life is the one in which we grew up, and when we veer away from that traditional model, we are tempted to see our behavior as deviant. Because it is not entirely clear to us yet how to go about creating a new family mode, we often try to do both.

We have chosen to be working mothers, but we have not yet been able to shed the old expectations. We still hope, secretly, to be both working mothers and traditional mothers. Simple physics should make it clear that such a combination is unworkable, but still we try. We shield our children from our working in feeble attempts to resemble, as best we can, our own at-home mothers. Because we are often guilty about working, we tend not to talk about it as often as we might, or in as positive terms as we might. There is sometimes a furtive quality about our lives, which inhibits us from making it clear in the workplace that we are working mothers who have responsibilities at home, or from making it clear at home that we are workers with responsibilities elsewhere. Thus we get into situations as Nancy, the doctor, did when she realized miserably that she was trying to be supermother and was failing: Although she was a doctor, *just like her husband,* she alone was taking care of the children, giving them enrichment experiences on weekends and simultaneously trying to cook a gourmet dinner for her husband's business associates—just as our mothers used to do.

Pick one, say the experts. Let the other go. Invest in the dual-wage or dual-career family and let the traditional family pattern go. Trying to be both a working mother and an at-home mother will lead only to frustration. This doesn't mean that you can't love your children just as much as your mother loved hers, or that you can't attend to their needs just as heartily. It means, rather, that you cannot expect yourself to be able to do all of the things that a traditional at-home mother can do.

Housework is a good example. We grew up in homes in which our mothers were good homemakers. It was among their most important jobs. They did not hire people to clean their houses for them, nor did they have their parties catered. They did not buy cakes at the bakery; they made them. They also made drapes, slipcovers, quilts, sweaters and Christmas presents. Because these mothers were our role models, we somehow expect that we, too, should be domestic wizards. We try to bake and have dinner parties and keep spotless houses, even though we don't have enough time to do it in. Because we are pressed, nothing is a pleasure. Worse, we fail, and feel bad about it.

There are standards of excellence and there are standards of decency. Strive for excellence where it matters: in communication with your children, in your job, in achieving a workable, loving partnership with a spouse. Allow yourself to accept a standard of decency wherever it is possible. A working mother needn't be a gourmet cook, president of the PTA and the main contributor to her child's school bake sale. If such activities are fun and stress-reducing, then fine. If they are not, then pare down. Make it clear to yourself first, and then to those who matter, why you are making your choices. A child who takes pride in the fact that his mother is a computer programmer and senses that she gets satisfaction from her work will be better able to come to terms with his disappointment that his mother cannot volunteer to drive the class on a field trip.

More to the point, a working mother should enlist the other members of her family in creating a nontraditional lifestyle. In the traditional family, the mother catered to everyone's needs. She did all the cleaning, all the cooking, all the laundry, all the shopping. Even today, women still perform these chores far more than do other members of the family. This anachronistic attitude that the mother should be the sole keeper of the home causes stress, tension and exhaustion in dual-wage and dual-career families. But change begins with the working mother herself. She must first be alert to her choices and the consequences of her choices, and communicate those perceptions to her spouse and to her children. In the nontraditional family, the home is the responsibility of all family members—including children. "I can't see household chores as a job anymore," said Mary Anne, the administrator. "This is 1985, and everybody has a little space and we all have to clean it. Isn't that the attitude now?"

• *Find the best childcare you can.*   Working mothers report that a key ingredient to feeling comfortable about their choice to combine working and mothering is the ability to find good childcare for infants, toddlers and preschoolers. Without it, they say, it is impossible to feel relaxed either at the workplace or at home. Concerns about what might be happening to the child during the mother's absence begin to encroach upon her work hours, often causing her to check up on the caretaker at too-frequent intervals, to steal time from work to get home early or, in some cases, to quit her job.

A disruptive change in childcare personnel is a serious problem for both the mother and her child. Most child specialists agree that a small child needs consistent love and care for the majority of the child's waking hours. Children form attachments to caretakers and can show signs of emotional disturbance if subjected to revolving-door caretaking —that is, frequent turnover in personnel. Mothers, too, find that the hiring and firing of many caretakers over a short period of time causes stress, both as they worry about the effects on their children and as they discover they must disrupt their work schedules in order to again find a suitable situation.

Choosing the right kind of childcare for your family, then, must be among a new working mother's highest priorities. This entails research, homework and planning well in advance of the date when childcare becomes necessary. Children, too, whether they be infants or toddlers, will need to be eased into a childcare situation. It is therefore advised that working mothers begin this process at least two months before their return to work.

This process, however, is an arduous task. If the working mother is the square peg, the round hole that she is trying to fit into is one characterized by a shocking absence of universally available quality childcare for all the children who need it. Unlike more than one hundred other countries, we have no national childcare policy. Worse, since 1980 we have seen a 21 percent reduction in federal subsidies for childcare. Even more alarming is the fact that childcare personnel, having realized over the last five years that they are both undervalued and underpaid, are beginning to leave the profession. A hopelessly inadequate situation—indeed, one which has been called "a national scandal"—is in danger of becoming shameful.

Consider for a moment the plight of the single mother, one who has to work in order to put food on the table. Of necessity, she has to find childcare. But single mothers can rarely afford nannies or full-time housekeepers. Often they cannot even afford or find full-time center day-care. Instead, they have to resort to patchwork childcare—a neighbor with children of her own for a few hours a day, an elderly grandmother for another few hours, a babysitter, perhaps, in the late afternoon. The child is shuttled from one situation to the other—not always a desirable circumstance for the very young. And single mothers are not alone. Fully 70 percent of all working mothers say they *have* to work to make ends meet.

Finding good childcare is not easy. But it is a task that needs to be attended to before a mother can feel good about her decision to return to the work force. In order to be a positive role model, certain practical matters must be solved. Childcare may be the hardest and the most vital.

There are several different forms of childcare a working mother may investigate before she makes her decision. As we have just seen, not all types are available to all mothers, however, either because of economic limitations or geography. In some towns and cities, center day-care may be too expensive or not available at all. In many urban areas, particularly in middle and upper-middle income pockets, family day-care is often not a possibility simply because there may not be enough at-home mothers to provide such services. Because of the disintegration of the extended family (and because many of our mothers have now joined the work force!), few of us are able to take advantage of extended family care. Fewer still have the resources to be able to hire a full-time nanny or housekeeper. Yet it is important to be aware of all the kinds of childcare that you may choose from so that when you begin your research you will have a broader picture of what to look for.

Center day-care. In center day-care, a child is cared for outside the home by a number of trained personnel. Care is consistent, in that the day-care center can't "get sick" or "quit," and it is usually open from about eight in the morning until six at night, when most mothers work. Center day-care tends to cost somewhat more than neighborhood mothers and babysitters and, of course, extended family care, but is usually less expensive than hiring a full-time housekeeper or live-in nanny.

The advantages of center day-care are that programs and care are geared to the age level of your child and in general are conducted by trained personnel. Children learn beginning skills and participate in stimulating projects and games. They learn how to share and how to cooperate with others. Children are seldom in danger of sitting idly in front of a television as they might be if cared for in the home of a neighborhood mother. Also, it is easier for the working mother to ascertain what actually goes on in the day-care center and to decide if this is the program she wants for her child. Often this kind of assessment is very difficult to make if one is relying on family day-care.

The disadvantages of center day-care are that in some centers the ratio of children to trained personnel may be too high and the individual needs of the children cannot be met. One-on-one care is not a possibility in center day-care, and some children may not thrive in a situation where it is necessary always to have to defer to the group. Some experts suggest that center day-care may be *too* stimulating for some very young children, and others wonder about the consequences of the lack of one-on-one care for infants. Some centers, in fact, may not take infants at all, requiring that the child be toilet-trained before entrance. Another disadvantage of center day-care is that children in day-care centers get more colds, rashes and flu than children who are raised at home.

There are licensing agents and regulatory boards for center day-care in all states, but the quality of center day-care varies. Some institutions operate only for profit and may not have the best interests of the child in mind when planning programs or buying materials for the children to work with. Some try to enroll as many children as possible, giving little thought to the best caretaker-child ratio. Still others, as we have seen in horrifying news stories, may subject a child to either sexual or physical abuse. In general, however, in my experience and in the experience of the mothers I have interviewed, childcare personnel in day-care centers do care about the children, do plan interesting and varied age-appropriate activities, and are alert to possible developing problems in the child. My own daughter formed a strong and loving bond with her day-care teacher, a young woman who had a great sense of humor and inexhaustible reserves of energy. I do not think my daughter's experience is unique; many other mothers have spoken to me of similar attachments. In fact, there is among the working mothers I have interviewed and known a tendency to feel that the day-care center chosen for one's child is the "best" in the area. I think this reflects a general satisfaction with center day-care, but I think it is also partly due to the need on the part of the mother to feel that she has done the best for her child.

Perhaps the greatest source of concern for working mothers is the guilt they feel over leaving their young children or babies in surrogate care—in an institution such as a day-care center, in another family's home, or with a nanny. Is it all right, they ask, to leave a child at a day-care center? How many hours a day can I be away from my child without harming him? Nancy, the pediatrician, says she often worries about whether she is doing the right thing when she leaves her two children and goes to work. "Kids are defenseless," she says. "They can't say, 'Mommy, I need two hours of your attention in the middle of the day.'"

The issue of the advisability of surrogate childcare—and how much —is a controversial one. Some experts contend that it is unacceptable to leave a child of six months of age in surrogate care for more than a very few hours a day. "So far, there is too little evidence of the effects of day-care on babies to make policy decisions," says Dr. Burton L. White, an educational psychologist and the author of *The First Three Years of Life*. "All the research implicates one critical factor: For the first several months, babies need loads and loads of affection and attention. They must have ready access for the majority of their waking hours to someone who's crazy about them.

"My ideal pattern is this. No substitute care for six months, with the exception of an occasional night out; part-time substitute care with parents equally sharing childcare the rest of the time.

"My opinion is based on a lifetime of doing research on what's best for babies. I'm not in the business of making life easier for young couples."[4]

John Munder Ross, a clinical psychologist in New York and co-editor of *Father and Child: Developmental and Clinical Perspectives,* has similar beliefs. He describes some of the children he has treated from two-career families as having "an anhedonic quality—a feeling of joylessness, an inability to experience pure pleasure."[5]

Although Dr. Ross cautions that all the factors in a particular case need to be known before making any generalizations, he is troubled by this issue: "You have to wonder about a parent who gives up his child to the complete care of another. Why do they put personal achievement ahead of the interests of their child?"

But many professional observers are concluding that women's anxieties about leaving their children in surrogate care are a reflection of fears rather than of reality.

"The research done has thus far not demonstrated adverse effects of quality day-care for infants and young children," says Lois Hoffman of the University of Michigan. "The face-value assessment of the data is very reassuring," she says, but adds that other factors must be taken into account, such as the nature of the individual mother-child relationship or the feelings a mother has about her employment. "You have to ask," she says, " 'What is the child experiencing? How would it be different if the mother were at home?' "[6]

Dr. Mary C. Howell, a pediatrician and developmental psychologist in Boston, is the author of what has remained among the most definitive reviews of the literature of the effect of maternal employment on children. "No uniformly harmful effects on family life, or on the growth and development of children have been demonstrated," she wrote of working mothers in the journal *Pediatrics.* "Maternal employment may jeopardize family life when the conditions of her employment are demeaning to her self-esteem, when other family members are strongly disapproving of her work away from home or when mutually agreeable arrangements for children and housework cannot be met. Otherwise, maternal employment seems to offer many advantages to family relations and for the lives of children."[7]

In the studies to date, there has been an impressive lack of any consistent data that shows that center day-care is harmful to young children. To the contrary, most data reveals that children not only do well in center day-care, but also may be ahead of their peers in social adjustment and learning skills. Alison Clarke-Stewart, an associate professor of education at the University of Chicago and a recognized expert in the field of day-care, reports in her book *Daycare* that in thirty studies conducted over the last fifteen years in the United States, Canada, England, Sweden and Czechoslovakia, day-care has had no apparent detrimental effects on a child's intellectual development. Children were found not only to hold their own when compared to at-home children; they often did better in a number of areas: verbal fluency, memory, comprehension, problem solving and writing their names. Their speech was discovered to be more complex, and they were able to identify other people's feelings and points of view earlier. They also scored twenty to thirty points higher on I.Q. tests than did at-home children. These results were found to be especially true for economically disadvantaged children, whose at-home care may not include basic learning skills.

Subsequent to her research, Clarke-Stewart directed the Chicago Study of Child Care and Development, in which she looked at 152 children from a mixture of backgrounds and a variety of childcare arrangements. The children ranged from two to four years old and included children at home with parents or a babysitter, in a neighbor's home, in day-care centers, in nursery schools and in combinations of nursery schools and babysitters. The childcare situations were ones that occurred naturally in the community and did not include exceptionally good or what are called "model" day-care facilities. The children were tested in a variety of skills: "to understand sentences, to name colors, fruits and animals, to remember numbers, to identify photographs of objects, to use play materials, to solve problems, to label pictures of emotional situations, to copy designs made with blocks, to visualize how things would look to another person and to communicate with a listener."

The results clearly favored the children in center day-care. "On all these measures of intellectual competence, a clear difference was found between children in home care . . . and center care . . . favoring those in center care. This occurred for children of all family backgrounds, for both boys and girls, after as little as six months in day-care," writes Clarke-Stewart.

"In sum, it appears likely that there is something about day-care centers and nursery schools that stimulates or maintains children's intellectual development, at least until the beginning of school. Remember, however, that these findings—however positive they are about day-care—do not guarantee that all children will benefit from being in a center. The centers that had these apparent advantages, though not at all 'exceptional,' were all of relatively good quality; poor-quality centers would not be expected to have such positive outcomes."

The studies comparing at-home children with day-care children also took a look at the child's relationship with the mother. Was the bond between the child and the mother diluted or injured as a result of the child's being in a day-care center for as many as eight hours a day? Clarke-Stewart found, in her research, that children in day-care were quite attached to their mothers, and that this feeling was not replaced by their relationship with another caregiver. "[Children] may also form an affectionate relationship with a childminder who is involved in their care for substantial periods of time, and this caregiver is preferred to a stranger, but day-care children still overwhelmingly prefer their mothers to this caregiver. They go to their mother for help, stay close to her, approach her more often, interact with her more, and go to her rather than the caregiver when distressed or bored. In the day-care center they do not greet the teacher in the morning with the same joy as they greet the mother at night. They do not behave as if the caregiver is a substitute mother, nor is this how caregivers perceive themselves."

Clarke-Stewart did report on one difference between the day-care children and the at-home children that at first seemed to suggest that the day-care children were less attached to their mothers, but on reflection appeared to indicate something else. In laboratory settings, day-care children did not go to or stay as close to their mothers as at-home children did. They did not seek as much physical contact and they were more likely to ignore the mother when she came back into the room. This, said Clarke-Stewart, seemed to represent, for day-care children, "an earlier or adaptive independence from the mother that is a natural and realistic response to daily separations from her and regular interactions with strangers. For day-care children, this pattern of greater distance is related to greater overall social competence, not to poorer adjustment. What is more, although these day-care children maintain greater physical distance from their mother, they are just as affectionate with her—or more so."

The research has also revealed that children raised in day-care centers tend to be more socially outgoing than children raised at home, to be friendlier and to be more socially mature. As they enter school, they are better adjusted, more persistent at their tasks and more likely to be leaders.

The longer the child is in day-care, says Clarke-Stewart, the stronger the effects are. But the differences between day-care children and at-home children appear to lessen after the first few grades of elementary school. "What day-care seems to do is to speed up children's intellectual development during the preschool period rather than to change it permanently," said the researcher.

Family day-care.   Family day-care refers to a childcare situation in which a woman, who usually has children of her own, also cares for the children of working mothers. This care is provided in the home of the neighborhood mother. The quality of the care will depend on the mother herself, her attitudes regarding the needs of infants and toddlers, the number of children she is taking care of, whether or not she favors her own children over her clients' children, and on the materials and facilities available to her. The advantages of this type of arrangement are that if the number of children is small (say, two or three children, including the caretaker's own), then an infant or toddler is able to receive more individual attention than he or she might in a day-care center. Another advantage is that such care is usually less expensive.

Unfortunately, however, the disadvantages of family day-care outnumber the advantages. In many states, family day-care providers must be licensed, thus insuring at least minimal standards of caretaker/child ratios and physical care. Yet even those family day-care providers who are licensed (and thousands are not) will only be as good as their own initiative and attitudes allow them to be. In many family day-care homes, children follow a routine similar to the one they might follow in their own homes: Mom does her chores while the children play together. Occasionally this mom might play games with them and read to them, or take them outside, but there is nothing that says she has to. Sometimes television sets are left on all day and the children spend a great deal of time in front of them; some mothers are more involved with housework than they are with the children. Occasionally clients' children find themselves coming second after the mother's own, learning that certain toys are off-limits and that the mother's hugs and kisses go first to someone else. Another disadvantage is that family day-care mothers can get sick, or their children can get sick, thus making them unavailable for childcare. One working mother said to me that she once figured out that for her to go to work, four people had to be healthy: herself, her child, her caretaker and her caretaker's child.

I have had two experiences with family day-care providers, one good and one bad, and both of which I feel represent the two extremes in the family day-care spectrum. The first caretaker my daughter ever had was a woman named Pat, who had one daughter of her own, and who, by her own admission, was "meant to have ten kids." She was a born mother. She was good at it, took pride in it, genuinely loved babies and could hardly believe she was getting paid for doing what she loved best in life. My daughter was four months old when she first went there— for three hours a day—and I remember with special fondness the way Pat would come to her the moment I entered the house and the way they would be playing together when I came to get her. My daughter seemed to thrive, and there were many days when I wondered if perhaps Pat wasn't a better mother than myself. But Pat got pregnant and delivered prematurely, and abruptly I had to find another situation. A friend of a friend put me on to a neighborhood woman whom I shall call Jean. I ought to have intuited something might not be right when I first visited her: Her house was immaculately clean, despite the presence of two children of her own. But I was ignorant then, and instead I was merely impressed. She seemed a nice enough woman, and I was in a pinch, and so I hired her. I have always regretted it.

When I would arrive to pick up my daughter (she was older now, and staying four to five hours a day), I would notice that she seemed withdrawn and quiet and almost dazed. I attributed this, as I attributed all new changes in her personality at that time, to a "stage" and didn't concern myself overly with it at first. But then, because something unexpected had come up, I went to Jean's home earlier than I was supposed to. When I walked into the room, my daughter and Jean's two children were sitting in front of the TV, watching not "Sesame Street" or "Mr. Rogers," or something I might have allowed even in my own home, but a soap opera. They had toys beside them, but the toys couldn't compete with the television. Alarmed, but not wanting to give offense, I suggested as discreetly as I could that Katherine didn't "do well" with too much exposure to TV, and that, if possible, I hoped that Jean would keep her away from it. Jean bristled. The TV, she announced, was always on, and who was I to tell her how to live her life in her own home? She had a point. On the other hand, I didn't have to keep my daughter there, and I didn't.

Extended family care.   Extended family care has two enormous advantages over other forms. It is usually free, and it has the potential to pair your child with someone who loves her almost as most as you do: a grandmother, a grandfather or another close relative. It does, however, have serious disadvantages. Extended family care does not cost money, but it does not come without cost. Being so in debt to one's mother or mother-in-law can strain family relations and can cause a new working mother to abdicate her responsibility in deciding what is the best kind of care her child should be receiving. Battles between mothers of different generations as to schools of thought about child-rearing can happen in any family, but they are most likely to surface in extended family care situations. You don't believe in playpens, but your mother-in-law does. You believe in teaching a child to feed himself, but your mother doesn't like the mess and insists on spoon-feeding the child. You believe a toddler should simply be removed from a situation in which he is misbehaving; your father believes in a good quick spank. Some older people have tremendous reserves of energy, but many don't. You may find that your child's caregiver, then, is a lot less active than you would ideally like.

Working mothers who decide to rely on a family member for child-care might do well to pay that person for the work that he or she is doing. Not only would such an arrangement give the mother a greater feeling of control and a greater ability to say what she thinks the childcare should consist of; it would also contribute to breaking the pattern of at-home childcare for no pay which has characterized motherhood for decades.

At-home care.   Those who can afford at-home care may employ a live-in housekeeper (sometimes referred to as a nanny) or a full-time babysitter.

Live-in help can be an unparalleled luxury for the working mother. Such a person can provide one-on-one care for infants and toddlers and will probably help with household chores as well. A working mother with live-in help needn't worry about rushing home from work to get to a day-care center before it closes, and needn't hire extra sitters for evenings or weekend nights when the parents go out. For the working mother who travels in the course of her business, live-in help makes it possible for her to do that with relative ease.

Nannies and full-time babysitters seem to be especially popular when children are infants. But as the child matures and needs more stimulation and more time spent with other children in play groups, the working mother will need to see to it that these needs are met. The nanny or babysitter may not stimulate your child in the manner you would like or may not provide him with enough opportunities to play outside with other children or at the homes of other children. And the childcare that you get will only be as good as the person you hire. Before children can talk and tell you what happened during the day, it may be hard to ascertain exactly how much time the nanny or babysitter is spending in direct interaction with your child. Some observers have been alarmed by the pods of nannies who gather at the park to chat to one another while infants and toddlers sit idle in carriages and strollers. Others worry that nannies and babysitters may spend more time on housework than they do with children. Still others have shown concern over language barriers between the caretaker and the child. While good mothering is not dependent on I.Q. or even upon a firm command of the English language, alert and active verbal and nonverbal communication is essential to the development of the child.

Choose your nanny or housekeeper prudently and wisely. In essence, this person will become a member of the family, and the child will almost certainly develop a strong attachment to her or him. In some measure, the caretaker will impart attitudes and values to the child, and you will want to make sure that those teachings are compatible with your own. And because of the potential of a bond forming between the caretaker and the child—and because of the possibility that the child may be hurt if the nanny leaves abruptly—exhaustive interviewing beforehand is essential. The unexpected may certainly arise—you may not like the caretaker's child-rearing practices in action, or the caretaker, for personal reasons, may have to leave—but it is best to keep turnover to a minimum.

• *Explore your options at the workplace.* Common sense dictates, and many psychologists concur, that the two or three years following the birth of a child are not an especially good time to *build* one's career or to take on more responsibilities than one has to in one's job. The infant and toddler years are joyous ones, but they are also characterized by many sleepless nights, constant attention to the child's needs and tremendous demands for physical energy. To be simultaneously trying for a promotion, traveling a great deal or taking on special projects that would require you to work longer hours than normal might be poor planning at this stage in your family's life as well as in your career. Only with a great deal of help, both from one's spouse and from a nearly full-time caretaker, could one hope to satisfy everyone's needs. And even so, such a mother might discover that she was shortchanging herself by missing out on many delightful moments with her child.

Most experts suggest that the infant and toddler years are ones in which a working woman might consider staying as flexible as possible, exploring all of the options available to her and perhaps reducing the number of hours she puts in during a given week. This may be accomplished by formal arrangements with one's employer, by plateauing (that is, by staying put in one's career and doing only what is absolutely required for a temporary period of time) or by a radical reorganization of priorities for two or three years until children are well settled in preschool programs.

It is not necessary to work full-time every day of one's life in order to experience the emotional, social and psychological benefits of working —or to model those benefits to a daughter or to a son. Although many employers still look askance at women who request part-time work during their children's early years and may cause them to feel uncomfortable, many women are discovering that self-esteem, competence and success are not intrinsically dependent upon an eight-to-five schedule. Priorities shift and change in a woman's life. At one point, in her mid- to late-twenties, career-building may take precedence, and she may feel most challenged and most alive in the workplace where she is testing her skills, making valuable social contacts and learning her trade. Later, in her thirties, she may shift her priorities to child-rearing for a fairly intense two or three years. This doesn't mean that she has *given up* on her career, as many are inclined to think: It merely means that her job or her career will shift to the back burner for a while so that she can fully experience motherhood during a time when her child and she both need to do that. In the *Newsweek* poll, more than half of the mothers who had part-time work said they had done so to be with their children.

Unfortunately, temporarily shifting priorities from the job to the home remains a radical idea in the workplace. Today, 71 percent of women have full-time jobs. Few employers are comfortable with the idea of giving new mothers part-time work, allowing them to cut back on their hours or relieving them of responsibilities that would require them to be away from their babies at night or on weekends. Nor are they reassured that if they were to make such accommodations for new mothers, that these accommodations would be only temporary. Employers feel that if they make allowances for working mothers, they will be flooded with requests for part-time work from all employees. And the discomfort is not the employer's alone. Colleagues and co-workers often express resentment and irritation when new mothers are allowed to reduce their hours. If handled poorly, part-time work for working mothers can often mean extra work for co-workers.

Because of resentment in the workplace and because working mothers have been exposed to too few women who have modeled innovative, yet workable, ways of combining working and mothering, many women feel confused and uncomfortable when they discover they are pregnant or immediately after the birth of a child. There are few models, either institutionalized or informal, to show working mothers how to reduce their hours successfully or how to shift priorities without feeling that they are losing everything that they have worked for. Faced with rigid employers, recalcitrant husbands and overwhelming longings to be with their babies, they think they must quit their jobs and their careers and become bona fide full-time mothers. Unfortunately, because there are no formal policies regarding this period of "time-out" that many new mothers feel they must take, and there are few, if any safeguards on their careers, some mothers do lose valuable ground when they try to return several years later. Other mothers, for economic reasons, have no options but to work full-time. Whether they want to or not, they must leave their children at the age of two or three months in the care of another person or persons for eight or more hours a day. For some mothers—but not necessarily for all—this abrupt separation from an infant can be stress-producing.

Ideally, women, spouses and company policies would recognize that both women and men need flexibility during the early years of their children's lives. To ignore the incontrovertible fact that universally available quality childcare is still not a reality in this country, that neither infants nor parents can experience each other if they are not allowed to be together, and that such a period of intense parenting is but temporary is to blindly and foolishly try to fit that square peg into that round hole. This isn't to say that new working mothers or fathers need to quit their jobs, or that a new working mother or father can't reliably and competently hold down a job when children are young. It simply means that there needs to be some recognition of the fact that working and parenting cannot be performed simultaneously every minute of the day—and that some exploration into the various kinds of options that might be made available to both women and men when they have infants and toddlers has to be made.

Some progressive companies have begun that exploration. On-site day-care, part-time work, job-sharing, flextime schedules, bringing the child to work, and partial at-home work are some of the new ways of working that couples and companies are trying.

When anxieties about childcare are alleviated, working parents not only become better workers, but they also become better parents. Although the need for on-site day-care (day-care facilities located at the place of work) far outstrips the availability, a few progressive companies have instituted such programs and have discovered that worker productivity goes up, absenteeism goes down and working mothers, as well as their spouses, appear to be less stressed than working mothers for whom no such quality facilities are available. At the Zale Corporation, a large, national jewelry-retailing company headquartered in Dallas, working mothers (or fathers) may have lunch with, or visit at any time, their children in an on-site facility which has proved to be nearly self-supporting. The center is cheerful, well-staffed and well-equipped. Forty percent of the parents of the children at the center say they took jobs at Zale primarily because it had such a center.

Vicki, thirty-five, a tax manager with Zale, put her three-month-old baby in the center. "I'd been working on my career for thirteen years," she said. "I couldn't think of giving it up." Having on-site day-care made it possible for Vicki to continue breast-feeding her baby. "I went over twice a day. I couldn't have done that if the center didn't exist. It brought the baby and me closer to each other."[8]

As the need for on-site day-care grows larger, more companies are expected to explore this option for their workers. Some 2,500 companies nationwide provide some kind of day-care assistance. About 150 companies have on-site day-care. Today, one city, San Francisco, has a law that makes developers of major new projects provide rent-free space or provide $1 a square foot for nearby childcare centers. If such support for childcare is not forthcoming among San Francisco developers, building approval is denied. In Massachusetts, a pilot program is in the works that makes low-interest loans of up to $250,000 to companies to set up their own day-care facilities. At the Polaroid Corporation in Cambridge, Massachusetts, parents with salaries under $30,000 are given subsidies for childcare. Women who plan to become pregnant, or who find themselves pregnant, might consider transferring to a company that offers on-site day-care or proposing the creation of such a facility within their own companies.

Part-time work may also be an option for some women during their child's infant and toddler years. "I went back to work full-time after three and a half months of maternity leave when Jeffrey was born," said Nancy, the doctor, who at the time was a staff physician at a child development center. "I didn't want to let my superiors down, and I was afraid they'd discover I could be replaced. But I was overwhelmed. I was miserable. All I ever did was work and do errands. I wasn't enjoying Jeffrey. Nothing gave me pleasure. I wasn't allowed to experience either Jeffrey or my career fully. But I didn't want to give up either of them."

Because of the stress, Nancy negotiated a four-day week. It was an improvement, she said. "I could take Jeffrey swimming; I could play with Jennifer. We could do things together. For the first time, I felt like a regular mother."

Nancy's boss was willing to accommodate her request for part-time work in order not to lose her. But had she not been such a valued employee, the same schedule might not have been offered. In the absence of company-wide policies, informal arrangements are made. Obviously, employers are more willing to accommodate workers whom they cannot easily replace. But these private accommodations, which allow some women but not others to benefit from part-time arrangements, may, in fact, be more damaging than helpful to women in general. For, according to advocates for women's rights, these policies have the inadvertent effect of satisfying—and thus silencing—the most talented women in the work force, those who might otherwise spear-head a change in policy.

This limited privilege for the especially talented also may cause resentment among employees for whom such accommodations are not likely to be made because they are not working mothers. Mary, the editor, fully expected to go back to work full-time after her maternity leave. But after she had her baby, her priorities changed radically—mostly, she says, as a result of "falling in love" with her daughter.

While she was on maternity leave, she requested part-time work, pointing out that she could make a valuable contribution during this temporary period in her life, and that she was prepared to commit herself to the company for many years. She was refused part-time work, but when it became clear that a full-time schedule was making no one very happy, her company allowed her to work part-time on a freelance basis. As such, she lost all her benefits and her seniority, but she was still willing to give it a try.

As time went on, however, Mary discovered that she was regarded as a second-class citizen by her colleagues and that the interesting and important work assignments went to others. She also felt a considerable loss of self-esteem as well as a good deal of guilt when watching others working long hours while she came and went.

Thinking that perhaps a job change was in order, she sought and found a three-day-a-week schedule at another publishing firm. Yet again, the response from colleagues was unnerving. "People would make snide comments such as, 'Well, we'd like to go home early, too, you know,' or, 'If you were in here more, you'd know what was going on,'" said Mary. "After a while, my self-esteem plummeted to an all-time low. I just wasn't able to get the job done. I didn't feel a part of the team, and I felt a lot of hostility from my co-workers."

Finally, Mary compromised and took on a four-day-a-week schedule. "Now I feel much better about my job," she says. "My work life is very important to me, and it was just suffering too much."

Finding the best mix of work and mothering is a personal formula that varies from woman to woman. For some, full-time work during their babies' early years is desirable; for others, it is a necessity. Other mothers, however, discover that they are happiest and most fulfilled if they temporarily modify their work schedules, sacrificing short-term career goals for the long-term goal of successfully combining working and mothering without stress and guilt. Firms that five or ten years ago had no part-time workers now report that as many as 25 percent of their female staff work part-time (fewer days per week or fewer hours in a day) in order to attend to the needs of infants and toddlers at home. It is encouraging that many of these companies are realizing that allowing new mothers to work part-time for a period of two to three years, with the understanding that the mother will resume her full-time commitments when the child is in a preschool program, promotes company loyalty and reduces turnover.

Another encouraging sign is the growing number of working fathers who are choosing four-day work weeks in order to share in the responsibility of childcare. A couple who is able to negotiate a four-day week for each partner need find childcare for only three days a week. Perhaps the father will have Mondays off with the child, and the mother will have Fridays off. The baby or toddler will need surrogate care, then, only on Tuesdays, Wednesdays and Thursdays. Aside from making some working mothers feel more comfortable emotionally and economically about the amount of surrogate care they have to provide for their young children, this arrangement also has the added benefit of making both parents committed to helping the other fully experience the dual roles of parent and worker. Such a couple may feel like a team —with no one partner accepting the bulk of the childcare responsibilities. When parents feel like a team and are pleased about their work and childcare arrangements, such well-being tends to mitigate stress and to communicate itself in positive ways to children.

Flextime schedules also allow parents to share work and childcare and to feel like a team. A flextime schedule is one that overlaps or dovetails with the traditional nine-to-five schedule and permits a parent to come in early and thus go home early, or to come in late and stay late. A couple who each had the benefit of flextime schedules could arrange their days so that the surrogate childcare was kept to a minimum. He might work from seven to three; she might work from eleven to seven. Childcare would be needed for only four hours a day. About 20 percent of workers—both male and female—have flextime schedules.

In addition to on-site day-care, part-time work and flextime schedules, some companies have allowed working mothers to pursue job-sharing, either with a colleague or with a spouse who works in the same field. (Job-sharing has always been a possibility among couples who are self-employed; artists, writers and couples with small businesses have often shared one job, two jobs or one and one-half jobs without calling it such. So-called "mom and pop" stores are a good example.) In a formal job-sharing arrangement, the partners may split the day into afternoon and morning sessions, may alternate weeks or may both work together, but on a schedule of reduced hours. Salary and benefits are split down the middle. Many smart employers are discovering that they tend to get two committed workers for the price of one, since the productivity of each member of the partnership often exceeds a part-time schedule.

Another option that a working mother might explore is bringing the baby to work with her. A few mothers have satisfactorily solved the working and mothering bind this way. For women who have private offices, or who work in an atmosphere where infants are appreciated and can easily be accommodated, such a solution may seem ideal. Pat, thirty-nine, the owner of a bookstore in a small town, often brought her new baby to work with her, keeping her on her lap while she was talking to customers and making sales, and saving paperwork for those hours when the baby slept in a Port-a-Crib in a backroom. Far from being a distraction, the baby seemed to enhance the homey atmosphere of the bookshop. "I enjoy having her here," said Pat. "And, ironically, it's great advertising. People come in to see how she's doing. She's meeting a lot of people and she's quite well socialized." Another woman, however, a college administrator, found that her job did not easily share itself with an infant on the premises. The baby tended to cry during important phone calls and to need to have her diaper changed in the middle of meetings.

One obvious drawback to this option is that such a solution is only temporary. When infants become toddlers and are no longer immobile, few work situations can accommodate them. "Basically it's getting harder to have her here as she gets older," said Pat. "She's more mobile now. I can't very well baby-proof the store, so I'll have to store-proof the baby for as long as this arrangement is feasible."

At-home work may be another solution during both the infant and toddler years. Many women are discovering that they work better and faster at home than they do in offices, where social contacts, lunch hours and meetings distract them from the business at hand. Still others have work that by its very nature lends itself to working in a home environment. I am obviously an example of someone whose work almost demands that I work at home, but there are thousands of women—women who work with computers, for example—who are able to do part of their work, or the bulk of it, at home. Working at home allows a woman to choose which hours she will work, thus giving her more flexibility regarding childcare. A woman with an infant may work during the child's naps and in the evening, thus reducing her need for surrogate care to almost nil. A woman with a toddler or preschooler may work when her husband is home, when a babysitter is present, or when her child is in nursery school, so that she is able to be with her child more hours of the day than she would if she were working in an office. Some women with full-time jobs work a portion of their hours at home; others work at home exclusively. At-home work may be temporary (during a child's infancy and toddlerhood) or permanent.

One drawback of at-home work, however (indeed the very characteristic that makes it so efficient and attractive for new mothers), is that it doesn't allow for social contacts, informal feedback or teamwork. A woman working in isolation, with little firsthand response to her work, may, ironically, begin to experience some of the loss of self-esteem that at-home mothers say they feel. Another disadvantage is that women who freelance, or who work on a piecemeal basis, often have no benefits and are paid low wages. Partial at-home work, or at-home work which is temporary, then, may be the best solution for some working mothers.

- *Let your child see that working and mothering can be combined successfully.* "If I had a mother who worked, my life would be so much easier now," said Mary, the editor. "I would have some idea how to go about doing this thing that we're doing."

Combining working and mothering has proven difficult for many of us because we had few, if any, role models to show us how to do it. Our children, however, will have role models—us. But as those role models, we will be effective only if we allow them to see both aspects of our lives and if we communicate positive feelings to them about both mothering and working.

In my interviews with working mothers, I was impressed by how often the mothers took their young children to their places of work— sometimes because work had to be done on weekends and it was easier to take the children along, but often because the mothers took pride in their work and wanted the children to see the workplace, in the same way our fathers sometimes let us explore the inner sanctums of their offices. "I've brought my daughter, who is four, and my son, who is five, in with me to work on Saturdays. They sit at the typesetting machine and type away. It gives them an idea of what I do," said Sue, the typesetter.

"[My daughter is] four now, and she's seen me working all her life. I've taken her to the library with me, and I'm always bringing a lot of books home," said Phyllis, the librarian.

"Recently, I took [Giselle] to work with me. We went on Sunday morning to the office, and she had the greatest time. She really enjoyed it. She played with the computers. She sat at the desk and called different people on the telephone," said Mayra, the financial comptroller.

All too often, we think that we will be better mothers if we do not let our work life impinge on our home life. To some extent this is true. A young child who has been away from you most of the day will need and want your full attention when you are in the home. Phone calls or paperwork which distract your attention from the child will often be met with resentment or demonstrative behavior on the part of the child. (What mother is not familiar with the common syndrome of a child who plays nicely and quietly by herself *until* the phone rings? The moment that the mother is on the phone is the moment that the child will suddenly decide she has urgent noisy needs that must be met right *now*.)

On the other hand, how is a child to see that working and mothering are both integral parts of a woman's repertoire unless you tell the child that this is so? Hiding your work from your child might, instead, convey the message that there is something wrong with working: If there weren't something wrong with it, why would you hide it? Feeling guilty about working, or feeling overly stressed, will convey negative feelings about combining the two to a young child. This is particularly important for daughters, who, if they see that combining working and mothering is too hard, may choose to avoid one role or the other when they mature.

A balance can be struck between not allowing work to impinge on time spent with children, and yet permitting them to experience you as a worker as well as a mother. Much of this balance can be achieved by talking to your children about work. Tell your children what you do and why. Describe to them where you go and what your tasks are while you are there, and if possible, take them along one day to see your work environment. When you have achieved something in the workplace—a promotion, a raise, a compliment from a boss for a job well done—tell your child. We sometimes think that children won't understand "adult" things such as promotions and raises, but regardless of a child's cognitive comprehension about the mechanics of wages, she or he will certainly understand that something good has happened to you—that you have been rewarded, complimented or have won a prize. These are positive feelings that the child can easily relate to, since she or he will have been rewarded for accomplishments, will have been complimented and will have won "prizes" for good behavior.

Likewise, you needn't shield the child from problems at work. To the contrary, the child may benefit from seeing that you can handle problems in a positive manner. Such modeling may be useful to the child in terms of learning how to handle her own needs, in learning how to negotiate, and in learning how to get along with other children. "My boss had one idea, and I had another, and at first we disagreed, but then we put the two ideas together and we shared them," you could say to a child. Or you may find that you are tempted to hide angry feelings or disappointment. But again, constructive anger or a heart-to-heart talk about disappointment may not only not harm your child, it may teach her valuable ways to handle such feelings herself.

• *Prepare daughters for a life of work.* If future demographic projections about the shape of the American family come true, girls will need to be prepared for a lifelong commitment to work in a way that was never before necessary in this country. Already 50 percent of the mothers of infants under one year of age work outside the home, and that figure is expected to increase substantially over the next decade. Single-parent households may reach staggering proportions as early as 1990. Even if these projections were only partially correct, the number of young women who would find themselves heads of households would be in the millions. To not prepare our daughters for a life of work borders on the irresponsible.

In the past, daughters were prey to two syndromes that often sabotaged their attempts to pursue lifelong work at which they might expect to find self-esteem, economic independence and satisfaction: the "Mr. Right" syndrome and the "drifting" syndrome. In the first, girls were taught—by their mothers, by their peers and by the media—that their destiny would one day appear to them in the form of a man who would sweep them off their feet and take care of them, both emotionally and economically. As a corollary to that, girls learned that preparing for the future would be a foolish and redundant endeavor, since, like as not, the man would have his own ideas about where the couple was headed, and the woman would be expected to drift until anchored by these stronger, more assertive, indeed *more legitimate* aspirations.

Deferring to a man crippled millions of women, who either found themselves trapped in claustrophobic marriages while skills they once took pride in atrophied, or, following a divorce or the departure of their children from the nest, out on the street looking for a job with a portfolio that consisted of diapers, dishes and dustpans. Others, with the benefits of the women's movement behind them as they emerged from college, tentatively tested their skills in the marketplace, usually beginning in lower entry-level positions than they were qualified for, and taking longer than their male counterparts to reach the upper levels if they got there at all. Because these tentative explorations frequently involved moving from the "helping professions" to careers in more male-dominated fields—as those fields began to open up to women— it often took a decade or more to feel comfortable in one's career, profession or trade. Such a delay often meant years of economic dependency on someone else.

Obviously the fact that you are a working mother will help prepare your daughter for a life of work, because she will know firsthand that work and achievement outside the home are among the range of possibilities for women. Beyond that, however, you should speak of future goals, jobs or careers to girls in the same way you would to a son. (Ironically, it may be even more important to help girls than boys plan for an independent economic future, since the vast majority of the projected number of single-parent heads-of-household will be women.) As your daughter matures, and vocational choices become more of a reality, help her to be alert to the consequences of her choices. Share with her your knowledge of the economic realities of certain vocations, as well as the trade-offs inherent in combining that life choice with the responsibilities of raising a family. Speak honestly with her about the benefits—as well as the difficulties—of being a working mother. Mothers in the past, through no fault of their own, promoted the myth of Mr. Right and fostered that myth in conversations with their daughters, inadvertently doing them a tremendous disservice. Honest talk about marriage and what it really entailed was rare—on the premise that one didn't want to disillusion a young woman. But to continue to shield our daughters from economic or emotional reality hinders their decision-making ability and forces them to make choices without enough information at their disposal.

• _Work toward easing sex stereotypes._ As we saw in Chapter 5, the sex-role stereotyping of young children starts from day one, is prevalent in schools, toys and the media, and begins to narrow, at a very early age, the range of possibilities for both girls and boys.

Sex-role stereotyping is ubiquitous and insidious: Even the most alert of parents may unknowingly treat girls differently from boys, in terms of expectations, promoting certain behavior, encouraging independence or dependence, and preparing them for adult life. Raised with traditional expectations ourselves, it is often difficult to rid ourselves of certain feelings or instinctual habits, even though we may intellectually swear by an egalitarian sex-role ideology. Remember the parents who said they encouraged their daughters to play with trucks and other masculine toys in order to erase certain sex-role stereotypes in their children, but who were unaware of the ways in which they subtly invited their daughters to be dependent and their sons to be independent?

The working mother may model for her daughters and her sons egalitarian behavior in the home and in her work life. A child's understanding of how things work in the adult world begins with you and your spouse, if one is present. If the child sees that both parents are nurturing and loving, both parents are assertive when assertiveness is called for, both parents share responsibilities in the home, both parents take care of the children and both parents earn income in the outside world, that construct will help to shape the child's picture of what may be possible for him or her when the child matures. A child who sees that his or her mother does not devalue herself will not be predisposed to devalue females in the world at large—unless someone or something else tells him or her that this is so.

For this reason it is not enough—although it is vital and important —to be a model for egalitarian behavior in the home. It is also necessary to pay attention to the messages the child receives in books, at school, from toys and in the media. Take a good hard look at the way in which your child's room is decorated, for example, or at the toys which fill the shelves in that room or at the books in your child's library. Do the toys in your daughter's room encourage passive rather than active play? Do the really interesting things in your child's books happen to boys, men or male characters? What TV shows does your child watch regularly, and what subtle messages do those shows convey? What about the ads in those shows? Do they portray girls with dolls and boys with bicycles? If this is the case, you needn't disallow all TV watching for children (although most child specialists believe in limiting and monitoring TV). Instead watch the shows and the ads with the child and occasionally mention to the child those portrayals which seem stereotypical.

Erasing sex-role stereotypes has proven to be easier for girls than for boys. Deep-seated fears prevent many of us from encouraging cross-sex behavior in boys to the extent that we allow it in girls. But encouraging cross-sex behavior needn't devalue boys or lead to confusion regarding their sexual identity. To the contrary, the goal of encouraging cross-sex behavior in boys is to widen their repertoire and to allow them to experience the nurturing side of their personalities without inhibition and fear. Dr. Lawrence Balter, in his book *Dr. Balter's Child Sense,* addresses this issue: "The central question is: How can we make it easier for a child to identify with proper sex roles and at the same time not be sexist or oppressed? Is that possible? It's an interesting dilemma. Your goal as a parent is to encourage your child to grow up comfortably in [his or her] physiological role. . . . You want your child to be comfortable with [his or her] own reality, but at the same time, you don't necessarily want to curtail any attempts to explore other roles, too.

"The answer, I think, lies partly in the way we explain play with tea sets or dolls or trucks to our children. You can say to a boy who is washing a doll, 'Isn't it nice you're pretending to be a daddy.' Not a mommy but a daddy—because fathers, too, give baths to babies. Why can't a boy do the same activity but pretend to be a daddy instead of a mommy? Why can't a boy serve food just as Daddy does? Doesn't Daddy ever cut up an apple and give it to him? Doesn't Daddy ever

pour the milk? Then the boy can identify with the father and still play
out a number of 'nurturing' roles. It will be clear to him that he's going
to grow up to be a man—like Daddy—and that fathers do lots of
things, many of which are loving and caring and giving."

Easing sex-role stereotypes involves a process of consciousness-raising
—for oneself, for one's spouse and for one's children. And it is just as
important to do this for boys as it is for girls. It is difficult for a woman
to achieve an egalitarian marriage or to feel comfortable in the role of
a working mother if she has grown up believing herself to be a second-
class citizen, but it may also be difficult for a man to achieve a successful
partnership with a working woman if he subconsciously feels that males
are innately superior to females or that males are instinctively more
active and assertive than females. Such a belief system does a disservice
to both boys and girls: The dual-career or dual-wage marriage—unquestionably the marriage of the future—is the one in which both our sons
and our daughters will have to feel comfortable.

• *Foster autonomy in your children.* It has been said by many who
work with and study children that allowing a child to grow into an
autonomous being is the most important gift a parent can bestow on
his child. Autonomy is the ability to choose how to be or how to think
for oneself. It implies a feeling of self-worth, of independence and of
confidence in one's judgment.

Girls in the past were often denied autonomy. Instead, they were
taught to defer to a man's judgment. They were encouraged to allow
others to determine their self-worth. Autonomy and deference aren't
a very good mix. Therefore, because women in the past have been
expected to be emotionally and economically dependent on men, girls
were not encouraged to be autonomous.

Working mothers who are striving to achieve autonomy in their own
lives can help to promote autonomy in their daughters'. Such a mother
will encourage her daughter to make decisions, will give her practice
in that decision-making and will teach her to take responsibility for the
choices she does make. One doesn't get to be a good decision-maker
without practice. Girls who have had no experience making judgments
and taking responsibility for those judgments—whether the decisions
be about people, about oneself or about work—may find as they mature
that they not only cannot make decisions in their best interest, but they
no longer even know what they really feel.

• *Plan time together as a family.* In Knaub's study of the children of dual-career families, she asked the children to name the ways in which the family was able to come closer together. Fifty-three percent of the respondents said that because time was so precious in the dual-career family, they planned their family activities together very carefully. When asked to specify what these activities were, 40 percent named travel, 33 percent named taking walks and talking together, and 26 percent named holiday celebrations. "They scheduled weekend and travel time together," said Knaub. "They didn't allow anybody to bring their offices or their work along. It was a rest from the outside world, a time when they could really concentrate on each other. One of the most important bits of advice I would give to such families, based on what the children had to say, is to make sure that they plan on a regular basis this kind of time away from household chores, the telephone, and the temptation to work."

Dual-career and dual-wage families live by schedules. Because they are, by necessity, busy families, scheduling is necessary in order to avoid chaos. There are schedules for work, babysitters, meal preparation and shopping. Some couples even report that they have to schedule sex together, because if they didn't, other chores, or simply the desire to sleep, would take precedence.

But making time to concentrate on one another, without the distractions of household chores or work commitments, can often be overlooked when forming the monthly or weekly schedule. It doesn't clamor for attention; it doesn't come with built-in deadlines. It's vague and quiet and can be put off until next week or until next month without impeding practical progress. Yet to put it off is to deprive yourself and your children of valuable time spent experiencing one another and communicating to one another. Without such time spent together, problems and questions that children have can get put on the back burner to simmer away unsolved and unanswered.

The dual-wage and dual-career family is not the traditional family. In the traditional family, Mom was always there to chat over milk and cookies in the afternoon after school, and if there was a problem or a question, it might come up then and at least get aired, if not resolved. But in the dual-career or dual-wage family, leisure time is at a premium and can get swallowed up by extra work commitments or extra chores or simply the desire to be alone to gather one's resources. Because uninterrupted time spent together can get lost in the shuffle, the nontraditional family needs to recognize this need and to plan, however formally or informally, to integrate it into their family life.

Unfortunately, one of the characteristics of the nontraditional family is that they often come together when each member of the family is most frazzled—at the end of a long work or school day when there are many cooking, cleaning and shopping chores to be performed just so the family can function. Facing such chores when one is tired and depleted can lead to frustration, stress and short tempers. If such tensions characterize the early evening hours of your family, it might be prudent to rearrange the schedule to allow for quiet time without chores when first coming together.

Perhaps the nontraditional family could create a ritual of a shared hour when they first meet each other after a long day. The focus could be on sharing some easily prepared foods, such as fruit and cheese and crackers (so that everyone won't be cranky from hunger) while spending an hour together just talking, if children are older, or reading to or playing with younger children. Such time together can be relaxing and delightful—particularly if it is understood that when it is time to do the chores, everyone will pitch in to make the workload lighter. Frequently it is the pattern in the dual-career family that one parent takes care of the children while the other prepares the meal. But such division of labor deprives the child of having both of his or her parents together, and deprives the parents of experiencing each other and their children together. Making one hour a ritual in the household—an hour when phone calls go unanswered, when the television is not allowed to be on and when chores go unattended to—might give both parents and children a much-needed anchor in their day.

• *Avoid the temptation to become a workaholic.* Some women become workaholics because they feel insecure about their careers or jobs and believe they need to work all the time in order to be adequate; others become workaholics because, as Celeste, the interior designer, put it: "My work pans out better than my relationships." Still others feel insecure about their ability to be good mothers and use the demands of work as an excuse to be absent from the home more than is strictly necessary.

Workaholism and the mothering of young children do not a happy combination make. Even older children—teenagers who were able to articulate their needs—expressed concern about mothers who appeared to work too hard and too long. One felt like a client who needed to make an appointment with her busy mother; another felt as if her feelings and her concerns had to be put on hold; still another, in an ironic role reversal, became the mother to her mother. She worried about her mother's physical and emotional well-being as a result of the mother's putting in so many hours that she was no longer able to take good care of herself.

The word workaholic, like its namesake, alcoholic, connotes an unhealthy addiction. And, like its namesake, it suggests excess and an escape from the realities of life. Work and love have been identified as the twin pillars of emotional health. But if one is allowed to encroach upon the other, emotional health may be in jeopardy. Such a condition in a working mother is clearly not conducive to being a good role model.

Workaholism may affect children in two ways. In the first instance, this syndrome—on the part of either parent—deprives that child of love and attention that is that child's right. (Workaholics who are with the child in body, but who are preoccupied with work concerns, may also deprive the child of alert, direct interaction.) In the second instance, a mother who is a workaholic runs the risk of turning her child off (a daughter in particular) to the world of work. If work is seen as consuming all of a woman's life and depriving her of leisure time or a satisfactory marriage and family life, combining working and mothering may loom in the child's mind as an unattractive option. The positive working-mother role model wants to show her child how to achieve a balance between working and mothering. A mother who is obsessed with her office will not be able to achieve that balance.

• *Raise the consciousness of your child's school.* The nontraditional family cannot exist in a vacuum. It cannot thrive in a society that still caters only to the traditional way of life. It needs recognition that it exists, and it needs support systems in order to function. To date, those support systems have lagged behind the need. There are still twice as many parents seeking quality day-care for their young children as there are slots available; in some areas, after-school programs either do not exist at all or cannot accommodate the growing number of children in dual-career or dual-wage families; and schools continue to schedule conferences, plays, sports activities and other school events during hours when working parents cannot attend.

Working mothers of school-age children now outnumber at-home mothers. One would imagine that if those mothers could get together to lobby for necessary changes in school policies, then accommodations would be forthcoming. Such an interest group would reflect the majority interest in the school population. But that, of course, is the problem. Working mothers cannot and do not get together for the same reason they cannot bake brownies for bake sales or show up for midafternoon parent-teacher sessions.

Working mothers can, however, effect change on an individual level when special conflicts or needs arise concerning their own children. Working mothers can raise the consciousness of teachers, coaches and principals by simply saying, when the occasion calls for it, "I am a working mother. I work from nine to five. I cannot be here during those hours, but I do not want to miss out on my child's sports activities or school conferences. Nor do I want my child to miss out because her mother cannot be here."

Guilt, confusion and worry over whether or not we are doing the right thing has kept many of us from simply stating the obvious. Because we are living nontraditional lives, yet are still trying to cope with systems set up for traditional families, we find it hard at times to say to teachers and to principals that we are working mothers. But such statements should be made, in the presence of our children, without guilt and without inhibition. If we believe in what we are doing, and we convey to our children positive feelings about our choices and our actions, our children will feel comfortable in nontraditional families. If, however, we shy away from identifying ourselves as working mothers —for fear that we will be looked down upon by school personnel—we convey to our children that there is something wrong with being this kind of a family.

• *Be a model for mothering as well as working.* Dr. Michael Bulmash, in a previous chapter, stated that "women have become increasingly uncomfortable in the role of nurturer." He added that the pressure on women to succeed in male terms and the concurrent pressure to become discomfited by the traditional role of mother have created a generation of mothers who lack confidence in their mothering.

The goal of the positive working-mother role model is to widen the range of possibilities for daughters and sons. As working mothers, we are in a unique position to model both working and mothering. But if our work life begins to impinge on our mothering, either in real terms or in terms of our attitudes toward the two endeavors, then we risk shutting off, before they've even had a chance to experience them, a wide and fulfilling range of choices for our children.

In an ideal world, a mother would be as highly valued as a doctor. She would find respect both in society and in the home. She would be paid for her work, might take courses in her chosen field, and might belong to a network (or union) of other mothers so as to mitigate the isolation that seems to go with the job. Because she was highly valued by society—both economically and socially—she would not suffer from a lack of self-esteem, would not be dependent upon a male breadwinner, and would feel competent and successful in her chosen career. Certainly there are a myriad of skills a mother could practice and hone and feel proud of.

It's a fanciful idea, and not one likely to shake the foundations of American society in the very near future. But from this portrait one can see clearly what doesn't exist for the American mother today. Because such respect is lacking in our culture, the working mother will need to be alert to the ways in which she herself, or her spouse, might be tempted to devalue that part of herself that is a mother.

10

The New Working Father

*M*ike's dad was a forester in Montana. He spent a great deal of time with his son on weekends and in the evenings, but the shared activities almost always focused on "men's" work: Father and son repaired and built around the home and in the yard. His father was a very important figure in Mike's life, but it was not his responsibility to attend to childcare duties or household chores. He didn't change Mike's diapers when he was a baby or get him dressed in the morning when he was small. He didn't cook his meals or keep his room clean. As was the pattern in the households of Mike's boyhood friends, his mother took care of the domestic side of life, while his father earned the living and attended to those chores that were considered to be male in character.

Now Mike is a father. He is, however, a different sort of dad from what his own was. "There's no part of the child-rearing that I haven't done," says Mike, whose daughter is six. "I come home from work two days a week at 3:30 so that I can be there when Caitlin gets home from school. I've always done at least 50 percent of the childcare—changing her diapers, feeding her, getting her dressed in the morning for school. I've never felt that it was my wife's job—after all, it's my house, my dishes and my child, too."

Mike is an independent producer of filmstrips and videotapes, and his wife, Judy, is a psychologist. Before they had children, they had worked out an egalitarian division of labor, because they believed together that such a sharing of chores was fair. Judy was an ardent feminist, and Mike shared her value system. Now that Judy works nearly full-time, however, this sharing has become imperative. Yet Mike's reasons for shared parenting are not entirely pragmatic. "My reasons for doing it aren't political or cultural. I do it because I love this kid and I like to be with her. I get a lot out of the relationship. I wouldn't be happy if I didn't have the time for her. It's very visceral. I felt it right from the beginning."

Over the last decade—and most visibly in the last five years—the character of the American father has changed dramatically from that of the traditional father of a generation ago. When we were children, most fathers did not change diapers, did not get us ready for school and did not pick us up from babysitters or day-care centers on the way home to bake potatoes and set the table for dinner. They may have read us stories at night before we went to bed, but they did not know where the pajamas were kept. They may have played baseball with us on Saturday afternoons, but they did not know how to get stains out of corduroys. They may have put a cool hand on our foreheads when we were sick, but they did not stay home from work the next morning because we could not go to school. They didn't have to: There was Mom to do all that.

Twenty years ago, fathers had a special and distinct role within the family that contrasted sharply with the role of the mother. The division of labor—and the way that division of labor defined the potential for intimacy with children—was clear. Although many fathers, like Mike's, spent time with their children on weekends and evenings, others remained shadowy absentee figures—gone the entire day and glimpsed behind large newspapers at night. These fathers were often strong figures in the moral and emotional development of their children, and important role models for intercourse with the world outside the home, but they were largely exempt from the pull and tug of daily family life.

The working father today is a changed species. No longer the rarefied authority figure of a previous generation, the new working father has —with considerable help—removed many of the barriers that prevented him from becoming an active parent and a co-nurturer to his children. Most men are still locked into demanding full-time jobs in which career modification is even less of an option than for women. But many fathers are not willing to be locked out of their children's lives. It is no longer unusual, for instance, to see a group of fathers at the playground, briefcases parked along the fence, pushing their kids on the swings and chatting among themselves about growth and development —not of corporations, but of toddlers.

Active parenting by men today starts with conception. Nearly as eager as women to learn about pregnancy and birth, and to cope with the powerful emotions that accompany such a milestone, they buy books on prenatal care and attend with their wives Lamaze or Bradley Method classes in which they are encouraged to be active participants in the birth. To the extent that their enthusiasm and abilities allow, they coach during the event, and a few insist on delivering the baby when she or he is born. New fathers report, with the same feverish language as their partners, the joy of the birth experience and the intense involvement they have in their newborns. It is rare today to find a father who prefers to pace in the waiting room; in fact, most obstetricians encourage fathers to be with their partners during labor and delivery and for the important process of bonding following the birth.

When their babies come home, working fathers also report that they revel in the hands-on approach to baby care. With some awkwardness, but with pride, they change diapers, bottle-feed infants, know where the T-shirts are kept and walk the floors at night to help settle colicky babies. "My father wasn't around for any of the births of his children," said Charles, thirty-one, a magazine editor. "He was on the golf course twice and at the racetrack once. He wasn't even near the hospital. When my wife got pregnant, however, there was never any question that I wouldn't be as fully involved as she. During her pregnancy, I did 90 percent of the cooking because she was working long hours and wasn't feeling well. I went to all of the childbirth classes; I even went to the class on breast-feeding by myself when my wife was sick. She had a fifteen-hour labor, and I was there every step of the way. The baby was on the bottle a lot during the early weeks after birth because of a medical problem, and I did all the feeding. In fact, I gave the baby his first bottle. Because my wife was often exhausted, I would do the feedings and change the baby several times during the night, even though I had a job to go to the next morning. I was totally involved."

As the babies grow, working fathers find they have the same urges and desires as working mothers: They want to be there when their toddlers take their first steps—they don't want to just hear about it when they come home from work. They take over childcare responsibilities for long periods of time when Mom is not available, and they rather like being seen in the nurturing role: at the park, at the supermarket or taking the baby for a walk in the stroller.

For some working fathers, during their children's early years, parenting, to their surprise, begins to take precedence over their career goals: Priorities shift and change. Some fathers have even stopped working for a period of time to stay home to allow their wives to pursue their careers. Others have negotiated job-sharing arrangements with their partners or with other colleagues in order to play a larger part in childcare. Many more are discovering that jobs which do not allow for time to be with their children simply have to be modified, despite the sacrifices. The fast track to success—which often carries with it the need to be at the workplace for ten or more hours a day—just doesn't stack up when compared to the ability to be there for your kid's childhood. "My daughter has definitely had a deep effect on my aspirations," said Jeffrey, forty-one, a journalist. "I no longer think of myself as having the desire to succeed in a demanding profession. I would rather have a position that was boring and unchallenging, but which gave me a lot of free time to be with her, than to take a job that demanded more of me."

And still other fathers, like Ansell, forty-one, a sculptor, are able to take on a large part of the childcare because they work at home. His wife, Dina, works full-time as the principal of an elementary school, so Ansell assumes the major burden of childcare. When their daughter, Samantha, was a baby and a toddler, Ansell took care of her while his wife was at work. Now that Samantha is of school age, Ansell minds her after school. Often, during their afternoons together, Samantha plays in her father's studio, giving Ansell the opportunity to continue his work. "It was difficult, exasperating and a lot of joy," said Ansell of the first few years raising his daughter. "I have a relationship with Samantha I wouldn't have had otherwise, and it certainly changed the way I see women. I empathize with the way they operate in the world. I'm doing essentially what is considered a female role."

The fathers' reports and perceptions of their changing role are confirmed by working mothers themselves. "My husband was brought up in a household where he not only had a traditional kind of family life; he had an absentee father," said Jackie, the university administrator. "His father was a politician and was in Washington all week. When his father would come home, he'd be the Weekend Hero. He took the kids out for Sunday outings and for trips to the zoo. His father did all the fun things, and his mother got stuck with the broken toys and the report cards.

"But when our daughter, Leigh, was born, my husband, Tommy, fell in love with her, and he had no trouble assuming the traditional mothering activities. He changed her diapers, he bathed her, he took her on errands—mostly because he was so thrilled to have this child that he couldn't spend enough time with her. I really didn't have to do anything in terms of childcare."

Many other mothers report that their husbands, too, share childcare responsibilities with them:

Mayra: "Her father and I share everything. There is really no distinct role for either of us. I take care of her. He takes care of her. Whoever is able to takes off from work when Giselle is sick."

Elaine: "Kate takes it totally for granted that both parents work and that both parents take care of her."

Pat: "Her father and I share child-rearing and household tasks."

Sandra: "My husband and I share housework and child-rearing. We each work four days a week. Each of us gets to take care of our daughter all alone for one day, and she's in day-care the other three days."

Laura: "We share child-rearing and housekeeping equally. It depends on who has more free time."

Shared parenting, the new working father is discovering, is a previously untapped wellspring of pleasure. Yet, not surprisingly, working fathers who take their childcare responsibilities seriously and who have made a commitment not just to be supportive but to share equally in the upbringing of their children report that they, too, are prey to many of the same syndromes that characterize the too-busy working mother: fatigue, stress and the desire to be Superdad. And others are finding out that the daily tasks of childcare are sometimes unrewarding and tough.

On the whole, however, fathers say that active parenting has made their lives richer, that they have an intimacy with their children they never would have had otherwise, and that the rewards of being a "present" father more than compensate for the sacrifices they have had to make. Being active parents, they say, has allowed them to develop the nurturing sides of their personalities in a way that was never before possible. "One thing that has really been accomplished by large numbers of couples is the idea that both partners are involved in child-rearing," said Dr. Sylvia Feinberg of Tufts University. "I think that men see it as their role to pick kids up at day-care centers and to change diapers. Twenty-five years ago, a lot of men would have been threatened by these activities: Now they're thriving on them."

That the concept of fatherhood in this country is changing is indisputable. This revolution, however, has been largely confined to child-rearing. It is still quite rare to find a dual-career or dual-wage family in which the working father spends as much time at *all* the family's domestic chores in a given week as the working mother. Often the discrepancy, in terms of hours spent, is quite large.

In 1986, the Boston University School of Social Work conducted a study of 651 employees of an unnamed Boston-based company. They discovered that women work twice as many hours on homemaking and childcare as men. This was true even if the woman's income was greater than the man's. When children were sick, it was the woman who was most likely to stay home. Married female parents spent eighty-five hours per week combining work and family life; married male parents spent sixty-five hours.

When Patricia Knaub questioned the children of dual-career families, in her study referred to earlier, she found similar imbalances in workload: 51.6 percent reported that their mothers assumed the major responsibility for the housework; 15 percent said that it was their father's responsibility.

Even when fathers report they share child-rearing activities with their wives, women usually put in more hours. According to a 1982 study conducted by Joseph Pleck, assistant director of the Wellesley College Center for Research on Women, men spend an average of fifteen to twenty minutes in direct participation with their children (and two to four hours indirectly) each day, and women spend twice that. In those families in which childcare responsibilities approach a fifty-fifty division of labor between fathers and mothers, fathers are found most often to "play" with their children, while mothers still assume most of the "caretaking" rituals.

Some observers who have pondered these statistics have suggested that the "new working father" is a species that is getting a lot of mileage out of a modest amount of input—an idea that many harried working dads would be quick to dispute. But the figures do suggest that the new working father is an evolving species, not yet fully developed. A number of obstacles—some initiated from within, some imposed from the outside—have hindered his ability to share fully in parenting and domestic chores.

One of the reasons that fathers do not put in as many hours as mothers is that they still have a reluctance to perform household chores. That men participate more often and to a larger extent in child-rearing than in domestic tasks should come as little surprise. The payoff, after all, is considerably greater for child-rearing than for housework. Men stand to gain something very tangible and wonderful if they make themselves available for their kids' childhoods: a newfound intimacy, an enrichment of their own personalities and a joy that can't be matched in the boardroom. Housework, however, is a different matter. Housework has always been a servant task—often dull, tedious and repetitive. It delivers very few rewards, intrinsic or otherwise. Being a good vacuumer or a good dishwasher doesn't carry with it the panache of being a good father. And it has so long been associated with the powerless that to invest in it may suggest a relinquishing of one's own power within the family. Since those who have power rarely give it up, men have been much slower to embrace domestic chores. Even if both partners in a marriage are sharing equally in child-rearing, the working mother generally assumes the majority of household tasks. Her domestic burden, therefore, is often larger.

And like the women of this transitional group, the new working father is also fighting old expectations. With few exceptions, the new working father was not raised to change diapers, do the food shopping or stay home with a sick child. For some men, evolving into a sharing partner has been a torturous journey—one in which they had to shed old beliefs and ideas about what it meant to be a man and to have the superior position in the household. To make *any* progress in this direction often brings with it excessive praise, distorting the reality.

The workplace has also hindered the evolution of the new working father. It is still very much easier for a woman than a man to ask for a parental leave, to request and receive part-time work or to abandon the workplace entirely for two or three years while children are young. Men who take parental leaves, who change jobs to be with their children or who leave the work force entirely are still so rare they make news. Economic realities account for part of the problem. If the working mother still makes only sixty-four cents to the dollar when compared to working fathers, then simple arithmetic might dictate that the mother reduce her hours rather than the father. A more formidable obstacle, however, is the fact that men's work lives remain considerably less flexible than do women's. When Catalyst, a national organization for working women, recently polled personnel directors about their companies' policies, 119 of them said they did offer paternity leave. But of those 119 companies, 41 percent of them later went on to say that "no time" was the appropriate amount of time a man should take off to be with his infant.[1] Men who would therefore like to be more fully participating fathers find that the policies of the workplace prevent them from doing so.

Progress in the workplace has been slow, but there are some encouraging signs. Less than a decade ago, almost no companies had paternity-leave policies, and a father who asked for time off to help care for a newborn was likely to be regarded with shock and suspicion. Today there is a bill before Congress mandating that employers provide parents of either sex with at least four months of unpaid leave at the birth or serious illness of a child with their jobs guaranteed when they return to work. Responding to pressures from within, some companies are beginning to think about more flexible work schedules for their male employees as well as for working mothers.

At the American workplace, working mothers have been the agents for change, paving the way, in many instances, for working fathers. They have also been the agents for change in the American home. While the women's movement and the subsequent evolution of the culture created an attitudinal climate in which it became acceptable to be a participating father, it wasn't until women entered the workplace in large numbers that men were compelled to embrace shared parenting. If mothers were still at home, as they were in the 1950s, it seems highly unlikely that men would feel enthusiastic about child-rearing to the extent they do today. The new working father is a direct response to the fact that the mother is no longer home all day.

"There seems to be a changing ideology and rhetoric prescribing a greater role for men _in_ the family to complement a greater role for women _outside_ the family," write Carolyn Pope Cowan and Philip A. Cowan in their paper "Men's Involvement in the Family: Implications for Family Well-Being."

"Mothering 'predispositions' aside, when economics makes exclusive motherhood too costly, fuller participation by fathers is likely to follow," writes Kathleen Gerson in *Hard Choices.*

Harvard anthropologists Mary Maxwell West and Melvin J. Konner found in a survey of the role of the father in eighty societies that when women's work other than childcare is considered essential and important, male investment in parenting increases.[2] "The highest degree of male parental investment can be expected when relationships are monogamous, when local warfare is absent, when the division of labor allows fathers access to their children and *when women's contributions are important.*"[3] (Italics mine.)

The presence of the working mother in the majority of households has necessitated the appearance of the new working father. He exists because she exists. And this new working father is no longer confined to the middle and upper-middle classes. Although the new working father began as a middle-class phenomenon, working-class men, too, are a part of this evolution. Union officials report that contract negotiations often include such topics as paternity leave, personal days to attend children's school events, and sick-child care leaves.

The changing nature of the father has also spread to the families of at-home mothers. As the culture has sanctioned the new fatherhood—in response to the presence of the working mother—the benefits of shared parenting have been contagious. In essence, then, the working mother has set off a chain reaction—all the elements of which affect our children.

THE EFFECTS OF THE NEW WORKING FATHER ON CHILDREN

Psychologists who study children tend to agree that two nurturers are better than one. A child in the home of two nurturing and working parents has two individuals to provide emotional and physical love, two persons who can offer creative and intellectual stimulation, and two role models from whom he or she can absorb vital information pertaining to both domestic intimacy and the life outside the home. "To the degree that greater flexibility allows men who are more nurturing to take it on, this is a very good experience for the child," says Dr. Kirsten Dahl of Yale.

Two nurturing parents may also contribute to a more relaxed home environment. When the energy level of one parent falters, there is the other to take up the slack. Direct interaction with a young child can be difficult to sustain for long periods of time—a fact borne out not only by the testimony of parents themselves, but by the results of time-use studies. Having a fresh recruit waiting in the wings, or being able to spell each other—no matter what the task—can help to mitigate the tension and stress that often accompanies the day-to-day dealings with an intractable two-year-old (or an intractable eight-year-old). It also helps to provide a richer variety of life experiences in the home, further stimulating a child's growth and development.

Having two nurturing parents appears as well to broaden a child's range of possibilities and to ease the formation of rigid stereotypes. Grace Baruch and Rosalind Barnett discovered, in a study they conducted of four-year-old girls, that the more involved the father was in childcare tasks, the less stereotyped were the child's views of men and women. "It seems that when a father takes on some of the responsibility of his child's care, not just 'helping Mom,' his daughter sees men as more caring and less aggressive. She also sees women as more independent, more capable of being 'in charge.' "[4]

Working fathers, mindful of the stereotypes that were in place when they were children, often make a conscious effort to provide a nonsexist environment for their daughters. Mike, for example, felt a sense of responsibility to involve his daughter in masculine endeavors. "I think there's a value to having more open-ended role models in terms of sex stereotypes. Caitlin, by and large, doesn't have a lot of rigid thinking. And I think that's useful for her. She doesn't feel, for example, that it's a woman's job to clean and cook, nor does she feel that because she's a girl that she can't fix things. I always include her when I'm fixing something or making something. She has a workshop in the basement, for example. Girls miss out on experiences that give them mechanical skills. And because of this, they end up feeling incompetent in the world. Because she's a girl I make an effort to give her these experiences."

Sons, too, benefit from having two nurturing parents. Fathers who show respect for women and for women's roles by not being reluctant to take on the traditional female tasks in the house not only allow their sons to develop the affective sides of their personalities, but also appear to engender similar respect for women in sons. "A child who witnesses his dad acting in a maternal role, as it were, learns something that another child has yet to learn," says Dr. Michael Bulmash, the child psychologist. "Because Dad can do this thing, it becomes a given in that home for that child. He's seeing it from the ground up. It becomes part of his possible."

Such a "possible" may be enormously liberating for a child. Nancy Chodorow in her book *The Reproduction of Mothering* explains: "[Traditional] roles have been functional, but for a sex-gender system founded on sexual inequality. . . . Fathers are supposed to help children to individuate and break their dependence on their mothers. But this dependence on her, and this primary identification, would not be created in the first place if men took primary parenting responsibilities. Children could be dependent from the outset on people of both genders and establish an individuated sense of self in relation to both. In this way, masculinity would not become tied to denial of dependence and devaluation of women. Feminine personality would be less preoccupied with individuation, and children would not develop fears of maternal omnipotence and expectations of women's unique self-sacrificing qualities. This would reduce men's needs to guard their masculinity and their control of social and cultural spheres which create and define women as secondary and powerless, and would help women to develop the autonomy which too much embeddedness in relationships has often taken from them.

"Equal parenting would not threaten anyone's primary sense of gendered self. . . ." adds Chodorow. "Personal connection to an identification with both parents would enable a person to choose those activities she or he desired, without feeling that such choices jeopardized their gender identity. . . ."

She concludes: "My expectation is that equal parenting would leave people of both genders with the positive capacities each has, but without the destructive extremes these currently tend toward."

Parents who share parenting and breadwinning appear to liberate young children from rigid roles and to allow them to explore more fully both their masculine and feminine sides. The question that remains to be answered, however, is whether or not nurturing fathers will beget nurturing fathers in the next generation. Do parents beget like parents? Will the men and women of the next generation look back to their fathers for both nurturing and achievement skills and to their mothers as well for both sets of behavior? Will Caitlin, for instance, use Mike as a role model for nurturing skills when she has a newborn and her mother as a role model for work-related skills at her first job?

Questions about the future are impossible to answer, of course, but a great deal of evidence suggests that an individual's range of possibilities, formed in early childhood, remains with that person into adulthood. The validity of this hypothesis is most dramatically observed in aberrant behavior—children of suicides statistically are more likely to try suicide themselves, for example, than are the children of nonsuicides. The same correlation shows up in children who were victims of child abuse. Styles of parenting—hardly likely to be reported to any official organization and thus show up as statistics—are more difficult to assess. Yet firsthand accounts from nontraditional parents seem to bear the hypothesis out. Women who had working mothers as role models say they are less conflicted about combining career and family life than their peers; likewise, men who were raised by nurturing fathers appear to have an easier time than other men sharing both child-rearing and domestic chores with their partners.

Whether or not these changed styles of parenting become the norm in society depends on several factors. Social change can really only evolve if it serves society in a pragmatic way, if the obstacles to this change are not insurmountable and if the people involved continue, at some level, to desire this change. "We live in a period when the demands of the roles defined by the sex-gender system have created widespread discomfort and resistance," writes Nancy Chodorow. "Aspects of this system are in crisis internally and in conflict with economic tendencies. Change will certainly occur, but the outcome is far from certain. The elimination of the present organization of parenting in favor of a system of parenting in which both men and women are responsible would be a tremendous social advance. This outcome is historically possible, but far from inevitable. Such advances do not occur simply because they are better for 'society,' and certainly not simply because they are better for some (usually less powerful) people. They depend on the conscious organization and activity of all women and men who recognize that their interests lie in transforming the social organization of gender and eliminating sexual inequality."

THE MOVE TOWARD ANDROGYNY

The transformation of the organization of gender and the elimination of social inequality, to the extent that it is happening in the culture today, is creating a move toward androgyny. To many, the word androgyny is a threatening term, a word that conveys a fearful lack of clarity about one's sexual identity. One conjures up visions of men who have somehow gone "soft," and women just short of Amazonian in their strength and control. The tall wife and the short husband, the henpecked father and the battle-ax in a skirt who heads the corporation are all caricatures in our imagination: disagreeable stereotypes that make us uncomfortable enough to laugh at them. So upsetting, in fact, is the word androgyny to some people that I was advised several times not to use the term in this book for fear "it will turn men off." Not insignificantly, the people who offered this advice were all male.

As noted in Chapter 7, we suffer in this culture from deep-seated fears about cross-sex behavior—particularly cross-sex behavior in males. While androgynous behavior is seen as adding to the repertoire of females—giving them something they never had—it is sometimes seen as subtracting from the repertoire of a male, taking away something valuable that only he should possess. Dr. Lawrence Balter, the child psychologist, has explained these fears by suggesting that subconsciously we think that males who engage in cross-sex behavior have given up something—a penis, to be precise—thus fostering anxieties about possible homosexuality in that male. Although these fears are wildly irrational, we still think that some essential part of a man's "maleness" is missing if he participates in behavior usually regarded as female.

Another explanation—less Freudian and more a result of sexual politics—may clarify why we usually applaud cross-sex behavior in girls but not in boys. For centuries, male activities have been regarded as superior to female activities. Being a warrior and protecting the home carried with it more power than tending the fires and cooking the meat. Being a vice president of General Motors gave an individual more clout than knowing how to separate colors in the wash. Being captain of the football team got you award dinners, special pats on the back from the principal and perhaps a scholarship to college. Being captain of the cheerleaders merely got you dates. If a girl made the football team, or a woman became vice president of General Motors, that was admirable. But if a boy joined the cheerleaders, he risked becoming an object of ridicule; if a man gave up the vice presidency at General Motors to stay home to separate the wash, he had better have a damn good reason. Society has long thought it a disservice to a man to make him more like a woman, whereas it's often been a credit to a woman if she's shown she has certain masculine attributes, such as physical courage and assertiveness. Because the culture tends to value masculine activity more than feminine activity, we think we are adding to a woman's development to have her take on masculine roles. Conversely, we think we are taking valuable time away from the man's natural masculine endeavors if he pursues so-called feminine roles. Substitute the word power for "valuable time" in the above sentence, and one can see the roots of the reluctance for those in power to upset the status quo.

Those who have power don't give it up—*unless they are forced to, unless they see it as in their best interest to do so, or unless formerly powerless activities and endeavors suddenly become invested with a new kind of power.*

Such has been the case with the new move toward androgyny. "A generation ago, the androgynous image was considered dangerous and frightening," says Dr. Pruett. "Today, however, it is seen as attractive, even chic."

The feminist writings of the 1960s—and the consciousness-raising movement of the early 1970s—encouraged androgynous behavior among women. Women were urged to become competent in a variety of formerly male endeavors: They could be bosses, lawyers, doctors, car mechanics and carpenters, they were told, if they wanted to be. They were encouraged to become breadwinners, to wear pants and to give up confining modes of dress—long fingernails, for example, which would make changing the oil difficult, or high heels, which would make a woman vulnerable to attack and also a sex object. The move toward androgynous behavior was seen as being "liberating" for women.

Initially, however, this "liberation" threatened many men. To be sure, some men who were politically motivated, during a climate of radical rhetoric, tried to embrace cross-sex behavior themselves. Some marriages in the 1970s, founded on egalitarian values, had men sharing domestic chores with their wives. In some households, men took on cooking and cleaning and minding the children as a matter of principle. A few even learned to like it. But progress was slow.

It wasn't until a majority of women entered the work force that large numbers of men *were forced* to enter the feminine domain. Because family life and marital relations threatened to break down if they didn't pitch in, men saw that it was in *their best interest to do so.* This was particularly true in the realm of childcare. If they perceived that family harmony was a by-product of sharing the chores, they liked the rewards of childcare even better. The intrinsic payoff, they discovered, was a large one. And then, subtly, becoming a participating father—a nurturing father who was just as involved with the day-to-day chores as his female partner—began to be invested with a certain *unique power of its own.* The new working father discovered that he was part of a new breed of men who were valued by society, who were admired by other women and sometimes even envied by other men. Thus the three obstacles to embracing androgynous behavior and giving up traditional power began to give way: Men were compelled to do it, they found it in their best interest to do so, and the act itself became invested with a kind of reverse power. What's more, they began to feel good about themselves. They were, they felt, doing the "right thing."

This androgynous behavior on the part of both parents becomes, in a nontraditional family, a model for a child. As a result, those who work with children are now seeing more androgynous behavior in the children of these families. Nursery-school teachers, for example, report that boys play in the kitchen and girls adopt masculine Superhero roles in fantasy play. And this androgynous behavior, say researchers, is thought to be a boon to children's emotional health.

The androgynous family experience liberates children from rigid molds. Both boys and girls find it easier to explore, to act on and to balance their masculine and feminine sides. Sandra Bem, a researcher at Cornell, who has been studying cross-sex behavior in both males and females, says that "for fully effective and healthy human functioning, masculinity and femininity must be tempered by the other and the two must be integrated into a more balanced, a more fully human personality."[5]

Bem arrived at this conclusion by a series of carefully controlled studies. She designed a scale by which both men and women could label themselves either masculine or feminine or androgynous. Individuals who scored high on a list of feminine attributes she provided for them to check off, for example, were feminine. Individuals who scored high on the masculine list were masculine, and those who scored high on both lists were labeled androgynous. She then offered payment to all three groups for performing certain activities and for advancing certain opinions. She discovered that rigidly "sex-typed" males and females rejected cross-sex activities (such as ironing a shirt or hammering a nail) even though that rejection cost them money. Moreover, she discovered that they felt nervous and uncomfortable when asked to perform these chores.

Another discovery was that women sex-typed as "feminine" were the least competent of all three groups. From this she concluded: "The major effect of femininity in women—untempered by a sufficient level of masculinity—may not be to inhibit instrumental or masculine behavior per se, but to inhibit any behavior at all in a situation where the 'appropriate' behavior is left ambiguous or unspecified.

"In other words, 'feminine' women can be paralyzed in any situation which requires a fair amount of independent decision-making or initiative."[6]

In her study, Bem found that masculine and androgynous subjects were significantly more independent in their opinions than the feminine subjects, but the androgynous male turned out to be especially interesting. "He performs spectacularly. He shuns no behavior just because our culture happens to label it as female, and his competence crosses both the instrumental and the expressive domains. Thus, he stands firm in his opinions, he cuddles kittens and bounces babies, and he has a sympathetic ear for someone in distress."

The enhanced emotional well-being of androgynous behavior in women has been well documented. Bem's studies confirm this and appear also to confirm what other researchers have felt—that androgynous behavior in men also has a salutary effect on their emotional health. Androgynous parental behavior, if modeled in the home for children to emulate, would appear then to be of enormous value to children, as it liberates them to explore more fully their masculine and feminine sides.

But some researchers have wondered if children won't become confused by androgynous role models. Do androgynous parents promote gender confusion, for example? Does the fact that Dad cooks and Mom comes home with a briefcase puzzle a little boy who is looking for markers to help him figure out who he is and what his role will be as an adult? Will interchangeable roles in the household promote a sense that both men and women are the same?

Studies suggest that a child's gender identity is not so fragile that a working mother or a nurturing father will fundamentally confuse it.

"Children adapt to change," says Dr. Ritvo of the Yale Child Study Center. "It wouldn't exceed the capacity of the child to understand who's doing what in the family. What creates more difficulties is whether or not the parents are conflicted about their roles. If the mother or father is troubled or unhappy about her or his role, and her or his function as a woman or a man, that might be a problem. I'm not talking about who works or who does the dishes, but rather about their own feelings of masculinity or femininity and their own sexual roles in a love relationship. If a mother projects a climate of being troubled or conflicted about her adult female role, then that could create difficulties for the child in establishing an identity that is adaptive for life."

Between the ages of eighteen months and three years, a young child works hard to make his psychology fit his biological givens. When a child discovers his own body, he begins to ask: What's my body all about? What can it do? How is it like Dad's? How is it different from Mom's? This search for gender identity is the result of the child's own researches and of the attitude that the parents, who know that the child is a given gender, have toward the child. Young boys, for example, in order to solidify their masculinity and their identity as male, have to find out those characteristics that are exclusively male and not female. The psychological work of a two-year-old is to latch on to those "markers."

But as these markers become more confused, as, for example, the issue of dress is for young girls ("Why should I wear a dress?" my daughter asked when she was three and I was somewhat frantically trying to get her into appropriate attire for a birthday party. *"You* never do."), will it be harder for today's children to find these markers than it was for a previous generation?

Dr. Dahl, the Yale anthropologist and psychoanalyst, dismisses the idea. Such gender confusion, she explains, is more likely the result of some extraordinarily profound disturbance in the mother/child relationship, and is not a result of the mother's job or of the division of responsibilities in the home.

Dr. Lawrence Balter points out that there have been cases of gender identification problems in children—in boys more often than in girls. "The little boys want to dress up like Mommy, and to wear feminine things, like earrings. But these cases usually have to do with a troubled relationship with the mother. We don't know why, but we usually see this in conventional homes, where the mothers don't work, and where traditional stereotypes are in place. We think that perhaps the boy fears the loss of his mother and may have to hold on to her by identifying with her characteristics."

Healthy children in healthy nontraditional families should not have difficulties in establishing their gender identity—that is, fundamentally knowing whether they are a boy or a girl. Discovering what is appropriate behavior for that gender, however, will involve a different set of explorations than was true for previous generations—primarily because children will have a larger concept of what a sex role is.

Child psychologists have long understood that young children view men and women as performing different roles in the world. If Mom and Dad appear to have interchangeable jobs, will differentiating sex roles be harder for them? "It may be harder than it was for our generation," says Dr. Phyllis Cohen, a child psychiatrist at Yale. "But children will find those things that are necessary for them to differentiate the sexes. If it's no longer cookbooks and wrenches, it will be something else—maybe something as basic as a tone of voice or a way of handling a child."

The Oedipal phase of a child's development, according to Freudian theory, begins at about three and usually resolves itself around five. During this period, the child is said to "fall in love" with the parent of the opposite sex and may begin to compete with the parent of the same sex. By the time the Oedipal stage is resolved, however, the mini love affair has come to an end, the child has formed a strong identification with the parent of the same sex, and he or she has begun to incorporate many of the attitudes and values of this parent—which form the basis of the child's identity and morality.

How does a mother who is both a breadwinner and an achiever affect a young child during this critical phase? "For girls during the Oedipal phase, there is a heightened identification with the mother," says Dr. Balter. "If the mother is actively involved in a predominantly male arena, the girl will incorporate this into her own personality. Little boys, though they identify with their fathers, will nevertheless see in their mothers a potential they might otherwise not have noticed in women. This may contribute to the mental image of what's appropriate for women, and the boy may be sensitized to the fact that women can occupy any number of different roles.

"Jobs that people have are quite different from what your gender is. There's no reason to mix up jobs and gender. It's just an arbitrary thing. There are, however, undeniable differences between adult males and adult females, like voice and physical characteristics. But a child can learn that *adults* can give baths or vacuum. It doesn't have to have anything to do with being male or female."

ANDROGYNOUS WOMEN, BUT TRADITIONAL MEN?

Mike is a nontraditional father. Judy is a nontraditional mother. Both parents leave the home, go to work, earn money and come home. Both parents share cooking and shopping and vacuuming. Both parents make accommodations at work to get home at 3:30 on alternate days to be there when their daughter, Caitlin, gets off the bus from school. When they are with Caitlin, they both take care of her. Mike makes an effort to allow Caitlin to see that men cook and that women can fix things. Judy, by the very nature of her work, allows Caitlin to see that women, like men, are workers and nurturers. Caitlin is a lovely, bright six-year-old. She does not have, as Mike has said, a lot of rigid thinking. She says with pride that she knows how "to fix lots of things," and in fact plans to be a carpenter when she grows up. Yet she is equally intrigued by the mysteries of pregnancy and birth. She is growing up in a household in which both parents exhibit androgynous behavior, but she is not confused about her gender (she likes being a girl and has many feminine attributes), nor is she confused about her sex role. Her sex role is an expansive one that incorporates tenderness as well as assertiveness, caring as well as competency. I know Caitlin, and I find her to be a remarkably healthy girl with an inquisitive and engaging disposition. Her self-esteem shows no signs of damage.

Caitlin is a lucky girl. Her range of possibilities is large because her parents model for her a wide variety of androgynous behavior. But Caitlin's family is not the norm in American society. As we have seen, even in homes in which working fathers share parenting with working mothers, mothers still retain a larger share of the domestic burden. In most homes, daughters observe that mothers work and take care of them and the house, thus providing them with the idea that they, too, will work and take care of the home as a matter of course. But in most families today, sons still see that their primary role model's job often takes precedence over the mother's, that Mom is responsible for the home and that childcare is often on the part of the father a less demanding occupation than it is for the mother. This evolving, yet still unequal, division of labor suggests that we may be breeding a generation of androgynous women and still-traditional men. It is an idea that concerns Dr. J. Brooks-Gunn, the senior research scientist at the Educational Testing Service, whose studies have been referred to earlier in this book.

Her research into the ways androgynous mothers and feminine mothers interacted with their young children first prompted this concern. She observed that while androgynous mothers promoted androgynous behavior in their daughters and feminine mothers did not, neither androgynous nor feminine mothers promoted androgynous behavior in sons. "Even though sex roles are changing, and androgynous mothers are promoting nurturing and independent behavior in daughters, they are less willing to promote both in sons," says Dr. Brooks-Gunn. "One could speculate that the next generation may be comprised of androgynous females but not androgynous males. Men, in other words, will still be socialized in the traditional way."

This line of reasoning omits the fact that nurturing fathers socialize sons to be nurturers. But this can happen only to the extent that fathers today model for their sons nurturing behavior. Because there is a significantly smaller population of androgynous fathers than there is of androgynous mothers, one can assume that the legacy of androgynous behavior will remain unequal for girls and for boys. Such a disparity could perpetuate the notion of unequal partnerships which characterizes so many dual-career and dual-wage marriages. Although the number of families in which men and women share the domestic burden equally is certain to be larger than it is today, we cannot expect that role conflicts in the home will be resolved in the next generation. The presence of the working mother has been a powerful force in the American family, but she cannot, by her presence alone, command an egalitarian partnership. The time-honored traditional division of labor and the residue of deep-seated fears about the androgynizing of the male hinder progress toward shared responsibilities in the home and in the workplace.

Yet progress is being made, and the population of androgynous role models for boys continues to grow. They in turn can be expected to model androgynous behavior for their sons and to have this behavior infiltrate the culture at large. While not a revolution, it is certainly an evolution—one which will continue to change the character of the American family.

There is a snapshot tacked onto a wall of my house that I put there five years ago and have never wanted to take down. It is a picture of my husband, John, cradling our daughter, who is only a month old, in the crook of his arm. She is a tiny package, in a soft white sleeping outfit, against his breast. She is crying, her little fists moving up to her face; my husband's head is bent toward hers, whispering to comfort her. He has come up from the cellar, where he has been trying to clean up his workbench, to be with her. His blue cotton shirt is rolled to the elbows, and his tanned forearms look massive in relation to the helpless infant. It is that image—the rough masculinity of the arms curled tenderly around the fragility of the child—that so appeals to me. It is not a posed picture—his face is not visible; hers, scrunched and reddened from her exertions, is not her best—but it is a moment of my husband and our daughter that I savor.

I savor it because it is reminiscent to me of all the nights he walked the floor with her, of all the songs he made up in the bathtub to distract her from a hairwash, of all the hours he spent feeding her and changing her and reading to her and showing her the world. For the first nine months of my daughter's life, my husband and I both worked at home. He was continuing, in a fairly relaxed manner, a freelance writing business he'd begun some years earlier. I, who had worked in the offices of a magazine in the city until the day I delivered, was just starting my own freelance business. My job—hustling and trying to get work—was the harder of the two. Because of this, John took over a somewhat larger share of the parenting during those early months. Ours was an unusual circumstance, and although we were always broke, I believe we were lucky.

By instinct, my husband is the more natural parent of the two of us. I'm not sure why this is so—although I suspect it's because his own parents, both his father and his mother, are exceptionally nurturing by nature. When I would be inclined to run to the books for advice, John would proceed by blind instinct and prove to have a soothing touch. When I was nearly in despair at my inability to stop a maddening crying fit our baby was having, John would take her from me and, in some mysterious way I have yet to fathom, ease her out of her discomfort and tease her into a smile. He had an extraordinary amount of patience, and he had a passion for his child that I think surprised him.

When Katherine was nine months old, we found ourselves spectacularly broke. Now it was my husband's turn to take a magazine job in the city. He minded the loss of his freedom and the commute, and he minded the suits and the traveling for business—but most of all he minded being away from his baby. He would call from the office to check up on her, and when he came in the door at night, he would look distracted until he'd found her. His time with her, now reduced to a couple of hours, was spent feeding her, bathing her and putting her to bed—a ritual that became his exclusive province. As she grew older, I would sometimes find them asleep together in her loft bed, my husband having drifted off with his legs dangling over the edge.

On weekends, he tried to teach her to play baseball. He bought her a Yankee jacket and gave her a toolbox. When I am away, they cook together, and once in a while they clean up the mess. Katherine is too big for him to hold in the crook of his arm now, but I have another picture in my mind that I savor just as much as the snapshot.

It is a summer evening and John has just come home from work. Katherine, in a huge yellow T-shirt of his that she sometimes wears for a nightgown, runs out onto the back lawn to greet him. But she discovers, en route, that the fireflies are out. Nearly levitating with excitement, she scampers all about the yard, in the dusk, to catch one. My husband quickly sheds his sport coat and his briefcase, and runs in his shirtsleeves with her. Darting in and out among the foliage, he waits until she finally catches one. Together they watch it glow in her small cupped hands, and then reluctantly she lets it go. He bends over and picks her up. Her long legs dangle from his embrace. She wants to know why fireflies glow. He walks with her over to a lawn chair and sits with her on his lap, telling her what he knows about fireflies, and making up the rest. They sit there together until his dinner has grown cold, her bedtime has long passed and even her yellow T-shirt is no longer visible.

11

The Single Working Mother

*A*lice was a child of the 1950s. She was raised, she says, to "get married and make decorative salads." In her childhood and in her teenage years, she learned that when she was a grown woman, a man would come along and she would fall in love. They would marry, she was told, and she would be taken care of. The idea that she might have to work for a living was never entertained. Consequently Alice didn't learn a trade or prepare for a profession. Instead, because she had artistic talents, she was encouraged to go to art school. Being an artist was a flexible pastime that wouldn't interfere with a future husband's career. It was a suitable pursuit for a woman who would eventually marry, have children and "settle down."

But there was in Alice an undefined rebelliousness. She wanted something more, yet she didn't know what it was. During her teen years and her early twenties, this rebelliousness found outlet in her art work and in the adoption of an offbeat style of dress. She thought of herself as "arty" and perhaps a bit wild and reckless.

Yet strong feelings of wanting to be independent and create her own life could not compete with the desire "to lie down and be taken care of." Thus, she found herself in her early twenties married to a man she did not love and pregnant with her son, Adam. The couple moved from New York, where Alice had grown up, to Michigan, where Alice knew almost no one. For two years, after her son was born, Alice struggled in her miserable marriage, trying to find some equilibrium as a good housewife and a good mother. But the marriage became suffocating. Scared, alone, penniless, yet knowing that emotional survival depended upon getting out, Alice left Michigan and her husband behind and returned to New York City with her son—a single mother in the days before such status had become nearly epidemic.

The year was 1970. She was twenty-eight and had a two-year-old. She had no money, and her former husband contributed only $17.50 a month in the way of child support. She was absolutely on her own, had no profession or trade and was the sole support of the child she dearly loved. She grew up fast.

Finding an apartment she could afford on the Upper West Side, Alice took a job as a glove designer and then as a waitress. She earned three hundred dollars a month, nearly half of which went to pay the rent. The rest was parceled out for food and for childcare. Seldom was there anything left over. She was isolated and intent on survival.

In time, she found support in the form of a consciousness-raising group—a group of eleven women who lived in her neighborhood who met to talk about themselves and the problems they had being women. Although no other women in the group were single mothers, their collective experiences—their struggle to find self-esteem and to become independent women in an era when the quest for self-knowledge was being encouraged by the women's movement—helped her enormously. "I went from being an infant to being a woman," Alice says succinctly.

Having neither a profession nor a trade was a handicap to Alice, but she was determined to provide a good home for her son. After several years as a waitress, she found a job selling accessories in a wholesale garment company, and then became romantically involved with a man who invited her to join him in a business he was just starting—a restaurant on the Upper West Side. The love affair disintegrated, but the business partnership remained intact. Today she is co-owner of the restaurant, and finally making enough money to send Adam, who is eighteen now, to college. But she has never remarried, and has been, for what seems like all of her life, a single parent engaged in an economic and emotional struggle for survival. "I had never taken care of myself in my life. Adam's father wasn't around, so I felt I had to be there for my child as much as I could. It hampered my ability to make a lot of money. I was very scared when I came to New York, but I also felt very positive that I could make it and that Adam and I would have a good life together. The first three years were the worst. I even considered leaving New York because I was so unhappy struggling. There were so many ups and downs. But although it was hard and often painful, I was very comfortable being a single parent. I became a mother with my whole being. I did as good a job as I could."

In 1970, when Alice first came to New York, she knew no one who was a single parent like herself. Today, however, her status is common. Between 1970 and 1984, the number of single-parent families in this country doubled. Today, one out of every four families is headed by a single parent, 90 percent of whom are women. It is estimated that by 1990 as many as half of all families in the United States may be headed by single parents. Put another way, half of all children born in the 1980s may spend at least some time in single-parent families.

A single mother, unless she is receiving welfare or ample alimony, is, by necessity, a working mother. And she doesn't make very much money. The median income of single mothers in this country is only $11,000 a year. The average weekly earnings of the nearly 6.5 million households headed by women is $297. For the approximately 1.7 million families headed by black women, that figure is $259. The net result of this is that more than half of all single-parent families fall below the poverty line. An even more alarming statistic is that one out of every four children in this country lives in poverty. For a divorced or never-married woman with children, working is not an option. It's a vital necessity.

The burden on the single mother is enormous. Hers is not an easy lot. Like Alice, many of the women who are single mothers today were raised to believe that they would marry and be economically provided for by their husbands. With that understanding, many of them gave up the potential for jobs or careers that could earn them substantial incomes, and instead had children and settled down—only to find themselves in divorce court. One out of every two marriages in this country ends in divorce, and with that divorce comes an almost inevitable shattering of a woman's former way of life. According to Lenore Weitzman, author of *The Divorce Revolution,* after a divorce, the disposable income of a man goes up 42 percent; but for a woman it goes down a shocking 73 percent. Most women find they have to leave the homes in which they were raising their families and seek housing elsewhere. Women who had never before been part of the work force suddenly find themselves having to get a job—often, because they had not prepared for this eventuality, in low-level entry positions.

Because full-time work is a necessity, full-time childcare also becomes vital. Yet with a low income, finding good-quality childcare is difficult. Few single mothers can afford full-time housekeepers or nannies; some can't afford full-time day-care. Instead, many have had to resort to patchwork care—a neighbor here, a relative there—piecing together adequate care for their children with the limited funds at their disposal.

Not all women, of course, are solely responsible for their children's upbringing; joint-custody arrangements now characterize many families following a divorce. But even if former husbands take the children on alternate weekends and for some vacations—and do provide child support—being a single parent for the majority of the children's waking hours can mean having to fill the gap felt by the loss of the other parent.

The emotional burden following a divorce can be devastating. Although many feel relief upon escaping from unhappy marriages and welcome the challenge of making it on their own for the first time in their lives, tearing apart a family—no matter how fraught with tensions that family was—is almost always a difficult, if not wrenching, experience. Not only one's own wounds, but also the hurts of children, have to be dealt with and healed. At a time when practical problems seem almost insurmountable—finding new housing, finding a job, making enough money to pay the rent—the single mother also discovers that she is the primary parent of a family in the midst of an emotional upheaval. In the months following a divorce, children often express their grief at the loss of the family in many troubling and unsettling ways—ranging from withdrawal to acting out both in the family setting and in school. Trying to help young children survive a divorce when one is coping with nearly unspeakable feelings oneself can seem an almost impossible task.

As if these problems weren't enough, the middle-class single mother also suffers from a kind of future shock. Having invested in the American dream of the nuclear family—with its happy marriage, breadwinning husband, domestic wife, suburban house and charming well-fed and well-cared-for children—many single mothers suddenly find themselves having to be good at something for which they were not prepared: being the breadwinner as well as the nurturer; being competent as well as affective; being the sole provider of warmth, love, income, repaired bicycles, cooked meals, holiday outings, birthday presents, mended clothes and fixed faucets. The basic training of her youth can seem woefully inadequate. The single mother finds she has to learn to do it all. Like Alice, she grows up fast.

The single working mother has practical problems that the dual-career or dual-wage working mother does not. For the single mother, survival is such an important issue that it tends to override—at least for the first year or two—other, more subtle issues, such as whether or not she is being an effective role model for her children. First things first. Food on the table, a roof over her head, a job to pay for the basics, adequate childcare and the wherewithal to cope with the emotional stresses and strains following a divorce are imperative issues that demand immediate attention.

The extent to which a single working mother worries about being a good role model for both her sons and her daughters may depend on whether or not the father is available to the children. Some fortunate single working mothers find themselves involved in responsible partnerships with former husbands who not only contribute significantly to the economic welfare of their children, but who feel compelled to be just as active fathers as they were before the divorce. The single working mother in this situation may not feel the additional pressure that some single parents feel to be both a father and a mother to her sons and her daughters, since there is a male role model very much in the picture.

Sue, the typesetter, interviewed in Chapter 3, has a four-year-old daughter and a six-year-old son. She works because she has to. "I am committed to my work. First of all, since I'm almost divorced, I have to be committed: I have to support myself, my children. We have to have a roof over our heads. That's my main motivation." She is lucky, however, in that her husband, from whom she is separated, is committed to the children and cares for them for half the week. She does not worry about her son having an adequate role model, because his father is still very much in the picture, but she does believe, by her example and by her teachings, that she has many important lessons to impart to her daughter as a result of her life experiences. "I think I'm a positive role model for my daughter in that I'm letting her know that a woman just doesn't get taken care of in life. She really has to go out on her own and make her own life. She has to make her own happiness."

Roberta, a black single working mother, has similar feelings: "Your life is what you make of it, and children will absorb those values that you believe are important and worthy of imparting. My job is a bigger one because I'm a single parent, but I think that things are exactly whatever you think them to be. I have not perceived single parenthood to be bad or good: It's something that happens. We talk about the divorce. I don't lie to the children. Their father and I didn't get along. Once a teacher said to me that my son was acting up because he was from a broken home. I asked her what she meant and she said, 'Well, you're divorced.' I said, 'What's that got to do with anything? My son has a father, and he has a mother. We just don't live together. If you think that because there's been a divorce the home is now "broken," well, that's your interpretation, not mine.'

"Our home is not broken. It's very much intact. I have a positive view about our family, and I tell my children that. That isn't to say it hasn't been tough at times—it has, but I teach them to like themselves and to feel positively about the family.

"I've also taught them that if they want to belong to this family, we all have to work together. My children support me. If supporting me means washing the dishes or washing the floor, then they do it. I don't want my children to be helpless, waiting for someone to come home and take care of them. My children know how to take care of themselves—my sons and my daughter. They know that hard times sometimes happen, but you don't just sit down and cry about them. It's 'Dry your face, girl, and get on with it' in this family. We all pull together. You have to decide what kind of a person you're going to be. You can be a winner and a doer, or you can sit around crying. My kids are winners and doers."

Roberta has a positive outlook on her family: Just because it doesn't conform to the traditional mold doesn't mean it's "broken." But other single working mothers whose former husbands have abandoned the family may worry about the effect of the absent father on the children and may feel compelled to "repair" the family in whatever way they can. Their concerns take on many colorations: They may feel that a son, in particular, has no primary role model to help him form his sex-role identity. This concern creates pressure on some single working mothers to find a replacement for the missing father in the form of a steady man, or better yet, a new father. Others try to fill the gap felt about the absent father by acting as both mother and father to the children. Having been raised in the traditional feminine role, they now find themselves reaching toward both extremes of the masculine-feminine spectrum: They strive to become stricter disciplinarians at the same time they try to give their children extra love and warmth; they feel compelled to master a number of tasks formerly executed by the absent father (assembling toys, talking to sons about sex, attending all the Little League games) while not shortchanging their children in the domestic sphere. If married, working mothers sometimes feel overburdened by the number and variety of tasks they must perform, for the single working mother who still retains traditional ideas about what men and women do in the world, the compulsion to be both mom and dad for her children is stressful. This is particularly true if the single working mother has felt guilty about the divorce and is trying to overcompensate for the family life she felt she "took away" from her children.

Trying to be both a mother and a father to a child, however, is most stressful and arduous for those women who on Sandra Bem's sex-role identity scale would define themselves as "feminine." For a woman who perceives adult roles as distinct, and who was trained to perform only one of these roles, taking on the other role can result in an awkward fit and uncomfortable feelings about one's identity. But women who have come to see masculine and feminine roles as blurred —who perceive the *adult* role as more androgynous than the traditional view—suffer less from feelings of inadequacy and from the need to compensate. A single working mother who takes it for granted that a woman can be both effective and competent—can fix scraped knees as well as temperamental cars—can add certain modes of behavior to her repertoire without excessive emotional strain and stress. Moreover, she teaches her son or her daughter valuable lessons about surviving in the adult world. "I think it's sexist to feel you have to be a 'mother' or a 'father' to a child," says Alice. "I was a human being. I was me. I gave everything I could. It came naturally to me to do everything. I never thought, A father should be doing this. It just flowed out of me.

"This isn't to say that Adam didn't have male role models. He did. I kept my dating separate from my home life, but Adam had my father, my brother and a wonderful neighbor in the building. This was his family, and he had a lot of wonderful love growing up.

"I sincerely feel there's no one way of doing a family. Adam had friends from homes that had a mother and a father and those families were sometimes horrendous. As long as I felt good about myself, I knew he would pick up on that and be okay."

Assuredly, the problems of single-parent families are unique and can affect children in harmful ways. The scars of a wrenching divorce may never be healed; children, suddenly plummeted into a lower standard of living, where just finding enough money for food and rent is a primary passion on the part of the mother, may begin themselves to become worried about finances; sons whose fathers have abandoned them may suffer from the loss of this role model and do poorly in social interaction and in school; badly pieced-together childcare may have a deleterious effect on young children, causing them to feel insecure and unwanted; and children whose primary parent is a divorced mother may have difficulty establishing the trust and desire necessary to form workable and loving partnerships themselves when they are adults. Getting divorced is one area in which you hope your kids *won't* follow in your footsteps.

Yet single-parent families cope—and some of them cope remarkably well. As the sole head of family, the single working mother can be an exceptionally strong and viable role model for both daughters and sons. The authors of *Lifeprints* found that the sense of mastery among divorced mothers was high. Out on their own for the first time in their lives, the discovery that they could deal with all of the problems that came their way was a heady and liberating feeling. A divorce forces a woman to become independent fast, to extend her reach, and to expand and grow as a person. Mastery in these personal areas, as well as in the more practical areas of finding housing and putting food on the table, can result in greater self-esteem. These lessons are not lost on daughters and sons. Daughters who see that their mothers can cope with a variety of life experiences inherit the potential for mastery in many areas themselves. Sons who observe firsthand the struggles of the single working mother have an opportunity to develop greater respect for the competency of women and greater compassion for their needs.

Alice, Roberta and Sue are all positive role models for their children. Each has struggled but each has survived. Each views her life and her family positively. Each has unambivalent pride in the job she is doing being a single working mother. And each feels, because of her life experiences, that she has important lessons to hand down to her children. None has a desire to shelter her children. To the contrary, each feels responsible to teach her children to take care of themselves—economically, emotionally and physically. Yet none of them promotes the notion of the desirability of living alone. Warmth and love, and a belief in the importance of the family, characterize each of these households.

One-parent families can be just as cohesive and warm as two-parent families. Although it has been said that two nurturers are better than one, it is also true that one good parent is better than two bad ones. And ironically, a child may get *more* attention in a single-parent family than he gets in a two-parent family. Undistracted by the tensions of a bad marriage—or simply by another stimulating adult who competes for her time—the single working mother may be able to devote more attention to her children than the married working mother.

The *presence* of the single working mother in nearly a quarter of American homes underscores certain vital tasks we face as individuals and as a society: *As working mothers, we must prepare our daughters for a life of work; as people who care about what happens to our children, we must create better support systems for single working parents; and as a society, we must learn to accept a new definition of the "family."*

If future projections come true, our daughters stand a 50 percent chance that they will, at some time in their lives, be single working mothers. To not prepare a daughter for a life of work, then, is to handicap her as an adult. By her very presence, the single working mother (and the married working mother) teach girls vital nontraditional lessons about the daughter's adult role. But working mothers need to be consciously aware of these lessons as well, in order to better facilitate this basic training.

Single parents have needs that traditional families do not. Chief among them is good childcare that they can afford. Women who take on the responsibility of raising their children by themselves are victimized first by a stunning drop in their standard of living, and, second, by an ability to earn only two-thirds of what men earn, even under the best of circumstances. Even when good consistent childcare, in the form of a day-care center, is geographically available to them, many single parents cannot begin to absorb the cost.

Single-parent families need more equal distribution-of-property laws in all states following a divorce, so that the standard of living for single mothers will not be so disparate from that of men. They need more emotional and practical support in the form of networking organizations, such as Parents Without Partners, a single-parent organization that now has one thousand chapters nationwide. They also need recognition at the workplace. Single mothers without good childcare, without benefit of after-school programs and without partners to share childcare responsibilities may not be able to work full-time schedules unless they reconcile themselves to leaving older children alone for several hours a day. Companies, mindful of the special problems of the single parent, might create more flexible working hours for such a mother. A few companies have recently instituted a policy offering working mothers work during school hours only. Thus the working mother can be home when her children get home from school and can spend vacations with them. Such a policy, if instituted on a large scale, could greatly relieve the tensions and stress on both the single parent herself and on her children.

Single-parenting does not carry with it the stigma that it used to, but because the necessary support systems for the single parent aren't in place yet, we suggest to the single mother that hers is an aberrant status. Yet the statistics tell us that this is not so. Indeed, the single-parent family is *more* prevalent in this society than the traditional American family of the breadwinning father and the at-home mother. We give lip-service to the idea of the "new family," but as a society we really don't believe it yet. Somehow we think this "aberration" will go away—the divorce rate will settle down, and we'll all get back to the business of being traditional families. But single-parenting is not going to go away. In fact, in the foreseeable future, it's going to increase. Not recognizing the single-parent family as just as viable as the dual-wage or the traditional family will hinder progress. As women in the early stages of the women's movement discovered, change starts with self-awareness. As a society, we must increase our self-awareness of what we really are before change can become possible. What we are is a nation of nontraditional families struggling for recognition and support in a system that has so far been remarkably slow to acknowledge our presence.

12

Looking to the Future

*A*t 3:45 in the afternoon, I go down to the corner to wait for the bus because that's when Katherine comes home from kindergarten. I sit on a rock next to an old barn that lists precariously to the west. The windows are cracked and broken. Raccoons live in there now, I'm told. I haven't been inside for years. As the seasons evolve, the vegetation surrounding the rock on which I perch changes from rust-hued leaves that I pick up to save for my daughter, to a brown mat that waits for snow, to the relief of daffodils that someone must have planted years ago, to a delicate froth of baby's breath pushing up through the cracks. I'm always tired at 3:45. I don't know if my daily rhythms dictate this or if I'm merely drained from the tussle with words that characterizes most of my days. I usually think, self-indulgently, that I could use a nap.

The bus comes lumbering up the hill, its lights flashing to a stop. I pick myself up from the rock, and an astonishing thing happens—no less remarkable because it happens every day. I begin to smile. I smile inanely at the driver as he opens the door, and at nothing in particular as I wait for my daughter to make her way up the aisle, carrying too much for her little arms—her lunchbox, her backpack, her jacket shed in the warmth of the bus, a sculpture made in school, a paper bag filled with assorted papers marked by her sturdy fledgling printing. I smile because she is a treasure to see. Her hair has fallen out of her ponytail, her hands are covered with smudges from colored pens, and the knees of her jogging pants are smeared with brown dirt and grass stains. I run my hand over the top of her head, because she has no free arms to hug me with, and I help her with her burdens. We walk up the hill together to the kitchen door, where, once inside, everything falls from her in a heap.

She always says she is hungry, so we sit together at the kitchen table while she eats a dish of yogurt or a banana. Sometimes she minds if I ask her to tell me what she did in school ("Do I *have* to?"), and sometimes she is voluble. Danny was being yukky today, she says, or Lauren let her have two of her Laughing Cow cheeses at lunch. Mrs. Potack said "Wowee!" when she handed in her writing paper, or Mrs. Potack took ten minutes off her recess because she got into a fight with Timothy. At five years of age, she is incapable of sitting calmly and squarely in a chair, so she is in constant motion, kneeing the chair from the side, standing beside it, finally sitting on one cheek. Then she is off. Outdoors to speed around on her High Rider, zipping through "traffic" and chattering into a pretend CB radio. Or digging in her garden, planting radishes in a cockeyed row. Or pretending to be a quarterback with a football she can barely get her hands on. Or upstairs to her desk to draw rainbows and hearts. Or to put all her stuffed animals in a row and indulge in the luxury of telling them what to do. I follow her around, and sometimes I suggest a game, but usually I just go with the flow. I like watching her. She tickles me.

I like who she is now. I'm not entirely sure what a five-year-old is supposed to be like, but she seems fine to me. She is comfortable with herself. She is not what I would call a tomboy, but she is not exclusively girlish either. She has never liked dresses, but she is determined to grow her hair down to her knees. She says her heart is "filled with love" for her parents, her dog and her stuffed animal "babies," but she is scrappy, stubborn and often given to long semi-rational explanations as to why things should go the way she wants them to. She is a Yankees fan, a Jets fan and a Knicks fan, but she likes Care Bear headbands and nail polish. She likes to earn money—cleaning up her room or picking up sticks in the backyard for a quarter. And she's still at an age when she thinks it's fun to help change the oil in the car or to empty the dishwasher. She is only just beginning to sort out that certain activities are characterized by the culture around her as masculine or feminine, but that seems to have little bearing on her future plans. It's never occurred to her that she can't be a pilot when she grows up, for instance, or a baseball player. Just the other day, she announced that she wanted to fly "the weightless airplanes." I'm not sure what she meant by that (possibly she was referring to gliders), but I did note that she didn't say she wanted to take a ride in one: She wanted to fly it herself. She has announced, however, that she doesn't want to be an astronaut because she might blow up, and she has asked me, please, not to be an astronaut either. Although it gave me pause to think the *Challenger* tragedy had affected her so, I was intrigued to observe that she thought it possible I could actually become an astronaut. Last week she told her father that she wanted to be a mother, a doctor, a scientist and a trapeze artist. She thinks she'll do them all simultaneously. At the risk of sounding as though I am editing the description of my daughter merely to nail down my thesis, I will tell you that I think she is comfortably androgynous.

When I think about her future, though, my brain refuses to function beyond a certain point. I am aware of the serendipity of life, of the way perfectly charming five-year-olds can become crack addicts at fourteen, or can be trapped in suffocating marriages at twenty. It happens. Life is not predictable. I don't have a strong sense of how she'll turn out. She could be a pilot of "weightless airplanes," or she could be the mother of six. She could be a physicist or a nurse. She could be a writer, like me, or a good businesswoman—not like me. I do think it's pertinent that neither she nor I have closed off, in our imaginations, very many options; but because of this, her future seems indistinct. If I had to guess, I'd venture that she'll probably work at a job and earn money all her life, and that at some point she will marry and raise children. If future predictions about the shape of American society in twenty years' time hold true, that's what most of the little five-year-olds will be doing when they're grown.

It seems to me that the job of a parent is to fit a child for the society in which that child will be an adult. If Katherine were a child of the Masai tribe in Kenya, my job would be to teach her how to make a mud and wattle hut, how to track down and find water in the bush, how to let blood from a cow's neck so as not to kill the cow but to make a potion of blood and cow's milk that is the staple diet. I would need to teach her that the woman's place is to bear children and take care of the hut, and that if she did not learn to acquiesce to the dominance of men, she would find herself ostracized by the tribe and hard-pressed to survive on the barren land alone. Her well-being would depend on these lessons, and as her mother, I would be remiss if I did not make sure she learned them.

But as Katherine is not a member of the Masai tribe, and is instead the child of a society in which she faces a 50 percent chance of becoming divorced, a 50 percent chance of becoming a single mother and an almost 100 percent chance of becoming part of a dual-wage family, I had better prepare her for a life of love and work.

As a working mother, I am in a good position to help prepare her for that future life. As we have seen earlier, children stand to benefit in many ways from having a working-mother role model. And yet, as we have also seen, these benefits are only possible if the mother is content with her role. But how can she be content with her role if she struggles constantly against the grain of society?

If the struggle to combine working and mothering in an individual home is too great, either because the mother is made to feel guilty for what she is doing or because she cannot find adequate practical support for her task, the children in that individual home may receive mixed messages: Women work, but it's too hard; I'm supposed to work when I grow up, but I don't want to be miserable like Mommy; or (worse) I don't want to work when I grow up; or (worse still), I don't want to have children when I grow up. In order to fit our children for the society in which they will live, society has to fit itself to the new nontraditional families that comprise it. The need to create support systems for working mothers, so that that struggle might be eased, is urgent. The need to recognize that most families in America today are nontraditional is immediate. It is not enough to throw up our hands and say, Oh, well, it will be better for working mothers when *our* children are working mothers. Conditions for working mothers must be improved now so that children will be better able to adapt comfortably to their adult roles. That process begins with the working mothers themselves.

In the past, there have been support systems for women. In the early 1970s, the women's movement provided an initial structure to help women to explore a variety of new roles. By 1973, some 80,000 to 100,000 women all across the country belonged to small women's groups, most of which met for a phenomenon that was called consciousness-raising. Consciousness-raising was among the women's movement's top priorities. Social change was not possible, it was argued, until women clearly understood they were oppressed and why. Because the political climate in the early seventies permitted radical thought, and because the women's movement provided a catalyst for introspection, self-examination and social change, consciousness-raising flourished. United by sex and by geography, women in groups of eight to twelve found their way to consciousness-raising either through the auspices of the National Organization for Women or by word of mouth. They each took turns holding the meetings in their homes and they talked, in an atmosphere of safety and freedom, about what it meant to be a woman. The purposes of consciousness-raising were clear: to break down barriers between women, to encourage open communication among them and to help them develop pride in their sex.

As a result of participation in these groups, women came to better understand themselves and to grow stronger. They struggled together for self-respect, for strength as a collective of women and for political awareness of the forces that united them. Once a week, they shared thoughts, feelings, fears and intimacies with more abandon than at any time before or since. They gave of themselves totally and were bonded together in the process. And when they were through, they had something that could never be taken away from them—tools to help them be women, workers, wives and mothers. Finding strength in numbers and in shared experiences they began to shed the second-class label and to have respect for their own struggles and for the struggles of other women. Fledgling hopes and goals that might have lain dormant or have been squashed altogether had they not belonged to such a group were given expression. By clarifying what it was they wanted to do, they took the first steps toward doing it.

But in time, consciousness-raising petered out—victim of a changing political climate, of expanding career opportunities for women, of shifting priorities on the part of the women's movement and of a subsequent lack of a sponsor. As the country became more conservative, the quest for self-knowledge gave way to self-fulfillment. As jobs opened up for women, and as women tried to combine careers with family life, the sheer struggle to succeed at mothering and working left little or no time for meeting with, or even thinking about, other women. The women's movement—having accomplished a preliminary goal of widespread education—moved reluctantly into a period of latency, shifting its priorities from consciousness-raising on a massive scale to activist issues on a smaller scale.

Today, ironically, because of the opportunities the women's movement in part made possible, women are again isolated. It is not the isolation of housewifery in suburbia that characterized the 1950s, but they are isolated nevertheless by the burden of trying to combine working and mothering in a society that has not made itself ready for them. Because trying to do both jobs without benefit of necessary support systems often consumes all of a woman's energy and time, she finds herself at a remove from a network of other women who have similar problems. This isolation has created a strong need for a second stage of consciousness-raising groups—this time focusing on how to combine motherhood and work. Despite the overload many women experience, the benefits would far outweigh the cost of an hour or two per week. Women could share feelings, thoughts and insights, and find strength in their commonality. As CR did for so many women in the early 1970s, women today might emerge with pride in themselves as working mothers, with self-respect for their struggles and with new tools to help them in their task.

Women need to talk to other women about what they are doing, and they need the emotional support they would find as a collective. The women's movement originally set forth the tenet that social change was not possible until women clearly understood why they were oppressed. The social change needed today to ease the burden on working mothers will not take place unless working mothers identify what it is they need and learn how to go about getting it. Social change for women has to begin with the women themselves. Solutions are possible—executed first on the personal level. Armed with an awareness of what those needs are, women can then begin to execute those solutions in the home, the workplace and in society at large.

At home, the task is to recognize the family as nontraditional. Recognition begins with the working mother, who then must raise the consciousness of the entire family. In the same way that consciousness-

raising allowed women to identify themselves as women, to have respect for themselves as women and to feel good about themselves, a
raised consciousness in the nontraditional family would allow that
family to identify itself as such, to gain new respect for itself, and to
have positive feelings about their way of being a family. As Patricia
Knaub and others have said, if Mom and Dad feel good about the
family and about their roles, these positive feelings will be communicated to the children, who will internalize them and take pride
in their family life. "To continue to define the dual-career lifestyle in
terms of deviance is clearly a disservice," says Knaub.

As models for their growing children, parents can talk about the
choices they have made and the responsibilities that go along with
them. In preparing their children for a life of love and work, they can
develop a commitment to share that will be observed firsthand by the
children, and can work to ease rigid sex stereotypes that have proven
to be so counterproductive to the nontraditional family. Together the
family can commit themselves to spend time with one another. By
developing a sense of teamwork—in which all members of the family
contribute to the running of the family—children will be able to
observe, from the ground up, how the family of their own particular
future operates.

Once that family has gained respect for itself on an intimate level,
it can then go out and demand respect for itself in the public sphere.
Families, linked together by networks of working mothers and fathers,
can lobby to raise the consciousnesses of those individuals in charge of
school policies. After-school programs for children of working parents
are a must, as is the rescheduling of school activities at which parental
attendance is desirable or required. Even more important is the development of programs that help prepare children for the economic and
social realities of their future. The old home-economics courses that
used to teach girls how to cook and sew might give way to the new
home economics: teaching girls *and boys* how to combine working and
parenting. Such courses might be made mandatory. In them children
would become exposed to the issues they can be expected to face as
partners in dual-wage or dual-career families: budgeting time as well as
money; sharing parenting; sharing domestic chores; creating more flexible work schedules and choosing among the differing forms of childcare. Such a course would be at least as important to them as chemistry

or French; one could certainly make the argument that such a course would be vital. In the space of a generation, the American family has transformed itself from the traditional to the nontraditional. Such a massive transformation cannot take place without educating the participants. We have learned our lessons the hard way—through trial and error. That need not be the case for our children. Why not give them the benefit of our mistakes and our insights?

The raised consciousness of the nontraditional family must be taken into the workplace as well. The task there is to obtain recognition that workers are parents, too, and that the needs of the nontraditional family are different. To date, the vast majority of American businesses and places of work are designed to accommodate only the traditional family structure—one in which the children are cared for by a parent who stays at home. Because such is not the case today, however, there has to be some *give* in the old design. Working parents are the keepers of a national resource: the children of this country. These children cannot grow up alone without those parents. Flexible ways of working have to be developed on a massive scale so that the nontraditional family can function without strain and stress. This flexibility must be made available to both men and women and must be offered without instilling guilt or without provoking punishment in the form of stalled forward momentum in the workplace. Shift work, flextime schedules, part-time work, modified hours, at-home work, on-site day-care and guaranteed paid parental childcare leave are but some of the options that might be made available on a widespread scale to American workers. The creation of a new way of being a family has necessitated the creation of a new way of working. But change starts with the workers themselves, who, once they understand their needs, can begin to communicate them to employers. Having gained self-respect as the parents of nontraditional families, women and men can begin to demand respect for these families in the workplace.

In society at large, the most pressing task for the nontraditional family is to secure universally available, good-quality childcare. The parents of the nontraditional family can be neither good workers, good parents nor good role models if they are troubled about their inability to find quality childcare that they can afford. Nor can they take steps to secure good childcare on a national scale if they are conflicted about the choices they have made, or if they shy away from identifying themselves as nontraditional. Networks of men and women who have raised their consciousnesses about what it means to be a nontraditional family and who put a value on their lifestyle might begin to band together to lobby for the reforms that are vital to their survival. Change starts from the ground up, from parents who feel the issue is urgent enough to put pressure on their congressmen to spend tax dollars on the country's children.

The debate as to whether or not mothers should work is not really a viable one anymore. Mothers do work and will continue to work. Children are not raised the way they used to be. Families don't look the way they did in the past. To continue to ignore the urgent need for reasonably priced, good-quality childcare will not make the American family resume its former shape. It will simply create a strain that may damage those families, may teach the children in those families confusing lessons about their own futures and may ultimately hurt the children in serious ways. We say we care about our children, but do we?

In the past, working mothers have not been a good interest group because they've been too busy. But can we afford to be so busy that we ignore our ability to effect change? Our numbers are large, and the needs are great. Creating idiosyncratic, patchwork solutions within individual families will solve immediate problems but not larger ones. Negotiating private accords with individual employers for more flexible schedules will help some highly valued women workers, but will not do much for working mothers as a whole. History has shown us that those who have power and who are invested in the status quo rarely make changes to benefit the disadvantaged unless pressured to do so. The pressure must come from working mothers themselves. The time spent would be an investment in the futures of our children—children who will then be better able to grow into their adult roles.

When one thinks about one's own child—and the children of an entire generation—it is impossible not to wonder how they will turn out. Although there is concern for how the child of five is getting along, there is also worry about how the young woman of eighteen, or the young father of twenty-five, will fare. Implicit in the thinking about young children today is speculation as to where they are headed.

There is no way, of course, to make any hard-and-fast predictions. We do not have a control group of eighteen-year-olds walking around who grew up under the same conditions as those of the three- and five-year-olds of the working-mother boom. Working mothers were not the norm in 1968, and the society in which these mothers worked was very different from today's. But despite this inability to say for sure how today's children will do, the available research does permit us to speculate.

The working-mother role model allows children to value women more highly than in previous generations. This higher value placed on women affects girls directly. It increases their self-esteem, their self-respect and their independence, and it gives them a primary role model with whom it is desirable to identify. Having a working mother increases the potential for a future of love and work in a daughter, and gives her a wider range of options to explore as an adult. Releasing her from a rigid, inferior and confining sex role, the working mother gives her daughter the potential for better mental health, a higher I.Q., and more domestic and political power. It allows her to better balance her masculine and feminine sides and confers upon her the ability to fulfill herself in ways previously denied to women. "The next generation of young women will start from a different place—a more confident place about what it means to be a woman," says feminist author Betty Friedan. "To be sure, they may face a new set of problems, but there won't be that automatic shrinking away, that sense of being something less. I believe women will enjoy better mental health and more political power and will relish both their careers and their motherhood. Their sense of possibilities will be lovely."

Having a working-mother role model allows boys, too, to value women more highly. Seeing women from the ground up as competent, effective, smart and capable of earning money and contributing to the family income causes sons to view women differently than in previous generations. Although the working mother may not be the primary role model for a boy, this disinclination to devalue women creates a tremendously positive potential in sons. The boy, and later the man, may see women as equal to men in the home, the workplace and in the political arena. In the home, a higher value placed on women may lead to egalitarian partnerships; in the workplace, a higher value placed on women may lead to increased respect for women as employees, colleagues and bosses; and in the political arena, a higher value placed on women may lead to important legislative changes. In the past, Congress and the Executive Branch have been composed of men whose mothers and whose wives, for the most part, did not work. But the next generation of lawmakers will have had mothers who worked, and wives who work. These basic domestic facts have the potential for sensitizing men more acutely to the needs of women. This possibility, combined with the increased number of women lawmakers and the increased pressure from nontraditional family voters, may finally help to bring about much of the legislation regarding childcare and work policies that is so urgently needed.

Almost certainly, our children will not experience the degree of difficulty in combining working and parenting that we have had. Many of the internal barriers to living the life of the nontraditional family—barriers rooted in the expectations of the traditional family—will have been eased. Our children will not be pioneers in an alien landscape. They will be the second generation, pushing further into a landscape already made familiar in their childhoods. They will benefit as children of the second generation do, from our mistakes, and they will have been assimilated into a culture that is growing and changing with them. To be sure, as Ms. Friedan has said, they may face a new set of problems —perhaps the emergence of a society that is comprised of androgynous women and only partially androgynyous men—but they will not suffer the guilt and conflict over creating a new lifestyle that so plagued our generation.

The dual-career and dual-wage family will be more prevalent in the future. The number of single working mothers will increase. Households in which both parents share child-rearing and share domestic chores will grow in number. Women will push further into male-dominated fields. More families will have a need for universally available, good-quality childcare. Women will probably return to a somewhat earlier age for childbearing—and the next generation of working mothers will very likely spawn another. These successive generations of working mothers will be better able to balance family life and work life than we have done.

"I think what has been learned is that both sexes can do both things," says Dr. Feinberg of Tufts University. "That women can indeed be lawyers and should be if they choose, but that there is still an enormous respect for child-rearing. The task for the next generation is one of fusing these two endeavors—not that one is better than the other. Whenever something is new, you abandon the old in order to embrace the new. I see what will come next will be figuring out a modification."

Paradoxically, our children will have more choices and fewer choices than we did. My daughter, Katherine, for example, won't have much choice about going to work: She will almost certainly have to, no matter what the future configuration of her family. She will, however, have more options as to what her job or career will be than I had, and she will have more choices available to her as to how to combine working and mothering. Already I can see that she perceives for herself a wider range of possibilities than I did at five, and that she has more self-confidence and a greater respect for her own worth as a female than I had as a child. I am not entirely responsible for these characteristics in her. Her father and the culture surrounding her family have also contributed to her sense of place in the world. But I do think, because I am a working mother, that I have shown her that loving and working and combining the two are possible for her—and that in both there is much to value and to treasure.

Notes

Chapter 1: "Am I Doing the Right Thing?"

1. Kathleen Gerson, *Hard Choices* (Berkeley: University of California Press, 1985), p. 214.
2. *Ibid.*, p. 70.

Chapter 2: But Mothers Have Always Worked . . .

1. Grace Baruch, Rosalind Barnett and Caryl Rivers, *Lifeprints* (New York: Plume Books, New American Library, 1983), p. 105.
2. Nancy Chodorow, *The Reproduction of Mothering: Psychoanalysis and the Sociology of Gender* (Berkeley: University of California Press, 1978), p. 4.
3. Kathleen Gerson, *Hard Choices* (Berkeley: University of California Press, 1985), p. 3, citing the works of Heidi Hartmann (1976), Anne Oakley (1974), and Neil J. and William T. Smelser (1963).
4. *Ibid.*, p. 3.
5. Helena Z. Lopata and Debra Barnewolt, "The Middle Years—Changes and Variations in Social Role Commitment," in *Women in Midlife* (New York: Plenum Press, 1984), p. 87, edited by J. Brooks-Gunn and Grace Baruch.
6. Gerson, *op. cit.*, p. 8.
7. Baruch, Barnett and Rivers, *op. cit.*, p. 234.
8. Gerson, *op. cit.*, p. 4, citing the work of Louise Kapp Howe (1977) and Valerie K. Openheimer (1970).
9. *Ibid.*, p. 4.
10. Diane E. Alington and Lillian E. Troll, "Social Change and Equality, The Roles of Women and Economics," in *Women in Midlife*, (New York: Plenum Press, 1984), p. 188, citing the work of M. Harris (1980), edited by J. Brooks-Gunn and Grace Baruch.
11. J. Brooks-Gunn, "The Relationship of Maternal Beliefs About Sex-Typing to Maternal and Young Children's Behavior," paper

prepared for the International Conference on Infancy Study, 1984.

12. Gerson, *op. cit.*, p. 7.

13. Lois Hoffman, "Maternal Employment and the Young Child," in *The Minnesota Symposia on Child Psychology*, Vol. 17, ed. Marion Perlmutter (Hillsdale, N.J.: Lawrence Erlbaum Associates, 1984).

14. Lopata and Barnewolt, *op. cit.*, p. 105.

15. Judy Long and Karen L. Porter, "Multiple Roles for Midlife Women," in *Women in Midlife*, (New York: Plenum Press, 1984), p. 41, edited by J. Brooks-Gunn and Grace Baruch.

16. Ronald J. D'Amico, R. Jean Haurin and Frank L. Mott, "The Effects of Mothers' Employment on Adolescent and Early Adult Outcomes of Young Men and Women," in *Children of Working Parents, Experiences and Outcomes* (Washington, D.C.: National Academy Press, 1983).

Chapter 4: Mother: The New Role Model

1. Diane E. Alington and Lillian E. Troll, "Social Change and Equality, The Roles of Women and Economics," in *Women in Midlife* (New York: Plenum Press, 1984), p. 196, citing the work of L. W. Harmon (1981), edited by J. Brooks-Gunn and Grace Baruch.

2. Patricia Kain Knaub, "Perceptions of Parental Power in Dual-Career Families," paper prepared for the National Council on Family Relations, 1984.

Chapter 5: The Effects on Daughters

1. Caryl Rivers, Rosalind Barnett and Grace Baruch, *Beyond Sugar and Spice* (New York: Ballantine, 1979), p. 32.

2. J. Brooks-Gunn and Wendy Schempp Matthews, *He and She: How Children Develop Their Sex-Role Identity* (Englewood Cliffs, N.J.: Prentice-Hall, 1979), p. 72.

3. *Ibid.*, p. 52.

4. Rivers, Barnett and Baruch, *op. cit.*, p. 31.

5. J. Brooks-Gunn, "The Relationship of Maternal Beliefs About Sex-Typing to Maternal and Young Children's Behavior," paper prepared for the International Conference on Infancy Study, 1984.

6. Rivers, Barnett and Baruch, *op. cit.*, p. 31.
7. Brooks-Gunn and Matthews, *op. cit.*, p. 145.
8. Rivers, Barnett and Baruch, *op. cit.*, p. 87, citing the work of Beverly Fagot (1977).
9. *Ibid.*, p. 89, citing the work of Lisa Serbin, Jane Connor and their colleagues at the State University of New York, Binghamton (1978).
10. Brooks-Gunn and Matthews, *op. cit.*, pp. 205, 206.
11. Brooks-Gunn (1984), *op. cit.*
12. Brooks-Gunn and Matthews, *op. cit.*, p. 194.
13. *Ibid.*, p. 199.
14. Rivers, Barnett and Baruch, *op. cit.*, p. 130.
15. Brooks-Gunn and Matthews, *op. cit.*, p. 189.
16. Grace Baruch, Rosalind Barnett and Caryl Rivers, *Lifeprints* (New York: Plume Books, New American Library, 1983), p. 236.
17. Rivers, Barnett and Baruch, *op. cit.*, p. 61.
18. Brooks-Gunn and Matthews, *op. cit.*, citing the work of Judith Schikedanz (1973), p. 175.
19. Rivers, Barnett and Baruch, *op. cit.*, p. 122.
20. Lois Hoffman, "Maternal Employment and the Young Child," in *The Minnesota Symposia on Child Psychology*, Vol. 17, ed. Marion Perlmutter (Hillsdale, N.J.: Lawrence Erlbaum Associates, 1984).
21. Ronald J. D'Amico, R. Jean Haurin and Frank L. Mott, "The Effects of Mothers' Employment on Adolescent and Early Adult Outcomes of Young Men and Women," in *Children of Working Parents, Experiences and Outcomes* (Washington, D. C.: National Academy Press, 1983).
22. *Ibid.*, p. 134.
23. Rivers, Barnett and Baruch, *op. cit.*, p. 72.
24. Hoffman, *op. cit.*, citing the work of F. A. Pedersen *et al.*, 1982.
25. Brooks-Gunn, (1984), *op. cit.*
26. Hoffman, *op. cit.*, citing the work of M. Golden *et al.* (1978).
27. Hoffman, *ibid.*, citing the work of F. A. Pedersen *et al.* (1982).
28. Diane E. Alington and Lillian E. Troll, "Social Change and Equality, The Roles of Women and Economics," in *Women in Midlife* (New York: Plenum Press, 1984), citing the work of S. L. Altman and S. K. Grossman (1977), p. 194, edited by J. Brooks-Gunn and Grace Baruch.

29. D'Amico, *op. cit.*, p. 134.
30. Alington, *op. cit.*, citing the work of Allen (1980), p. 194.
31. D'Amico, *op. cit.*, p. 145.
32. Rivers, Barnett and Baruch, *op. cit.*, p. 266.
33. Baruch, Barnett and Rivers, *op. cit.*, p. 75.
34. *Ibid.*, p. 268.
35. Hoffman, *op. cit.*

Chapter 7: The Effects on Sons

1. Patricia Kain Knaub, "Growing Up in a Dual Career Family: The Children's Perceptions," paper prepared for the National Council on Family Relations, 1984, citing the work of L. W. Hoffman and F. I. Nye (1974).
2. J. Brooks-Gunn and Wendy Schempp Matthews, *He and She: How Children Develop Their Sex-Role Identity* (Englewood Cliffs, N.J.: Prentice-Hall, 1979), p. 157.
3. Kim Brown, "Do Working Mothers Cheat Their Kids?," *Redbook*, April 1985, p. 77.
4. Lois Hoffman, "Maternal Employment and the Young Child," in *The Minnesota Symposia on Child Psychology*, Vol. 17, ed. Marion Perlmutter (Hillsdale, N.J.: Lawrence Erlbaum Associates, 1984).
5. Brooks-Gunn and Matthews, *op. cit.*, p. 157.
6. Dr. Lawrence Balter with Anita Shreve, *Dr. Balter's Child Sense* (New York: Poseidon, 1985), pp. 167–71.

Chapter 8: Stresses and Strains

1. Patricia Kain Knaub, "Growing Up in a Dual Career Family: The Children's Perceptions," paper prepared for the National Council on Family Relations, 1984.
2. Anita Shreve, "What the Baby Books Don't Tell You," *Redbook*, April 1984, pp. 90–91.
3. *Ibid.*, p. 91.

Chapter 9: A More Positive Outlook

1. Grace Baruch, Rosalind Barnett, and Caryl Rivers, *Lifeprints* (New York: Plume Books, New American Library, 1983), p. 143.

2. *Ibid.*, citing the work of Abigail Stewart.
3. Lois Hoffman, "Maternal Employment and the Young Child," in *The Minnesota Symposia on Child Psychology,* Vol. 17, ed. Marion Perlmutter (Hillsdale, N.J.: Lawrence Erlbaum Associates, 1984).
4. Anita Shreve, "Careers and the Lure of Motherhood," *The New York Times Magazine,* November 21, 1982, p. 46.
5. *Ibid.*
6. *Ibid.*
7. *Ibid.*
8. *Ibid.*, p. 56.

Chapter 10: The New Working Father

1. Gail Gregg, "Putting Kids First," *The New York Times Magazine,* April 13, 1986, p. 50.
2. Caryl Rivers, Rosalind Barnett and Grace Baruch, *Beyond Sugar and Spice* (New York: Ballantine, 1979), p. 20.
3. *Ibid.*, p. 21.
4. *Ibid.*, p. 27.
5. *Ibid.*, p. 108.
6. *Ibid.*, p. 112.

Bibliography

Diane E. Alington and Lillian E. Troll, "Social Change and Equality, The Roles of Women and Economics," in *Women in Midlife*, (New York: Plenum Press, 1984), edited by J. Brooks-Gunn and Grace Baruch.

Dr. Lawrence Balter with Anita Shreve, *Dr. Balter's Child Sense*, (New York: Poseidon, 1985).

Grace Baruch, Rosalind Barnett and Caryl Rivers, *Lifeprints: New Patterns of Love and Work for Today's Women*, (New York: Plume Books, New American Library, 1983).

Thomas Berndt, "Peer Relationships in Children of Working Parents: A Theoretical Analysis and Some Conclusions," *Children of Working Parents: Experiences and Outcomes* (Washington D.C.: National Academy Press, 1983).

Jean Bodin and Bonnie Mitelman, *Mothers Who Work: Strategies for Coping* (New York: Ballantine Books, 1983).

J. Brooks-Gunn, "The Relationship of Maternal Beliefs About Sex-Typing to Maternal and Young Children's Behavior," prepared for the International Conference on Infancy Study, 1984.

J. Brooks-Gunn and Wendy Schempp Matthews, *He and She: How Children Develop Their Sex-Role Identity* (Englewood Cliffs, New Jersey: Prentice-Hall, 1979).

Nancy Chodorow, *The Reproduction of Mothering* (Berkeley: University of California Press, 1978).

Alison Clarke-Stewart, *Daycare: The Developing Child*, Cambridge, Mass.: The Harvard University Press, 1982.

Ronald J. D'Amico, R. Jean Haurin and Frank L. Mott, "The Effects of Mothers' Employment on Adolescent and Early Adult Outcomes of

Young Men and Women," *Children of Working Parents, Experiences and Outcomes* (Washington D.C.: National Academy Press, 1983).

Kathleen Gerson, *Hard Choices* (Berkeley: University of California Press, 1985).

Dolores Gold and David Andres, "Developmental Comparisons Between Ten-Year-Old Children with Employed and Unemployed Mothers," *Child Development* (journal), 1978.

Lois Hoffman, "Maternal Employment and the Young Child," in *The Minnesota Symposia on Child Psychology*, Vol. 17, edited by Marion Perlmutter (Hillsdale, N.J.: Lawrence Erlbaum Associates, 1984).

Patricia Kain Knaub, "Perceptions of Parental Power in Dual-Career Families," paper prepared for the National Council on Family Relations, 1984.

Patricia Kain Knaub, "Growing Up in a Dual-Career Family: The Children's Perceptions," paper prepared for the National Council on Family Relations, 1984.

Judy Long and Karen L. Porter, "Multiple Roles for Midlife Women," in *Women in Midlife* (New York: Plenum Press, 1984), edited by J. Brooks-Gunn and Grace Baruch.

Helena Z. Lopata and Debra Barnewolt, "The Middle Years— Changes and Variations in Social Role Commitment," in *Women in Midlife* (New York: Plenum Press, 1984), edited by J. Brooks-Gunn and Grace Baruch.

Caryl Rivers, Rosalind Barnett and Grace Baruch, *Beyond Sugar and Spice* (New York: Ballantine, 1979).

Sandra Scarr, *Mother Care/Other Care* (New York: Basic Books, 1984).

Anita Shreve, "Careers and the Lure of Motherhood," *The New York Times Magazine*, November 21, 1982.

Anita Shreve, "The Working Mother as Role Model," *The New York Times Magazine*, September 9, 1984.

Index